3/03

Y0-BXX-384

3 00534 1378

FIC W
Cox, William Robert, 1901—
Comanche moon
Bath : Chivers Press, 2003.

Discarded by
Santa Maria Library

5/03

GAYLORD MG

COMANCHE MOON

Twelve men and two women. Trapped in an isolated stagecoach station in West Texas. One of them is 'White Eye' Pierce, who lived with the Comanches for eight years, and now sells their scalps for a living.

When the yellow moon rises, the Comanches will take their revenge on 'White Eye' the Indian hunter, and all those who are with him. The men. The women. The innocent. The guilty.

Some will die fast. Some will die hard. And some will live to envy the dead.

William R. Cox was born in Peapack, New Jersey. His early career was in newspaper journalism. In the late 1930s he began writing sports, crime, and adventure stories for the magazine market, and he made his debut as a Western writer with "Night of the Blood Bucket Raid" in *Dime Western* in the January, 1941 issue. It is worth noting that his Western story debut was with the first of several stories to feature a series character, Terry Glenn. During the 1940s Cox created a number of other series characters for the magazine market, most notably the Whistler Kid who appeared regularly in *10 Story Western* and Duke Bagley whose adventures usually were featured in *Star Western*. "The short story form was blissful until there were no markets," he once recalled. In the 1950s and 1960s Cox turned to television and wrote at least a hundred teleplays for such series as "Broken Arrow," "Dick Powell's Zane Grey Theater," "The Virginian," and "Bonanza." He also won a host of readers writing original paperback Western novels, the best known of which are novels about the adventures of two series characters originally published by Fawcett Gold Medal: Cemetery Jones in a series published under his own byline and the Tom Buchanan series which appeared under the house name, Jonas Ward. Dale L. Walker in the second edition of *Twentieth Century Western Writers* (1991) commented that William R. Cox's Western "novels are noted for their 'page-turner' pace, realistic dialogue, and frequent Colt-and-Winchester gun play. The series of novels built around the strong West Texas character, Tom Buchanan, are very typical Cox Western." Among his non-series Western novels, among his most notable titles are *Comanche Moon* (1959), *The Gunsharp* (1965), and *Moon at Cobre* (1969).

COMANCHE MOON

William R. Cox

GUNSMOKE

This hardback edition 2003
by Chivers Press
by arrangement with
Golden West Literary Agency

Copyright © 1959 by William R. Cox.
Copyright © 1962 by William R. Cox in
the British Commonwealth.
Copyright © renewed 1987 by William R. Cox.
All rights reserved.

ISBN 0 7540 8207 5

British Library Cataloguing in Publication Data available.

Printed and bound in Great Britain by
BOOKCRAFT, Midsomer Norton, Somerset

This book is dedicated to Bob Chenault, who came to me with the title Comanche Moon *and an idea about a bounty hunter who sold Indian scalps to the Mexican government.*

From this grew a screen treatment in which Pierce, the scalp taker, became the central figure. Other folk took form, the entire Comanche nation on their annual Moon Raid became involved, and the story gained proportion.

From the screen treatment came the book. Bob had done research for years, new data became available from various sources, the people developed on paper, the theme resolved itself through the people. It was pure pleasure to write the manuscript.

WILLIAM R. COX

Chapter 1

♦♦♦

The moon had not yet come to full when Pierce and his two companions rode down from the Sierra Diablos westward across the plain. It was late in August and the heat waves danced on an expanse of wild grass and the two men sucked too often on their canteens. They were a sorry pair.

They were, however, the best Pierce could get. He needed someone to keep his back protected in case of a fight, although he did not expect a pitched battle, ever. He worked in his own way, a single-purposed man known far and wide for his proficiency.

Too well known, he thought, and in too many places.

He was medium-sized, burly, with wide-spaced brown eyes and tight-coiled hair on a round skull. He wore cavalry drill trousers, a hickory shirt, and a loose vest, and his boots were hand-stitched from a good shop in El Paso.

He rode a grullo horse, built for endurance and speed, and across the Texas saddle rig was a large, soft, peculiarly shaped saddlebag. His hat was flat-crowned, black, destined for many uses. He was armed with a Remington rifle, a Remington .44-40 revolver, a bowie in a sheath, and a curious small, curved, sharp blade in his belt.

They had been gone from the towns for some time, and the pack animal trotted under a light load. They were heading for some foothills on the horizon which had no name but were well known to Pierce.

The Kid swigged at the water again and Dutch swore at him in thick gutturals. The Kid was stupid. He had been a great killer in Kansas towns at the age of eighteen. He

1

could not read or write, nor do anything else, much, except shoot off a revolver with uncanny speed.

Dutch was from Bremerton originally. He'd been a butcher and he looked it. His wife got to fooling around with a cowpuncher from one of the big outfits and Dutch had waylaid him one dark night with a cleaver. There was some talk about serving said cowpuncher up in the chopped meat before they found out about the murder, but Pierce discounted this. Dutch wasn't that imaginative.

They rode through the afternoon into the sun, tilting their hat brims, maintaining a slow, steady pace. They came to the hills before dark and reined in.

There was a smudge of smoke in a gully that Pierce remembered. He said, "Hunters, maybe."

"Or Comanches? They got to be around some place," said Dutch. "It is almost the time, no?"

"They might show smoke this far out," Pierce nodded. "If they are headin' this way. It's off their path."

"They come," said the Dutchman. "That Kiowa don't lie. Not after I fix, he don't lie."

Pierce would rather not think of the Kiowa. They had needed the information to preserve their lives, but the way the Dutchman used his knife—and the eyes of the Kid, watching with glee—these things still disturbed him.

"We'll go in. Stay behind me. Don't make a move unless I give you the sign."

They rode on into the shade of the trees. There was a stream which he knew, where they replenished their canteens and the Kid gibed at Dutch because he had water left and Dutch did not and Pierce had to shut them up.

The smoke worried him. Years on end the Comanches had raided south or southeast from the Staked Plains, but never in this direction. This was off their beaten path. If the smoke meant a scouting party then someone was care-less, and Comanches were never ones to overlook such details. If it was a war party, the entire nation might be some place around and this would have a meaning, proba-bly one of economy, since they were not superstitious. They bought horses, slaves, lives, as cheaply as possible, they were merchants of death.

It was, of course, the time for the Moon Raid. Maybe the cavalry was going to try and do something about the raid this year. U. S. Grant was in the White House and there were rumors in the settlements and in the Army, too, that the forts were to be reinforced.

Times were changing, Pierce thought. Maybe for the better, he hadn't an opinion. He wanted to get this business over, make sure of the size and location of the raiding Comanches, and then he wanted to be rid of his two companions and ride for the stage station, which was his immediate destination.

A few days, he thought, would do it. The only kind of loneliness he ever experienced was woman-loneliness. He'd been out too long this time. He couldn't think much of women because he had been out so long. It was embarassing.

He quieted the Kid and Dutch and they remounted and rode around the first hill. The smoke was gone from the sky. The gully, he recollected, was wide open on the north, then narrowed, and the fire must have been in the shade near where the rivulet wound from its source.

He decided to leave the horses in a grove of pecan trees, and had some trouble about this with Dutch and the Kid. They were dirty and lazy, he thought, to the point of danger. The odor of their unwashed bodies was sickening.

They climbed the second hill and peered out from a thick copse of brush. The Kid started to say something and Pierce had to clamp an iron hand on him. He motioned for encirclement.

Dutch whispered, "For what should we make the trouble?"

"Because I say so."

They had a routine when attacking a camp. He had drilled these two, coaxed them, almost whipped them. It was like training wild animals. They finally had a general idea of the procedure, although they never knew the reasons for his caution.

They moved off, one right, one to the left. They moved with some degree of skill but he knew that they would be careless, feeling that their lives were not in danger. Only fear could spur them to real effort. He looked down at the tiny camp on the edge of the stream below.

There wee two old men and a young one who could have been a boy or a girl, scrawny and lame. There was a spavined horse, but no dog, which probably meant that the meal in the pot over the fire was canine stew. These three might have been ill and turned out of the main body of Comanches to make a leisurely return to the Staked Plains.

In that case, thought Pierce, the war party might be either near at hand or gone on toward Mexico, he had no way of knowing. What he did know was that these were Indians and their hair was unmistakable. No one could fake Indian hair. It had to be real and then it was worth two hundred dollars Mex, no matter whose head it came from.

The only way it was profitable was to buy Mex goods with the Mex money and take it easy to Kaycee or St. Louis, and then you had to know your markets. They never thought of the business end of it, the people who would not talk with him, or who would have attacked him if they dared. It wasn't an easy way to make a living. A man wouldn't try it except for a lot of other things.

Always when he was ready for the deed he let the gates of memory open. He felt the elbows of Comanche squaws, the ingenious indignities which were worse than beatings. When they killed his folks and carried him away he was adolescent and the squaws knew how to take advantage of that.

Slavery was a condition which man had learned to endure through the ages, but the Comanches had approaches to it which few other nations managed to evolve. The Kiowas would torture a man into a bundle of writhing nerve ends, emasculated, armless, legless, eyeless, but in the end, he had to die. The Comanche allowed him to half-live, but knew how to attack the soul.

Few escaped with their reason. He knew no woman who had endured it and again faced civilization, although he had heard rumor of one who managed it, and married later on and did well. He would like to talk privately to that woman someday and understand her philosophy. It might help.

The red rage began to ignite within him. He held the rifle tight in his hands. The curving lines which extended down from his nostrils and spanned his mouth became channels for his sweat. The insects of August buzzed unnoticed around his head.

He could see nothing of Dutch or the Kid. He should have some sign. There was something astir which he did not like.

It was too late, because the rage had taken hold, the remembrances. He could no longer wait. He lifted the gun.

There was a shot from the left. That was the Kid, trigger-happy as always. The young Indian, boy or girl, was driven several feet by the force of the bullet.

Pierce shot the first old man through the body. He went over backward, grunting. He then aimed at the second old man, and maybe the Kid or Dutch fired at the same moment, because the Indian tried to go in two directions at once, spinning around, finally falling across the banked fire, which flared under its ashes and licked at his ragged buckskin shirt.

Pierce went down the hill fast, not relinquishing his rifle as he took the curved little knife from his belt. He bent over the first old man, taking the scalp lock in his left hand, making a small, quick incision with the knife, lifting. If you were not careful, you got too much skin, and it made a mess. There was a knack to it.

Holding the scalp, he looked for Dutch and the Kid. He opened his mouth to call to them, then the last of his high rage died and he knew what had happened. The Kiowa had, under torture, told the truth about the Comanche Moon Raid.

He took the older man's scalp with a lightning motion, decided to let the young one lie, ducked across the fire and back up the hill. Because the Comanches had come in the open mouth of the gully, and had taken time to stalk Dutch and the Kid, they were not yet aware of him. Otherwise, he would be dead right now.

It would take them time to figure it all out. He knew

them . . . how well he knew them. He ran over the second hill.

He got to the horses. His grullo was the only one worth saving, so he cut the throats of the others to keep the Indians from utilizing them. There was nothing in the other bags nor the packs worth saving. He took all the ammunition. He could always jettison it if the chase became too stern.

There was one thing in his favor. The Comanches were natural-born kidnappers and thieves. The capture of Dutch and the Kid would keep them exulting for a while. They would also have a little of cruel fun in their glee.

If his companions had been watchful, as he had taught them, they would not have been caught, Pierce thought, sourness in his throat. Now for a while they would pay a terrible price. It would be an hour or so before the captors began using their wits, casting about for trail. Then they would track him with care and some caution. This had to be a small advance party.

This also had to be the scouts of a main body, because it was late in August. For over a hundred years they had been following a pattern. The Kiowa had told the truth, all right. They were raiding east of El Paso for some reason.

He rode onto the plain, estimating the remaining sunlight. They couldn't track him in this phase of the moon, that part was sheer gain. On the other hand, he had only one direction in which he dared ride, south to the stage station.

Maybe Gloria would be there. She was a restless, impatient girl, always rushing things. He rode hard across the plain, figuring out the stage schedules in his mind. She'd be there, he decided, staying in one of the rooms the Mannings had in the back of the place.

It made the ride more worth while.

He didn't open the saddlebag until the horse needed a blow. He took a couple of wire hoops and stretched the fresh scalps on them, fastening them on sharpened hooks of his own design, and put them into the bag with the others. It would stink up the saddlebag, but he couldn't help that, he was not going to throw away four hundred dollars Mex.

They added up to twenty scalps, an even score of them. The hunting had been good enough. Splitting with the other two would have forced him to further effort, but now it was all right. The country would be full of Comanches and maybe he'd get a crack at them yet.

If he survived, that was. He remounted and the grullo niggled along. The sun was going down behind those hills and he thought he saw tiny figures flitting. Maybe a few of the young braves had been smart enough to look for him right away.

If there had been an opportunity, he would have been tempted to dry-gulch them. The young ones were simple-minded enough to try anything and their disregard of life and limb had provided him with many a hair-piece in the past. However, the country was rolling and wide open and there was no place for concealment. He rode steadily into the twilight with his thoughts.

It was always the same, the anger dying in the deed. Then that peculiar thing occurred—an emptiness, a hollowness manifested itself in his middle. There was relief in part, but there was no solid satisfaction.

If he could scalp the entire Comanche nation with one stroke of the sharp little knife, maybe that would do it.

On the other side, what would be left?

He could buy a ranch, stock it with some cows, settle down. He could get some steers, throw in with a trail herd and try it out north some place, like Montana. He could do a lot of things.

He didn't want to do a lot of things. He wanted to kill Comanches and take their hair.

He could still see and hear his mother and father when they had been torn to pieces before his eyes and Josie's eyes. He could still see Josie as she had been and then he could see her as she was now and then the picture would black out and leave him with the shakes in the night.

Then he would see it again and remember his pony, which he had loved. The Comanches had taken it along, abused it, finally eaten it. By that time he had been glad to get some of that half-cooked horse meat. He was skin and bones by then and matted hair, and all over him were scars where the squaws had poked him with sharp sticks.

Eight years, he had been with them. They thought they had him, by then. They had Josie and they thought they had him.

He had chosen the time carefully, with two horses staked out secretly on the plain and food and water painfully cached through the weeks of planning. He had killed Iron Head and two of his three sons before getting away in the night.

Their teachings had enabled him to escape the Staked Plains without recapture. Their own ways had made him a great scout for the cavalry later on, when he began harassing them. They had come to know him very well, oh, very well indeed, in the years since.

"White Eye," they called him, because of the rage which made glass of his eyes when he caught them unprepared and killed them and took their hair. They hunted him and he hunted them, and so far as he was concerned that was proper and the way it had to be. There would never be an end to this so long as Josie was alive and with them, never.

He fought down an uncertainty which he could never admit, which he could never quite dismiss. Josie was his sister, she loved him, he brought this into the front of his mind and tenaciously nailed it there.

The trouble was, the nails didn't always hold fast.

Chapter 2

◆◆◆

Comanche Station was halfway between Pecos and El Paso, on the Weyland Stage Line. It was built of adobe, the walls were thick against the heat. The building was square, with slitted windows for protection against siege. The morning sun gave it a washed, cleanly appearance which was somewhat spurious, although Myra Manning kept things better than most way places.

There was a well between the station and the barn. There were chickens in the yard, a bit scrawny but agile and loud. There was even a single skinny shoat. Manning wasn't much account, but he kept food for travelers, he could smoke a ham, he could quarter a beef.

The barn was ample, with hay in the loft and spare horses for the stage. The gear was oiled if not polished. Manning puttered a lot, many things seemed half-finished.

The road came down from the hills to the west, ran through the flat, and disappeared on a turning toward El Paso. The view was uninspiring but vast. The sky made a bowl here and the land needed care and irrigation and people of faith. Myra Manning felt these truths dimly, read her Bible, prayed a little, and faced middle age with no fond memories and no hope of the future.

Miguel and Silo were the hostlers. The former dragged his left leg, a memento of Comanches. Silo was himself the son of a wandering, lusty brave of that tribe. They squabbled eternally and Manning shrilled at them. There were two stages due that day, the first from the east, the second from El Paso way, to the west.

Manning went inside, a fair-haired man with protuberant

blue eyes and moist red lips. Gloria Vestal was at breakfast, sipping coffee. He knew Myra could look from the kitchen and see him, but he couldn't help pausing at the table.

Gloria was an ash blonde with dark skin which allowed her to withstand the rigors of Texas without fading too fast. She was twenty-four and she had lived maybe a hundred years but it didn't show on her. She wore gray serge for traveling and frills at her throat and fancy high shoes. She had pretty ankles and wrists and hands.

Dodge City had known her, and Abilene and Hays and El Paso most recently. She sang in a dubious contralto and she shook it up and when the price was right she would go upstairs. She wasn't common and had never been in a house. She always thought vaguely that she might own a house some day, a posh place, maybe in Kaycee, but it had never entered her head to go into one. She was above that, she considered.

In fact, since she had met Pierce she had taken to ways that were almost virtuous. He made enough money to keep her in clothing and food. The extras she made as occasion seemed to demand, but she was always at his beck and call. She felt a certain nobility in being loyal to Pierce, considering the way many people spoke of him.

Truthfully, she had never thought very much one way or the other about his business of collecting Indian scalps for pay at the hands of the Mexican government. She knew vaguely that the Mexicans could not protect themselves against the Comanches and the bounty was an effort to buy American aid. This satisfied her that Pierce was in a legitimate line of trade and further speculation was needless.

Besides, Pierce was a hell of a man. To realize that this was true she needed only to look at Manning, a failure, with ill-concealed lust in his watery eyes and on his woman's lips. She said, "Pierce should be along tonight or tomorrow."

"He better make the next eastbound," said Manning darkly. "I don't want Pierce around here."

Gloria smiled, showing even, white teeth. "Are you going to tell him that, Manning?"

"I don't look for trouble. If it comes, that's one thing, but I don't go searchin' for it. People don't like Pierce, that's the facts of the matter."

"What people? There's only Miz Manning and Silo and Miguel hereabouts."

"We got folks comin' and goin'. We got stages that stop here with all sorts of people aboard." He gulped. "You hadn't oughta be tangled up with Pierce, a girl like you."

She laughed, good-humored, genuinely amused. Myra Manning came from the kitchen at the sound and stood looking at them, a wooden mixing spoon in her hand. Manning sensed her presence and his shoulders moved in petulance.

He said, "Folks don't take kindly to bounty hunters. It's been said Pierce ain't too particular whose head the scalp comes from, long as it's Indian-black."

Myra Manning said in a dry, flat voice, "I'll need some help with the potatoes."

For a moment it seemed he would rebel, then Manning turned and walked with what dignity he could command to the kitchen. Myra moved a few steps toward the table, staring.

"That's a new-style travelin' dress. It's mighty pretty, Miss Vestal."

"Got it in Surrett's Shop in El Paso. You like it?" She got up and modeled it, twirling about. "You only have to wear one petticoat, specially in this weather." She twinkled, whispering, "Between you and me, it's a little too warm, so I left the drawers off, too."

Myra Manning gasped, then controlled herself with some effort. "It's very stylish, I can see that."

"Well, we'll be going to Kaycee and I wanted to look nice. I've got hopes it might be my wedding gown." She giggled. "Don't mention that. Pierce don't know it yet."

Myra tried hard not to look shocked. "He—he hasn't asked you?"

"For two years now he hasn't asked me. Oh, he's good to me, nobody could be better to a girl. It's just the sound of wedding bells drives him star-eyed."

"Star-eyed?"

"Off on another of his trips," said Gloria without rancor. "Don't get me wrong. I'm not begging anybody to marry me. I get along fine."

"Yes, I'm sure you do." Myra looked out one of the narrow windows at the expanse of flat land rolling to the western hills. "I ain't seen a town in over two years."

"Nothin' to them," said Gloria promptly. "Men and dogs and women with dirty kids. Whisky and gamblin' and cowboys stinkin' either of cheap cologne or cow dung. Gimme a nice place outside the city, a farm, maybe. Or a little ranch." She forbore to mention the house in Kaycee which nestled in the back of her dream factory. This was a second, fanciful vision, which she knew in her heart to be false but which sounded good when speaking with a faded character like Myra Manning. Gloria, whatever her faults, strove always to be kind.

"There's a church," said Myra. Her voice was soft. "There's Wednesday night prayer meetin', and strawberry socials and Ladies' Aid. There's singin' on Sunday, so pretty."

"Er, yeah, that's right. There is church." How long since she had sung in the choir in the Midwestern town? How long since the preacher's son had caught her in the organ loft on a day something like this, real hot, and her without her drawers then, too? Seven years, she counted, seven years of making it on her own. She was very proud of herself, when you came right down to it. She had done all right for a ruined woman.

The conversation died. Myra went back to the kitchen with thoughts of church in her mind. Gloria moved to the bar and rummaged around and dug out a beer, which was not cold but was better than warm. It fizzed a good bit when she loosened the wire holding the cap in place. It was early for beer but there wasn't anything else to do around the stage station.

It isn't an important station, which is why Manning is allowed in charge, she thought. Manning is one of those men who cannot stand up to the world, therefore he finds a little place of his own where he can boss a half-breed and a crippled Mexican. Even here he is afraid of Myra.

Through experience she knew why he was scared of his wife. He was lecherous and his wife was religious. That put him in the wrong, at least in his own mind. She had seen state senators older than him and more randy and she had seen young, starved cowhands off a trail drive who could give him cards and spades. But these hardy souls thought nothing of it. Trouble with Manning was that he believed in sin as conceived in the mind of his barren, pitiful wife.

Gloria took the beer to the window and stared out, speculating on Myra Manning. She amused herself this way quite often, imagining people under certain circumstances foreign to them. It was a game, like, suppose Myra was in the El Paso saloon called the Golden Nugget, singing in her choir-girl voice, dressed in short skirt and low bodice. Could she make it?

There was no law about dance-hall girls going to church. Even the whores went sometimes, to show off.

Myra was kind of long in the tooth, but when you thought about it, she wasn't such a bad build. Flat Nose Kate was older and uglier.

Would she do all right? No, she wouldn't, Gloria decided. It's not how you look, it's how you feel. To Myra it would be a bad thing. To Gloria it was a necessity, a living, and you might as well make the best of it. Count your blessings. Be glad you're not forced to stay in a house and take on anything that came along, no matter how dirty or smelly.

She wrinkled her nose. She hated bad smells.

She took a drink of the beer, tilting her head, and when she looked out the window again she thought she saw a speck against the horizon. She closed her eyes tight, opened them and squinted. It was something moving out there. Not many riders came this way, so maybe she ought to call Manning.

Maybe Manning would get the wind up, and go for his rifle. He had a regular armory on the place, because he was a frightened man and it gave him assurance to have arms. Maybe he would shoot too quick and hurt some innocent cowboy. You can never tell about the Mannings, she knew. She had seen them yank out a bowie or a six-shooter and kill when there was no reason.

She leaned her elbows on the wide adobe sill and watched. The figure grew larger in the rippling haziness. A little beat of excitement stirred her. Could it be Pierce?

Then why was he alone? He had two men with him. She had a letter about those two. Pierce had been disappointed, she had felt. He never told her anything straight out, but in two years she had learned to read between the lines even when he was talking to her.

She started to go outside where she could see batter. She stopped, because that was another thing about him, he hated any public demonstration, no matter how small. He never wanted her even to touch him where other people could see. He wasn't like that when they were alone. No, indeed, quite the contrary. She chuckled to herself.

It could be Pierce and it could be someone else.

It could be one of those other two men. He could be riding in to report that something had happened to Pierce, she thought. It could happen to him any time.

She sat down at the table. There was no use getting panicky. Pierce wasn't the whole world. She had enough money to get the stage to Kaycee.

Only she wouldn't be able to do anything there, not anything to her taste, that is. Better to go back to El Paso and work the saloons and save a stake and then go to Kaycee and see about protection and open her own place. How long, five years? She'd be almost thirty in five years.

She did hope it was Pierce riding in.

Chapter 3

♦♦♦

Caked with dust, his canteen empty, the grullo broken down to its knees, Pierce pulled in between the corral and the barn, in the shade. He slid down from the saddle and his legs buckled once, then straightened. Miguel, spouting Spanish, came on the run. Inside the barn door Silo raised an arm and gave him a rare smile.

These two, for far different reasons, understood him. He said to Miguel in Spanish, "Yes, they jumped us. There's an army out there, all right. Tracked me a good way, farther than necessary."

"Comanche Moon," wailed Miguel.

"Sure, the Moon Raid. Perhaps they will not come here, though. They strike for the haciendas, you know that."

Miguel knew it, all right. That's where they had stuck an arrow in him when he was a scrawny boy and had overlooked him in their haste to plunder and rape. Miguel had lain under the drain of the barn in horse manure and urine for two days before he could crawl out. By the time a doctor got to attend his leg he was maimed for life.

Meantime he had heard and seen the things that Pierce knew about so well. They shared this.

"They will come," Miguel mourned. "I had a dream, señor. Once marked by them you are never free. They will come for you and for me. Let us take horses and ride, señor."

"Where to?" asked Pierce in English. He had been thinking about nothing else since he learned how many Comanches were in this section of Texas. "To the *bandidos?* El Segundo rules the border with his thieves."

Miguel wailed on a minor key. He uncinched the saddle as Pierce took rifle, saddlebags, and bedroll from the horse's back. Silo came to help and Miguel shrilled at him, "Your father's people, you pig. They'll take you with them. You'll be a big chief and eat dog and have the women. They'll love you, son of a Comanche."

Silo ignored him. He was a handsome young man, olive-skinned, with Indian hair and long, smooth muscles. He said, "Pierce got scalps?"

"Plenty," said Pierce. He indicated the soft bag. "Got a couple need hangin'."

Silo opened the bag and took out the dried but odorous fresh ones on the wire hoops. He grinned at them. He carried them inside the stable and hung them on hooks to dry. Miguel brought handfuls of straw to rub down the grullo. Horses in the corral neighed and the grullo managed a weary snort.

Pierce picked up the saddlebags and started toward the station. Silo shouldered the bedroll and took the rifle in hand walked alongside, as an equal.

Pierce asked, "You had any word?"

Silo nodded. "Along the border to the south El Segundo rides. No good. Out there"—he waved the rifle—"Comanches. Plenty Comanches."

The breed had ways of knowing things and he generally told the truth, Pierce knew. A wandering sheepherder, a stray cowhand—sometimes, he thought, even the coyotes—talked to Silo.

"It's plenty bad."

"There are no horse soldiers," said Silo. "There should be more horse soldiers."

"The 6th is busy chasin' Apaches up north. Cochise is takin' up their time."

"You got Apache scalp?"

"Apache, Kiowa, Comanche. One Arapaho."

Silo was pleased. He had very nearly gone out with Pierce this time, only his Mexican blood prevented him. He had few fears but one of them was to fall alive into Comanche hands. He knew all about the way they treated half-breeds. They were worse than the Kiowas with their own mixed blood because they thought they owned all offspring and this made one not dwelling with them an escapee.

He asked, "Dutch and the Kid *muerto*, eh?"

"They got snagged without even givin' me a warning," said Pierce. "They were no good to begin with and then they couldn't keep their eyes open in a pinch."

"Captured?" asked Silo in Spanish.

Pierce nodded. Silo made a sign of the cross, impeded by the rifle. They went inside the station.

He saw Gloria sitting at the table, all pretty and smiling and happy. He put the saddlebag down in a corner and Silo took his bedroll into the rear, where the sleeping rooms were located. He stood looking at the girl, grinning. This was good, seeing her so clean and bright.

She said, "There's a beer. I saw you coming." She wanted him to know she had not run out and made a scene because that was the way he liked it.

"Thanks, Gloria." He sat down opposite her and the beer sluiced down his throat.

She said, "You got a smell on you like a goat."

"It could be worse. I'm just lucky I ain't smelln' like a corpse."

"I figured. When I saw you were alone."

"Those two." He finished the bottle of beer. "I swear I'll never go out like that again."

"You lose everything?"

"Nothing," he said with satisfaction. "I had all the hair in my special bag. We were goin' to split after Kaycee, you know, after the tradin'."

"Then it's all yours?" She had almost said "ours."

"Yep. Four thousand Mex."

"Four thousand." It was a nice, round sum. She wondered how many American dollars it would add up to. If the trading was good, maybe about even.

Manning came padding in, his eyes wide with fear. "You've gotta get outa here, Pierce. Right now. You got to go. I'll give you a fresh horse, anything. But you got to go."

Pierce said mildly, "Without a bath?"

"Miguel told me. It's the Comanche Moon Raid. They're trackin' you. They'll hit the station if you're here."

Pierce tipped back his chair, looking up at Manning.

"They're out. And they're raidin'. Maybe they did come this way to take a shot at me. But you been in this country long enough to know that now they're here, they'll hit you if they take a notion. Whether I'm here or not. They want horses and women, Manning."

"I've never had no trouble with 'em. I wouldn't have it now, wasn't for you. You got to go."

"I'm aiming to go. On the eastbound stage." Pierce stood up. "If the eastbound gets through, we'll be on it, Gloria and me."

"If—if it gets through? They ain't that far south. It will get through."

"O.K. Then why all the fuss?" Pierce frowned and his voice hardened. "I've got money for a bath and a meal. You're runnin' a way station. Get some water into a tub back in one of the rooms. You better make it quick if you want us to catch that stage."

Manning's throat worked. "You got no call to bring trouble on me and my wife. We get along with people. No Indians bother with us."

"You ain't seen anything but blanket Indians—yet," said Pierce. "Better get that tub ready."

Manning's hands waved, his wet lips writhed, but nothing intelligible came from him. He turned and ran into the kitchen.

Gloria said seriously, "I could ride sidesaddle if you think we ought to go on. Wouldn't it be better to ride into Mexico and catch the stage on the way back? Or maybe drive a wagon with the trade stuff?"

"It sure would. Only the Comanches would get other ideas. Or El Segundo would do likewise. No, we got to get East, then take a wagon and circle back. I got some money in a bank in Kaycee if worse comes to worse. We can wait out the Moon Raid if we have to."

"You couldn't get through alone? I mean, if I went on to Kaycee on the stage?"

He looked straight at her. "Honey, you ain't goin' no place alone. Not for a while you ain't."

She almost blushed. He was a hell of a man, all right.

Manning splashed water from buckets in his agitation and Pierce winked at her, then went to help. He took the tin tub and went back to the quarters with Manning stumbling behind him.

She would have liked to go back and scrub him, but he didn't want that, either. He was a very finicky man in some ways. It was really right nice of him not to act up in front of the people. She would have shocked the Mannings with pleasure, but that was not Pierce's way.

He was funny about that and a lot of other things, too. Some of it was due to his upbringing among the Indians. Some of it was bred into him by his folks, who had been God-fearing people from somewhere in Texas, ranchers doing well until the Comanches got them.

She knew his story, or almost all of it. There was something held back, no one knew of this. He carried it around with him, and, whatever it was, this was what kept him going back for scalps, even more than the money or the revenge, she thought. If he could get rid of it, whatever it was, maybe she could maneuver him before a preacher.

Maybe, that is.

Chapter 4

♦♦♦

The stage to El Paso lurched along without very much speed. It was an old Concord with a four-horse hitch. One of the hanging steps was broken and the black paint was peeling. Hump Foley was driving and Shotgun Beemis was the messenger. Like the coach, both had seen better days.

They came to the steep downgrade leading to Comanche Station. Hump set foot to the brake. He said, "Them wasn't Apache smoke signals."

"It's got to be Apaches. It's their country."

"Just the same, it wasn't. I know them little red skunks, I know 'em good."

"You don't know 'em any better'n me," said Shotgun.

Hump stared off at the Baylor Mountains. There was another column of smoke plastered against the sky. It shifted, was diminished, rose again. It was blanketed off, then increased beyond its first stage.

He took his foot off the brake. The coach lunged forward and the amazed horses began to run. Shotgun cursed, hanging onto the iron stanchion on his left. "You dumb fool. You wanta kill us all?"

The road was straight enough, but Sonora Pass was narrow and forbidding, shut off form the sunlight by overhanging rocks and a thick growth of stunted trees.

"I wanta get through the pass," shouted Hump. "Ain't no Comanches gonna cut me off before we hit the flats."

"You got Comanches on your dumb brain. Them's Apaches and they ain't about to come down this here far."

Inside the stage the passengers grabbed the straps and tried to ride with the storm. Two of them rode facing forward, a big, wide-shouldered man and a short fellow in a checkered suit and a derby hat. The cavalry sergeant wearing a 6 above crossed sabers rode backward, bracing himself with sturdy, outthrust legs, his red face stolid.

Ebenezer Tyler, the big man, was enjoying all of it, in spite of the discomfort, the terrible food, the lack of decent sleeping conditions, the interminable time it had taken to get here from New Jersey. He had wanted to come West as much as Brother Bob. He had remained home until the old folks died because it was his duty, and now he was seeing the elephant for fair.

It was too bad about Brother Bob getting himself killed by a bucking horse, but then Bob never had been as good with animals as Ben. He couldn't feel too sorry about it. Bob's ranch was now his ranch and he had a little money—little enough—from the auction back in Jersey. He could maybe fix up the place and make it work. If he knew anything about his late brother, it would be run down.

Bob was the oldest and he had always been somewhat of a hog. Grabbing everything for himself, that was Bob. When he got the neighbor's daughter in trouble, had he married her and tried to do the right thing? Not Bob, he had run off to the West.

So it was up to Ben, and he knew he was caught and he married Dolly. The baby never got born and Dolly was sickly for years. When she died it was like a shadow leaving the crowded old house. He missed her but it wasn't uncomfortable without her.

Then the old folks took sick and it was work and worry, bills to be paid, nothing but trouble. He'd even gone to Newark and brought doctors all the way to Long Valley in the carriage, but nothing helped. Nobody seemed to know just what was the matter, Ma and Pa just faded away.

There was nothing wrong with New Jersey, only it seemed empty with everyone gone but Ben. Got so he was hitting the applejack jug for something to do. He owed a lot and when he got the news about Bob he was glad to sell out, pay the debts, and embark for the West at long last.

"It sure is a big country," he said for the tenth time

since Pecos. They had come through the pass and were rolling along flat land again.

Alongside him, Luke Post said with amusement, "She sure is."

The cavalryman grunted. "I seen plenty of it in the war."

"East, you saw," Ben protested. "You said yourself you'd never been West."

"Enough, I seen, from a horse's back. Pennsylvania, Virginia, Mississippi, Georgia. The Carolinas, Maryland and Virginia again. Mainly, though, I seen Pennsylvania. Too much Pennsylvania."

"And now you're gonna see Texas. And New Mexico and Arizona," said Luke Post. "You're gonna see Apaches and Kiowas and Comanches. You're gonna wish you was back in Pennsylvania."

"Not never," said the sergeant. His name was Callahan. "Though it don't much matter. Hardtack and beans. I was with the 6th in the war. I'm lucky to be with the 6th again."

"What I don't see, is how come you're makin' it this way," puzzled Luke Post. "The 6th headquarters in Arizona. Seems like you'd go by Tucson or thereabouts."

"Orders," said Callahan indifferently. "What's the difference? Arizona, Texas, no matter."

The little man adjusted his derby, grinned at Ben Tyler. "This hombre's got a lot to learn, Ben. This soldier is gonna get educated about Texas and Arizona. *And* New Mexico."

Callahan looked out the window, a beefy man, simple as the alphabet. Orders were orders and he had his service record to bolster him, six campaigns and never a black mark against him. He'd fought the Rebs and he'd put in the years since then doing whatever they asked, nothing interesting. Now they sent him to fight Indians and he'd as soon as not.

Luke Post continued to look at Ben Tyler. He was like a lot of small men, always intrigued by a large man with muscles. He had met Ben in Kaycee, where he had just increased his stake by several thousand dollars and was unfortunate enough to attract the attention of the River Gang.

It was a narrow one, at that, he thought. They had waited until he was coming from Flo's, where he had taken on a bit too much of the bubbly. He wasn't much for drink, it being bad for his business, but sometimes after a session with the pasteboards he liked to relax with a woman and bubble wine, the kind you couldn't hardly get in the West most of the time.

So they had bushwhacked him on a dark street. He had outed the equalizer, all right, he was never slow about that. They were coming in several directions and he was figuring how to blast a way through and make a run for it. They had those cheatin' guns, double-barreled, throwing a .41, which at twenty paces or under could tear out a man's guts. It was going to be nip and tuck.

Then big Ben blundered into it. He saw several bullies closing in on one lone little man and that was enough. He let out a whoop and sailed in.

Of course he would have been ventilated within ten seconds except that Luke had the Colt ready in his hand. The River Gang had made a serious error there. They saw the tailored checkered suit and the hard hat and no visible pistol in his belt or under his arm and thought he was a cinch. So, he had the advantage of surprise and he began picking them off.

That distracted them, he remembered with huge satisfaction. That got them milling around, and then Ben began knocking heads. He never had seen anyone quite the equal to Ben when it came to slamming heads together. Two at a time, pick 'em up, whack 'em together.

He had almost forgot to choose his targets, watching the big farmer.

The way it turned out, the River boys being city thieves, ratlike, unused to open combat, didn't lay a scratch on either Luke or Ben. They had congratulated each other and returned to Flo's.

There were no flies on the farm boy when he got into the rosy lights and the champagne, neither, thought Luke with pleasure. He'd made them come to order, all right, after a couple of bottles. He had those frails dancing attendance. Nothing like a smooth, tanned skin and big muscles in a Kaycee whorehouse, so long as there was the *dinero* to spread around, and Luke was spending.

The tenderfoot was all right, though, he'd do to take along, the little gambler repeated to himself. Game as buttons, he was, and honest as the day.

Luke put a great store by honesty. His own beginnings as a successful man had not permitted strict consideration of this quality, yet he had doggedly fought to where he could pursue it in good faith.

· He had been orphaned early, a working cowhand at fourteen. Yet he had never learned to adore manual labor. Some quirk in his nature had made him aloof to the going principle of early to bed, early to rise. Late hours and cards seemed more attractive and he always had a knack with cards.

He had been winning in a Denver hall when a friend, Lon Harker, a short carder, managed to accumulate a good stake. Luke had prevailed upon Lon to pool their money and buy a couple of barrels of dubious whisky. This they had conveyed in a wagon to a spot adjacent to an Indian reservation.

Strictly against Federal law, but with enthusiastic approval from the noble red man the boys had set up a grogshop in the rear of the wagon. The profits were enormous. True, a few braves became ugly when buffalo robes gave out and thirst continued, but Luke had always been gun-quick. They started their own burying ground in a nearby copse of cottonwoods and the Indians learned respect.

They were on their tenth barrel, having made several trips to Denver and return, when the Army moved in. Poor Lon had tried to fight it out, being somewhat under the influence of their own dynamite brew. Luke, worrying a mite about the private cemetery and the fact that someone might discover a fresh grave and do some excavating, managed to get to the swift mare he had always saddled and ready. He was gone before he could be identified.

When Denver knew him again he had ordered the first of his fancy suitings and he was wearing the hard hat. One or two larger men had ventured to take exception to this unorthodox costuming and had suffered the death, but all in all people began to respect the rights of the diminutive gambler who played cards on the square and usually won.

The odd habiliments were accounted for by two things, a former cowhand's delight in such furbishings and a shrewd instinct for self-advertisement. It was a time when a man could be a gambler by profession and suffer no criticism by bankers, lawyers, storekeepers, nor by womankind in general. When Luke entered the business, he made no bones about it, he wanted everyone to know. He liked loud clothing and he wanted competition. His theories had been proven correct. He was twenty-five years old, he was fairly wealthy, and his reputation was such that no one challenged him to a gun fight. He hadn't a scar on his body and was healthy as a steer.

He said to Ben Tyler, "Comanche Station ain't much. We just eat and change horses and keep goin'."

"It's the food that kills me," Ben confessed. "Back in Jersey we always eat good. Never did realize how good."

Callahan said, "Eat good in Pennsylvania, too. Only goddam thing about Pennsylvania is any good."

Ben looked at him thoughtfully. "Sergeant, seems to me Pennsylvania can't be all that bad. You musta had a terrible time there, one way or another."

"Huh," said the sergeant. "You ever heard of Gettysburg?"

Luke said, "That was in the war, wasn't it?" and winked.

Callahan fixed him with a cold gaze. "I suppose you was a Rebel in the War. I suppose you goin' to tell me all about how the Rebs woulda won if they had shoes and guns."

Luke said innocently, "Well, wouldn't they?"

"They never woulda won," said Callahan heavily. "They didn't know how to fight a war. They played like it was a game. Only one of 'em knew anything, old Forrest. Get there the fustest with the mostest. That's war. You need men to fight a war, lots of men. And you need to know it's a war, not a pukin' game of one ole cat."

Luke said, "You may be right. On t'other hand, there's a few thousand damn redskins don't believe it."

"And they're goin' to be wiped out."

"Sure. Only in the meantime they're havin' a lotta fun, which is what war is to them, mainly, and a lotta fool white people is losin' their hair. And the friggin' U. S. Army ain't doin' such a great job of it, neither," said Luke. "You'll learn, Sergeant. You'll learn . . . if you live."

Callahan lifted a heavy shoulder. "The 6th is a good outfit. That's all I care." He turned to Ben. "You were right. Gettysburg wasn't everything about Pennsylvania. There was more to it. I just don't wanta talk about it."

He sort of did want to talk about it, though, Ben thought. On the long journey the three of them had spoken of things to each other that they would not have dreamed of telling a relative or a close friend. Callahan had been the most reticent but maybe now he was feeling left out of it. He'd talk, if there was enough time. This was one of the things which fascinated Ben about travel.

He had a great sense of human relationship and he had a large bump of curiosity. That is why he had always wanted to leave the narrow confines of Long Valley for another world. In him was the desire to meet people and move about. Maybe Bob's Texas ranch would provide him with a home base from which he could roam about this big, wide-open country.

He had already made a friend in little Luke, he knew. They were looking forward to a bountiful time in El Paso, one of Luke's favorite towns. Then Luke would go out and look over the ranch with him, give him some advice. There was nobody in all Jersey like this little gamecock with the drawling humor and the ready revolver.

Not that Ben held with shooting people. It was one thing he meant to eschew, this passion for the short gun. He could shoot a rifle with anybody, he'd done plenty squirrel hunting and target practice for fun. Revolvers, however, were the weapons of the criminals back home.

The River Gang, that had been different. Luke had a right to kill as many of them as he could hit, because they were crooks and they meant to get Luke. Ben was right glad he had busted a a few skulls for them.

It was the shoot-out stories which Luke had related with such quiet approval that dismayed him. He just couldn't imagine going out to meet another man, a man like himself, each bearing a revolver in a holster, each determined upon destruction of the other because of a fancied insult, or for that matter a real insult.

For himself, he'd meet any man with bare fists. After it was over and the blood stanched, the opponents would be just as well satisfied as those fellows with guns. Fact is, he'd lost a fight, once, and had lived to discover he was wrong in choosing the man in the first place. Supposing it had been a gun fight and he had won and *then* found he was in error?

There was silence in the stagecoach for a little while. They were on the straight road leading to Comanche Station and the horses were running free at a pace swifter than was the custom.

Up on the box, Shotgun was craning around, his weapon clutched in his hands. There were two puffs of dust far on the eastern horizon.

Hump said, "Two of 'em scoutin' because we're so near to the station. The rest in the hills. Gee-up, there you mangy dogs."

"It don't look like no Injuns," said Shotgun. "They wouldn't ride the road like that."

"You seen the smoke signals. The Apaches wouldn't ride the road. Comanches are different."

"There ain't no Comanches," said Shotgun. "You got Comanches stuck in your craw."

"Giddap, you pizzle-strung brutes," said Hump, snapping his whip over the heads of the lead team.

Chapter 5

♦♦♦

In the kitchen it was terribly hot. Manning put the last of
the potatoes in a pot of boiling water and muttered to
himself. Myra looked at him, then turned to the oven
where she was baking sourdough biscuits after a recipe of
her own.

"Just a few decent people and maybe a nice picnic once
in a while. It wouldn't be much, but it would be heaven
after this."

"We've got a livin' here," he said doggedly. "This
here is my place to run the way I want. Few more years
and we'll save enough to buy."

"We did that once. We bought a ranch. You remember
our ranch. Two cows and a pig and some chickens. You
couldn't make anything grow."

"I'll buy a store, this time."

"Yes. You'll buy a store."

"I'll show you how to run a store. I got ideas."

"Yes, you have ideas," she sighed. She went to the
window and looked across the dry land. "You always
have ideas."

"You got no faith, woman. You got no faith in nothin'!"

"That's almost funny, isn't it? I have no faith?"

"I ain't talkin' about the Bible. That don't get you
nothin', readin' that Bible. You're still complainin' and
sufferin'. What good does it do you, that Bible?"

She didn't bother to answer him. He hadn't the capacity
to understand. She had made her bed and she would lie in
it, and there wasn't any use complaining, he was right
there. She turned wearily to the task of preparing the meal
for the incoming stage passengers. Manning went out and

she knew he would be spying on Pierce and the woman of the saloons.

She had been town-reared and everything had been hard, all of her days. Her father had been a hell-fire preacher and her mother a subdued, mouselike little creature, afraid of her shadow and convinced of eternal damnation. Manning had come with his fair skin and his big talk and it seemed an escape to Myra Forsythe.

Children, she thought, would have helped. In poverty, bankruptcy, disillusionment, she would have had something to which to cling. You'd think a man as lecherous as Manning would have the seed to provide offspring.

She went to the open window, shooing the flies with her apron. There was a slight breeze off the plains and she sucked at the air. Her face was flushed and she pushed back a stray lock of the brown, rich hair which she wore too tight around her skull.

There was a man outside the window, dusty, sweaty, a short man in a lightweight town jacket and nankeen britches and low-heeled boots and a shirt amazingly clean. Beyond him she saw a vehicle which looked like a delivery wagon, such as the butcher used for deliveries in the town of her youth. It was completely covered with tarpaulin and hitched to it were a pair of weary dun ponies.

The man said, "Your pardon, ma'am. May I beg the use of your conveniences for my animals?"

She said, "This is a stage station. You can get anything you can pay for."

"Oh, I can pay." He smiled and his face was not young, but youthful. He had greenish eyes and his mustache was trimmed narrow across a broad upper lip and his speech was tinged with a drawl not native to Texas.

Struck by his mild and pleasant presence, she said, "I didn't mean to be unmannerly. It's just that this is our business. I mean, this is a public place."

"And I am fortunate indeed, ma'am."

"You can get a bath if you want. The westbound stage'll be in and we'll be servin'." She wanted to encourage him, to be friendly toward him. He looked a little lost with his peculiar rig and his formal ways, as if he didn't belong in this Godforsaken part of the country.

"That'll be nice," he nodded. He did not return his dilapidated wool hat to his head until he had smiled again and turned toward the wagon near the barn.

She was slightly flustered, using her folded apron corner to crack open the oven door while she peered in. People came and went as shadows through the way station and she never had communication with them. She always felt as though she were scarcely present, that this was a purgatory in which she half-existed. This strange little man had, oddly, incongruously, unbelievably, reached out with a few words and a smile and had touched her.

Immediately she was frightened by her thoughts. She bustled about, not noticing the heat, performing the myriad tasks necessary in preparing food for so many.

She heard Manning's loud voice, heard the stranger introduce himself as "Wade Lamkin, sir, of Savannah, Georgia." A Southerner, of course. Her father had been from Georgia, from the hill country. This man was of gentler antecedents. The sort of man she should have known before she met her husband.

Shocked, she realized that never before had she allowed such a thought to enter her mind. She must be going crazy with the heat, the hard work, the disappointments, everything. She felt tears in the corners of her eyes and angrily dashed them away with the edge of the apron.

Yet, when she heard the sound of the stage coming in, she went out to see it, something she had not bothered to do in many a long week.

She saw them descend, the massive Easterner, the quick-moving, knowing little gambler, the cavalryman in his unseasonable blouse. No one of much interest, she thought. They were like hundreds of others who had gone through.

Hump helped Miguel and Silo with the horses but Shotgun came stomping in, carrying his weapon, glowering. "Apaches, I say. No damned Comanches."

He saw Myra and tugged at his hat and said, "Sorry, ma'am. Didn't mean to cuss in front of you. That Hump, always with his own notions. Comanches."

Pierce and the girl came from the back rooms. The stranger named Lamkin must be having his turn at the tub and Myra knew she should get more water, but Pierce's expression held her as he intercepted Shotgun's progress to the bar.

"What's this about Comanches?"

"Ask that loco Foley. He'll tell you all about 'em. He's got 'em on his dumb mind."

Pierce went swiftly outside. She heard him greet the passengers, heard the names mentioned. She went to the stove and began bailing hot water from one of the big pots. Manning came in with the pails. She filled them and did not listen to his grumbling, going to the window as she reached for dishes to serve the company.

Hump was saying. "You know, and I know, there's a difference. These was Comanches. Couple of them come sky-hootin' down the flats behind us. Reckon they got discouraged, anyway we lost 'em."

Pierce's mouth was tight. "They're west and north, I knew that. If they made the big circle—"

He broke off, turning away. The cavalryman was staring at the odd wagon. The Easterner and the gambler were looking curiously about.

The soldier said, "Seen one of them things before, all right. Seen it at Bull Run, seen it at Antietam. Called it the 'whatizzit wagon,' some did. Little beady-eye man name of Brady had a big tube of a camera, allus takin' pictures. Make a man hold still three minutes while he took a picture. Dangest thing, the way they come out. Had one took myself at Antietam."

"I had one taken, in New York," said Ben. "Put a clamp behind my head, hurt like the devil. Man looks like a stuffed owl in one of them tintypes."

"That there's the wagon he develops his plates in," said Callahan proudly. "I watched him." He stuck his head under the canvas. "Yep! Got the same stink. Must be one of 'em around some place. Picture-taker, like Brady."

So that's what he did, the gentle-faced man. He took pictures. Myra thought for a fleeting moment that she might sit for one; then she remembered Manning and put aside the idea. There was no sentiment in Manning.

The gambler was laughing. As she went about her tasks, his voice came clearly to her.

"Last year up in Denver there was a fella, he had a regular layout for picture-takin'. Butch Raymond, Kid Bovey, Alligator Simms and Mort Graham come into town, havin' some fun. They'd held up a bank or two and were feelin' frisky. Got loaded with redeye and all went in and sat down and had their picture took. Two weeks later there was dodgers out on every one of them. Had to hit their shebang in the hills and stay there, what with everybody lookin' to collect the big rewards on their empty heads. Funny part of it was, they looked like a bunch of choir boys, all dressed up for that picture. To see 'em, you'd never believe they was the worst bunch since Quantrill."

"You forgettin' the James boys?" Callahan said. "They still get around a heap."

Luke said, "I never had any truck with that crowd. They don't play in my back yard. If I was to rate 'em off what I hear, though, Butch's crowd would give 'em cards and spades."

They went out of hearing, amiably debating the efficiency of rival outlaw gangs. Manning came rushing in, anxious to set up the table, now that money was in sight. It would be hustle and struggle to get them all fed. The noon hour was past and by night she would fall apart in the bed, and have to fight off Manning at that, she thought; he always got excited when there were people around.

She was bringing in the biscuits and some loaves she had baked yesterday when two riders pulled in. She had seen them before. They had a pack animal, so she expected they'd been in the Baylor Mountains prospecting. She knew their names, the slant-eyed one was Sligh and he looked like his name sounded, untrustworthy. The other was called Adobe and was loud and bullying, a powerful man with red hair, scarred from knife fights and hard living.

These were the kind of men she feared. They had no home, no rhyme nor reason for anything they did except the moment's necessity. The frontier was full of them, they had run away from something in the past and were going no place in the future. Their lives were based on violence.

Sligh had been in trouble with the sheriff in regard to a stage holdup, she remembered. He had a slickness of manner which indicated that he might possess brains. Adobe was all animal, a brute who did everything hard, took everything the toughest way.

Pierce was questioning them. She listened.

Adobe said in his scratchy, offensive manner, "It was us behind the stage, all right. The pack horse slowed up some. That damfool Hump run plumb away from us. Hell, we only wanted to warn him about the Comanches."

"They're north and east from here, then?"

"You bet your boots they are. We seen more damn Comanches than hell will hold, the past few days. Had us runnin' like rabbits. Had they been really lookin', they'd of got us, of course. They got other things on their mind. We're headin' west, pardner, pronto."

"I wouldn't, if I was you," said Pierce.

"You're crazy if you think not."

"You'll be dead as a mackerel if you try it," said Pierce. "They just run me in from that direction."

There was a moment's silence, then Sligh spoke. "You mean they got this place circled?"

"They haven't missed."

Adobe said, "Then we'll head for Mexico. The hell with it. I ain't fightin' no Comanches unless I got to."

Pierce said, "El Segundo is ridin' the border, lookin' for loot and a quick getaway before the Moon Raid."

Adobe said slowly, "Well, I be joe-damned. Anybody else know about this?"

"I'm about to inform them," said Pierce.

Myra felt the heaviness in the bounty hunter's tone as if she had been struck a blow. She went into the kitchen and looked out of the window. Everything seemed the same. Silo and Miguel were arguing. Was there a shrill, keening fear in Miguel's accents?

The chickens squawked, running in their stupid, aimless

fashion. The horses in the barn were nuzzling their grain, those in the corral moved indolently in the sun. The horses were what the Comanches wanted.

And women.

And vengeance. There was Pierce, whom they called White Eye because when he was angry his eyes reflected light as in mirrors. He had killed scores of them and peddled their scalps across the border.

This station had never been raided. Apaches riding through were always on some dour errand which did not allow for side excursions. The wild-riding Comanches operated from their homes on the Staked Plains. The Moon Raid started from there, thrust into Mexico, returned there.

Everyone had heard about the Moon Raids, she remembered. At first she had thought them based on superstition, but now she knew they were designed merely to give the thieving Comanches the light of the strong, enduring harvest moon for their attacks and long retreat across the Rio.

She tried to lose her fear by busying herself with toting hot food to the dining room, but it persisted. The sight of Wade Lamkin, polite smiling, as he mingled gracefully with the others, did nothing to release her. She was scared of Indians, of any violence.

Pierce, she noted, was silent, brooding. Only her husband was loud and aggressive.

"You'll see," said Manning. "The eastbound'll come through with the news that all's well. Nobody'll make me believe the Comanches are around here."

That was Manning, she thought, always wrong.

She moved toward the window, pushing back the curtains which were so difficult to keep clean and starched. Miguel and Silo were sitting, backs against the wall, and she could hear every word they said. They were speaking in Spanish and English, and she could understand them well enough.

Miguel said, "In two nights the moon will be full. Then you will see."

"So. We will see,' said Silo.

"For a hundred years it is so. The Moon Raid. We are like rats in a trap.''

"A cornered rat, he will fight."

"You will fight your own people? Not you, Silo. Maybe you are here to open the door to them, no?"

"Loco. You are loco for sure."

"Your father, he is Comanche, yes?"

Silo asked mildly, "You know your father, Miguel?"

"No matter my father. He is no Comanche."

"*Sí*. Mother, father, no Comanche." Silo laughed. "Run from Comanche. Run like rabbits, hide. No good, Comanche find. Take your father's hair. Take your mother's you-know-what."

"Comanche take your mother's you-know-what."

"*Sí*." said Silo placidly. "Now maybeso I take Comanche's *cojones*. I take them, hang in barn. Pierce take hair. I take *cojones*, put them with Pierce's hair."

"Your father's *cojones*, maybe." Now Miguel was laughing and Myra knew she should not be listening, but could not refrain from listening. "You take your father's *cojones!*"

"That would be good. That be very good thing."

Like two bad boys, thought Myra. Scared, but also excited at the prospect of a fight. Her mind ached with fear.

Chapter 6

♦ ♦ ♦

Pierce sat in the corner, from whence he could observe the large room. Across from him, Gloria said, "Are you sure, honey?"

"If the eastbound gets in, I'm wrong."

"Comanches," she said. "I never thought much about them. The only Indians I ever saw were drunk and dirty. Hangin' around the towns, looking for a handout."

"There's all kinds." He was estimating the crowd. He saw the big clodhopper, Tyler, taking sneak looks at Gloria, saw him ease into a chair nearby with the gambler, Luke Post. He knew about Luke Post.

Gloria said, "Honey, couldn't we take off?"

"No."

"Well, look. We got to make plans."

"Leave it to me."

"That sounds all right. Only you always have those Comanches on your mind. I swear, honey, there's no time you haven't got them on your mind." She lowered her voice, "Even when we're alone."

He looked at her hard, his eyes taking on that brilliance she knew so well, his White Eye stare. "You got any complaints?"

"You know better than that." She paused. "I did think we were goin' to be married this trip."

The light dimmed in his eyes, he moved uneasily. "Maybe I got Comanches. You—you got wedding bells on your mind."

"Why not? Is it good, the way we're livin'? Do you like it?"

"It ain't what you like in this world. It's what you get."

He was back at his examination of the company. Sligh and Adobe were rough citizens, and untrustworthy. He knew their kind. Former cowhands, too restless to stay in one place, looking for easy money. Prospecting without any real knowledge of the country's geology, they'd steal anything not nailed down.

She said, "A person can try and get what's good. I don't ask for a whole hell of a lot, honey."

"Sure. You're all right." The sergeant was a soldier, which meant he'd fight whichever way things went. The photographer was a Rebel and you could usually depend on them. Manning was no good, never would be any good.

She said, "We'll have some money for a stake. You know that for me it's only you, honey. Why can't we settle onto something?"

"We will, someday." He was thinking about a defense if the fight had to be made. The adobe building was stout. There ought to be food. They should be getting in water right now, but he knew better than to try and start anything. They didn't want to believe the truth. They wouldn't make a move because it would be admitting that they were surrounded and cut off from escape. They would wait out the eastbound stage come hell or high water.

Everything depended on how they took the bad news. He heard Callahan tell Manning that there was nothing to worry about, that the 6th Cavalry would be in the country. That was a soup bowl of cow dung if he ever heard it, but it perked up Manning considerably.

She said, "There's no time like the present. We're not gettin' any younger. Some day the Comanches will get you. Or some drunk cowboy will let loose in a saloon and I'll catch a stray slug."

"You got to play out your string," he said absently. With Silo and Miguel, there were an even dozen men. Up in the Panhandle in June at Adobe Wells there had been a notable fight. Billy Dixon and twenty-eight men and one woman had been in that one. For fifteen days they had held off seven hundred Kiowas, Comanches, and Cheyennes.

The thing was, the Indian force at Adobe Wells had not

been well led. Quannah Parker was there and Little Wolf, but it had been a wild, all-out testing ground without a real goal. Also, the white men were buffalo hunters with needle guns and old Sharps rifles and plenty ammunition, and they could shoot the eye out of a running horse.

This affair would be different. They wanted White Eye. There were more of them and they were headed for Mexico on the Moon Raid. They wouldn't waste any fifteen days hereabouts. They wouldn't need to, he added to himself.

She said, "I been playing out my string for too long, honey. Wasn't for you, I couldn't have gone this far. Now I want to get along, make headway."

The eastbound stage, he thought, that'll do it. Maybe too late, but it will set them off. They'll get scared and then maybe I can make them be sensible about the water and some way to prepare for a fight. There'll be a mess of Comanches out there. It won't do much good, but we got to make a fight.

He said, "Sure, Gloria, I know what you mean."

"You know, but you ain't aiming to do anything about it," she said shrewdly. She became aware that the wide-shouldered man at the next table was listening and turned to stare him down.

His eyes were brown and round and friendly and he had good teeth and a wide smile. She couldn't bring herself to scowl at him, found small, answering softness around her lips as she quickly looked away. She had to always keep in mind that she was back with Pierce, otherwise she would be betrayed into flirtation when she saw a man like Ben Tyler.

Pierce wasn't actually paying any attention to her, so she fell silent, again playing her little game of imagining people under certain circumstances. If this wide Eastener, now, came into a saloon, and she was working, she'd know right away. He'd know pretty soon, because she would let him see that she was interested. Those big, easy-looking men were shy and gentle sometimes and this looked like one of them. It was possible to have both pleasure and profit with this kind of man.

Luke Post would be looking after him. Luke had a softness in him for big men. Wyatt Earp was a friend of his, that tall, skinny operator who knew how to make money and stay on the right side of the law most of the time. He was a sharp one also, that Luke. She'd seen him in Dodge when a would-be gun-slinger challenged him. Luke gave the man first shot, just laid his pistol barrel along his forearm to get steady aim and hit the shooter right in the belt buckle. He was a cool customer, all right.

Callahan was a soldier and she knew nothing good about the breed, mostly the scum of the Eastern cities. Lamkin, now, there was a strange little one. She wouldn't ever know about anyone like the Southerner.

The others were as an open book not worth reading. She let her mind wander back to the big farmer from New Jersey.

Ben Tyler hadn't been paying close attention to Luke's story of the big Indian fight up in the Panhandle. Names like Billy Dixon, Bat Masterson, the Dutchman, didn't mean anything to him. He could not quite comprehend a fight with a band of wild Indians. Matter of fact, he wasn't interested.

He was interested in Gloria Vestal. What Luke had told him about Pierce had been shocking. He would never understand a man collecting scalps for money, this was beyond his ken, he thought. It was a shame this pretty girl was mixed up with such a man, and from what he could hear no good was going to come of it. Pierce seemed to be evading the issue of matrimony. Yet he must have promised her. Otherwise why should she be here, such a nice-looking, well-mannered, tastefully put-together girl?

He saw the neat little Southern photographer go into the kitchen and talk with Mrs. Manning. She was a sweet kind of woman for her age and everything, too.

He remembered Pierce's warning just before they sat down to eat. It didn't make sense. He'd bought a ticket on the Weyland Stage Line to El Paso. In an ordered world, they were responsible for delivering him to his destination. It just wasn't possible that he would have to stay here and be attacked by an army of Indians.

He had no desire to fight Indians. What he'd really like, he'd like to get to know the pretty girl a lot better. And to get to the ranch and see what it was like and start this fascinating new life. Why, a man could be killed trying to fight off all the Indians Pierce claimed were out there.

Luke was saying, "Take them two hombres, Adobe and Sligh. Never seen them afore in my life, but I can tell you everything about 'em. Drifters, rustlers, could be road agents. They got plenty of sand, they got muscle. What they ain't got is brains. Or maybe it's just they don't know how to use what brains they have got. In about a minute they're goin' to get nervish-like and suggest a card game."

"How do you know, Luke?"

"Seen 'em pick up a fresh deck and start fiddlin' with it. Could be they're markin' it. If they are, it'll be so easy to tell that even you could see it."

Ben said idly, "Oh, I could see it, all right. I played me some poker around Jersey. Uncle Tiger had an apple mill."

"He had a what?"

"A mill. Made cider and applejack."

Luke shook his head. "A man gets around, thinks he knows a few things. What's applejack?"

"Whisky distilled from apple juice." The girl's eyes were sort of violet and round and the lashes were fringed like petals.

"I be damn," said Luke. "Whisky from apples. Them folks in Jersey, no wonder they call 'em apple knockers."

"Never heard the expression," said Ben. "Lots of people stopped at Uncle Tiger's mill. Drummers, teamsters, all kinds thinkin' to catch a fool."

"They play poker?"

"Poker, euchre, anything they thought would take hard-earned money away from us poor farmers."

"They do themselves any good?"

"The real smart ones sometimes looked like they was." Ben grinned reflectively. "Then Uncle Tiger would switch 'em to the stone fence."

Luke was completely absorbed. "Now you tell me, what's a stone fence?"

"Applejack and hard cider. A few of them under their belts and it was who threw the rock."

Luke judiciously observed the two saddle tramps absorbing redeye at the bar. "Took the city slickers, huh?"

"They never had much," Ben shrugged. "It was more for fun than otherwise. Uncle Tiger was a card himself."

"He must've been."

"Drunk a gallon of apple a day, I reckon. When he was eighty-one he fell down some steps and broke his hip. Like to kill him."

"I heard that's bad for old folks."

"Oh, it wasn't the broken hip. Sittin' around like he had to, he drank more. Last I saw him he was gettin' to be a reg'lar lush. Didn't hardly make sense any more, and him only eighty-three, now."

"Ben, you should of stayed in Jersey," said Luke, wagging his head. "You ain't gonna find nothin' out here the likes of your Uncle Tiger."

"Oh, I dunno. He was gettin' bad, there." The girl was aware of him, he sensed that. Her man, Pierce, was sitting there, staring, as though his mind was far away. Husky sort of a fellow, but untrustworthy, it seemed. It was a shame.

Luke was right. The two cowboys or prospectors, or whatever, were calling for poker players. Luke nudged him. Manning kept running outside, looking for the eastbound stage, and Callahan was reading letters, and the others were at one thing or another. Maybe there'd be some fun playing cards for a while, at that. He'd follow Luke's lead and see what happened.

He already felt a beginning of recklessness in this Western way of doing things. An Indian fight was something he hadn't counted on, but if a man was in a country he had to go the way of the customs. Maybe the Army would come to the rescue, maybe Pierce was just sounding off, maybe it was all a mistake. He followed Luke to a round, large table at one side of the room.

Adobe and Sligh had been drinking too much, he thought. It wouldn't be much of a game, with him and Luke working together. Pierce wouldn't join them, but Hump, the stage driver, took a hand. They settled down and right away Ben saw that the cards had been thumbnailed. In a few hands he would be able to read them.

Luke winked at him and he nodded. They began playing for a dollar. Right away it developed that Adobe and Sligh believed that nobody knew anything about poker except Texans, and that they hadn't caught on to who Luke really was and that they had a vast contempt for Ben, a tenderfoot.

That didn't bother him, due to his experience with the men he had met in the apple mill. What did make him a mite nervous was the big revolvers they shifted around to where they were awful handy to their reach.

Chapter 7

♦♦♦

In the kitchen Myra was pouring tea, the last of her precious store, and Wade Lamkin was saying, "This is very kind of you, ma'am. I do reckon tea's a scarcity hereabouts."

"It's a real comfort," she sipped her cup. The dishes were stacked and she should be about washing them, but the little photographer held her. "I don't get to meet a Southron very often."

"You do not, then, consider Texans as Southerners?"

"They ain't," she said frankly, then flushed because she had slipped in her speech. She knew better, but living with Manning had led her into bad locution. "They're a breed apart, Mr. Lamkin."

"I find them so," he nodded, smiling. He had small, even teeth, well kept.

"I was in Savannah when I was a child," she said. "It was mighty pretty. Azaleas all over. Palm trees, too. Big oaks with Spanish moss dripping from every limb. It was warm and peaceful." Her father had broken the peace with his revival tent and his shouting and storming and sending people into fits of singing and dancing and screaming for the Lord to have mercy on them.

"It's a sleepy little port now. Broken, too, the niggers sitting in judgment, ruling all." He shook his head. "There is nothing left of the old ways."

"Did you take pictures in the War?"

"Yes. In New York after the War I met Mathew Brady. He is the greatest photographer who ever lived. The Congress has not yet bought his collection of memorable war prints. A pity." He sipped the tea. "Brady gave me the

43

notion to come West. I must say, he knew nothing about
the hardships.''

''Why do you want to take pictures of Indians? They're
not very pretty.''

''They are different,'' he said. ''Also, they are fashionable. Back East they will buy my prints. The War left me
with nothing but my camera.''

She understood that. For a few years she and Manning
had suffered under carpetbag rule. Texas had thrown it off
quicker than other places, she supposed.

He went on, ''Then it also gives me a purpose. A sense
of being part of history. The Indian is doomed, of course.
He won't last in his present state. I hoped to find a wild
tribe hereabouts.''

She said, ''It's a plain wonder you didn't. They'd have
killed you quicker'n a minute.''

''So they tell me. I had thought there was peace. My
information from Washington was precise about this.''

''Washington? What do they know? Indians are never at
peace. They're only careful not to start anything unless
they can hit and get away safe. Little troops of cavalry all
up and down the country keep them watchful. But it would
take a whole army of cavalry to do the job right.'' She had
heard this discussed by experts.

''Then that is why I didn't see any of them,'' he said.
''They were preparing for war?''

''The Moon Raid.'' She told him about the ancient
custom of the Comanches.

''Ah, the moon. It affects even the poor Indian,'' he
mused. ''Dogs, lovers . . . and Indians.''

She wasn't quite sure of what he meant, but when he
said the word ''lover'' a warmth stole over her not induced
by the tea. He was a gentle little man, unhandsome but
kindly, and what they would have called unashamed in the
South, ''sweet.'' She was enjoying herself as she had not
in years. Sitting in her own kitchen, she was having a
good time.

Manning rushed in and she started guiltily, but he was
stuffing hard money into his greasy buckskin poke and was
so wrought up that he wouldn't have noticed anything even

if there had been something for him to resent. He was
sweating and his hair floated wildly and his face was too
flushed. He was not a drinking man and a couple of stiff
ones could upset his equilibrium.

"Migawd, woman, the dishes . . . When the eastbound
gets in they'll wanta eat. . . . Got to get some more
whisky for them card players. . . . You all right, Mr.
Lamkin? Anything you want, just ask for it. . . . Long as
you can pay—haw, haw!" He fumbled and produced a
bottle. "That Comanche scare, don't pay attention. Just a
few of 'em chasin' that Pierce. Sergeant says the cavalry's
around some place. You wouldn't of got through if there'd
been Comanches. It just don't stand to reason."

He rushed back to collect more pay and she knew shame
for his avidity, his speech, his appearance. She felt herself
apologizing. "He's had a hard day. We don't get people
to stop along like this. Usually it's eat and run."

"Yes, I imagine it's pretty lonely," said Lamkin with
understanding.

"Well, a body can make out." Why did she have to
defend the miserable existence? "There's sunrise and sun-
set. There's plenty chores to keep a body busy. And I read
a lot in the Bible."

'I'll help you with the dishes," he said. "In payment
for the tea."

"Manning didn't mean anything about the tea." She
blushed. "He's not that bad."

"Of course not." He saw the way it must be for her and
was gentle. "I had sisters at home. I know about dishes.
Can I fetch some water?"

He put her at her ease without further effort. Up and
down the land he had met others like her. Perhaps, he
thought, he should do a brochure on the frontier woman
before that breed, like the Indian, was gone into history's
pages. It would not be pretty but it would provide a
background for the West.

This one was more comely than most of them, with their
leathery skin and toil-cracked hands and bent shoulders
and sagging paps. No children, that was the answer. Usually they bred like flies, lost the weaker infants, raised the

sturdy. A new, raw race was being born; it should be photographed for the record if not for art's sake.

More interesting than the men, he thought, dipping into the soft soap, feeling the sting of lye in a small cut on his index finger. They were a motley crew, many of them criminals, more of them fugitives from poverty, full of dissatisfaction, all with unrest in their souls.

This short gun which had come into use during the War, the Colt's or Remington or whatever this had come to be called "the equalizer." It made big men out of those small of stature or small of soul. Inaccurate at any considerable distance, it was a fine tool for murder. Formerly it had been the knife, and he had seen bowie fights which had made him vomit at sight of the blood. The revolver was neater and quicker.

He was a man who detested violence, yet always he seemed in the path of shocking events. Perhaps they had a hypnotic effect upon him which he did not recognize in its inception. Or maybe the course of his profession carried him unerringly to the place of desperate deeds.

He had seen duels under the Oaks of New Orleans. He had seen rapine and burnings in Georgia before the war. He had survived the sinking of a river boat when hundreds had perished. All during the military battles he had stood unscathed under fire which had killed its scores of hapless gray-coated, ragged soldiery.

Yet he now pursued the Indian, with his own red record of fighting and plundering. Was it a sense of history that drove him? Was it something more, some aloofness which he strove to palliate?

He had, with many other well-to-do Savannah boys, attended the university at Princeton, and with the others had returned to the South in '61 without finishing the course. He wished he had been allowed to remain in college. There was so much he did not know.

He saw through the kitchen door that Adobe and Sligh, those two primitive men, were at the bar, cracking Manning's fresh bottle of booze, speaking privately between themselves, certainly up to no good. At the table Luke Post was talking out of the side of his mouth to the big Jersey farmer, Tyler.

He sensed an approaching crisis, looked down at his wet hands in the soapy water, then at the woman, pink-cheeked, alive, smiling to have company at her chore. His hands were shaking. . . .

Luke was saying to Ben Tyler, "They know we must be on to them, but they can't figure out what to do. So they'll start a fight."

"They got nasty tongues in their heads. I don't mind fightin' them."

"You ain't heeled," Luke said blithely. "They fight with six-shooters."

"They wouldn't shoot an unarmed man?"

"One of 'em will throw you a gun. They don't know me, so that's the way they'll do it."

"I be damn," grumbled Ben. "You seem to be enjoyin' it. I'm like to get my head shot off and you set there grinnin'."

"Look at 'em put away that redeye. We used pepper, even snakeheads, in what we sold the Injuns, but it wasn't no worse than Manning's brand."

Ben fingered the winnings in front of him. It wasn't much, but probably about all the would-be cheaters had on them. Hump had also repaired to the bar for refreshment and didn't count. How would they come at him? He wasn't exactly scared, because he depended on Luke, but he was uncomfortable and strange.

The six gun, of which he knew so little, seemed clumsy; long-barreled, heavy, awkward to handle. Luke had told him some tall tales about fast draws and sharpshooting, about Wild Bill Hickok and Ben Thompson and a murderer named John Wesley Hardin. He didn't believe them.

Luke had done good in the fight with the River Gang, at point-blank range. He was cool and he aimed his shots and at that distance he didn't miss. For himself, Ben would take the rifle any day. A man could use two hands and aim a rifle and be pretty sure he was going to hit something. Far as close work was concerned, there was the shotgun. He'd seen Sheriff Buchanan go after a wife murderer in Peapack and cut the fellow right off at the pockets with a double load of buckshot. Grisly sight it had been, too.

Now here came this pair and the rules were different and he wasn't sure how to act. He'd just have to let Luke make the play. He wished the gal would get out of there; why didn't Pierce have sense enough to see that trouble was brewing?

His eyes on the wobbly approach of the booted man, he did not see Pierce make a quick estimation, then reach for the rifle which was ever within his arm's length. The girl merely altered her position, so that Pierce partially shielded her from the direct line of possible fire, her eyes interested and a bit compassionate as they recognized Ben's plight.

He did not see the reactions of the others in the room because he was paying close attention to Adobe and Sligh. A theory was forming in his mind. When they sat down and he picked up the cards for his deal it began to take concrete form.

Hump returned to the game, caught on right away, when Adobe, the bully, started complaining. Hump was scared but there wasn't any place for him to run, so he sat tight.

"You got a real slick way of dealin'. For a tenderfoot."

Ben said, "They play cards where I come from."

"I reckon they do," Adobe snarled. "I reckon they know a whole hell of a heap about cards wherever you come from."

"Yep. They sure do." Ben's grin and gesture toward the money in front of him was not designed to promote peace. He knew he was in for it, so he figured to play it out. No use showing the white feather now, he thought.

Luke just sat there. Adobe and Sligh probably thought he was a drummer, or a short-carder beneath their notice. Maybe their brains were so fogged by the liquor that they could hold only one idea at a time. They wanted their money back and they were enraged that an Easterner was beating their game. They couldn't understand why nobody played when they had good hands, but bet into them when the marked kings, queens and aces lay on the other side of the table.

Truthfully, they were not very bright. Adobe said, "I seen a whole heap of tenderfeet come out here and try to run a blazer. They wound up dead."

"Everybody winds up that way sooner or later," said Ben.

"I open for five," said Luke.

Hump scarcely looked at his cards. "I'll set this one out. Reckon I'll take a short one, meantime." He skedaddled to the bar. Ben saw by the backs of the pasteboards he laid down that he had at least aces paired.

Sligh folded his hand. Adobe glared at Ben, then at his cards. He turned them over. He shouted, "You see that? These here cards are marked. That's how he's been winnin' our *dinero*."

It was obvious, but very sudden. They had been smart enough to figure that after the carnage the deck might be examined. They wanted to clear themselves and regain their money and avenge themselves on Ben.

The chairs went over backwards as Adobe and Sligh moved. Adobe took the lead, standing with shoulders hunched, his hand clawed over the butt of his six-shooter. Sligh hauled sideways, flanking the room, but not drawing as yet. He caught a glimpse of the rifle in Pierce's hands and blinked.

Adobe was shouting, "Give that tenderfoot, mothercheatin', no good yellabelly a gun. I'll learn him he can't come into Texas and steal."

Luke made a casual gesture. From under the skirt of his elaborately tailored, rather full coat, he produced a revolver. It had nestled there, unnoted, in a special leather-lined pocket. He laid the barrel on the table and said, "Here's a gun."

Adobe, taken by surprise, batted his eyes.

In that instant, Ben applied his newly formed theory. He came off his chair, lunging forward. He dove into Adobe as that worthy dropped his right hand to the gun butt.

Sligh, under Luke's observance, dared not move.

Ben came up from a crouch. He had done quite a bit of fisticuffing in his time. The farm boys spent hours at a game called "boxing hats." This was a New Jersey sport which required skill and footwork to prevent an opponent from knocking your hat into the dust.

He had learned from a traveling farm hand and sometime pugilist that the shortest distance between two points is a straight line. Allowing for the dip of the gunman's hand to the butt of the revolver, he shot his right fist at the exposed chin.

Adobe took the punch, staggering. Before he could clear leather, a left hook banged against his jaw. He found himself windmilling for balance, shocked and hurt.

Ben shifted and led with the left. He caught the bridge of Adobe's nose. He snapped it in again, then crossed the right. Adobe, going backwards on high-heeled boots, caromed off the bar. Ben followed closely, aiming to prevent another grab at the revolver.

Adobe canted into him. Ben lowered his sights and lustily pumped both hands to the body. His knuckles were hurting and he had no desire to break a bone, so he lifted his shots above the studded pistol belt, getting to the short ribs, where he dug a right fist which buried itself deep.

Adobe went up on his toes. Then he bent forward, the whisky vomiting from bleeding mouth. Ben lowered the edge of his big fist on the nape of the neck. Adobe flattened out on the floor like a rug.

Luke murmured, "There ends lesson number one, Sligh. Don't go around pickin' on strangers when neighbors are near."

From outside, Miguel was yelling, "The stage! It comes, the stage."

People forgot about Adobe and Ben, running to the door. Luke held down on Sligh for another moment.

He said, "In case you got any ideas, we been playin' your marked cards right along. When he comes to, you better advise your boy that it wouldn't take much for me to ventilate him and you too, just to teach you manners. Adobe, he got off easy. I think he'll live. The way I play it, nobody's goin' to be walkin' around. Any questions?"

Sligh said, "Reckon there's been a slight mistake."

"No harm done," said Luke. He picked up the money, handed Ben his share. They moved to follow the others outdoors. Adobe slept on the floor.

Chapter 8

♦♦♦

Callahan said, "The 6th got in behind the Indians all right. They can't do nothin' when the 6th is in the field agin them."

"That stage was comin' awful fast when it went outa sight behind the trees," Pierce muttered.

"You can hitch up," Manning said to Hump. "You oughta been on your way long ago. Way behind schedule, now."

"You run the station. I run the stage," Hump growled.

The tension had been just beneath the surface of everyone's consciousness. There was a sigh of relief in all of them, even Pierce. Luke remained to one side, keeping an eye on the door in case Adobe should come to and begin blazing away, but he was smiling in that detached way of his, Ben saw.

They could hear the pounding hoofs of the horses, now. There was something disturbing in the cadence. Mrs. Manning and the little photographer came from the kitchen and stood in the background, engrossed in conversation, as if they alone were oblivious to the event.

Silo moved to Pierce and whispered in his ear. The bounty hunter nodded. He still retained his grip on the rifle. The girl looked at him with raised eyebrows and he shook his head. Ben began to feel nervous.

The stage hurtled into view. The horses were running wild, the ribbons hanging loose. On the box, the driver swung with the rattle and bang of whiffletrees. There was no sign of the shotgun. Silo and Miguel crept into the road, staring.

The horses knew the place. They slowed down. Miguel and Silo had no trouble with them.

Hump yelled at the driver, "Hey, there, Matson, what's the news up ahead?"

"To him that's 'back yonder,' " said Shotgun. "How you makin' it, Matson, any old way?"

The horses took their last step, halted. The harness creaked as the backing straps took hold, bringing the stage to a stop.

The driver turned his back to them. As he toppled, full length, turning over, they saw the arrow driven into his spine.

Pierce jumped for the door to the tonneau. He ripped it open.

A trickle of blood seeped over the sill. There was no sound, but there was a definite odor. They all recognized the smell of death.

Myra Manning cried out and turned toward the station, Lamkin supporting her. Gloria Vestal swallowed hard, changing color, then said, "You need help, honey?"

"Nothin' to help," Pierce said. "It was a runnin' fight. Funny they didn't shoot the horses."

There were two men, a woman and a child in the stage, Ben saw. They were all jumbled together where they had been tossed as the driver had made his wild run to escape.

Luke said, "Maybe the messenger gave 'em more'n they wanted. Maybe they didn't know they got the driver. Maybe they just plumb don't care, now they got us surrounded."

Pierce nodded. "Yeah. Somethin' like that."

"Better get us a spade or two," Luke suggested. "I been in one of these things when we didn't get to bury the corpuses. It ain't healthy."

"Yeah," said Pierce. "Shovels. That's right."

"Over by the trees, I'd say." Luke waved an arm. "Not too close, but close enough."

"Yeah," said Pierce. "Might need to use it again right soon."

"I figure," said Luke.

"The Army didn't come in," said Manning dully. He

had trouble taking his eyes from the dead in the stage. "They've got us cut off. The 6th didn't make it."

Callahan said, "They'll make it. All we got to do is get ready. We hold out awhile, they'll make it."

Pierce seemed to come newly alive. He said crisply, "Get these horses into the barn. Start pumpin' water and fill everything that'll hold it. Break out whatever guns and ammunition you got, Manning. Start totin' up the fodder. You, big fellow, get shovels from the barn and start diggin'. Reckon me and Luke better take care of these." He indicated the bodies.

Everyone moved to obey. They had to be doing something, all of them, and Pierce's assumption of leadership seemed natural.

Finding the shovels gave Ben Tyler time to collect himself. The fight and the reaction and then the terrible disappointment of learning the truth about the Indians had left him with his wits addled. He saw Gloria Vestal rummaging in the barn for milk pails and went to help.

She said, "Thanks. I guess all this is new to you."

"Not any barn, that's not new. I'm raised in barns, you might say."

She smiled. "Well, I can't say Indian fightin' is anything I had much experience with. Fact is, I never saw an Indian who'd do more than beg for a drink or some grub."

"You don't seem scared."

"Oh, I'll be scared enough, when I have time to think. If Pierce wasn't here, I'd be plain panicked. Pierce, he knows all there is to know about Comanches."

"So I hear."

She detected the note of disparagment in his voice and said, "All these people here will be glad enough to take orders from him, you saw that. And let me slip you a word, brother. There's worse than Pierce, and could be we got some of them along on this shindig."

She swung out with the pails. He found the second shovel and went to where Luke and Pierce were dragging the bodies beneath the sparse growth of stunted trees. He lined up six feet for each with his eye and began to dig.

Pierce shouted for more help and surprisingly, Manning came. Hump found a short-handled spade and turned to.

Pierce said, "I know it sounds bad, but we ain't got much time. The sun's westerin' fast. I suggest you dig a trench, maybe three feet deep."

"A person's entitled to his six feet," protested Ben. He looked at the bodies lying neatly in a row. "There's a woman and a little girl. It don't seem right."

"They won't know they're sleepin' with men," said Luke. "Pierce is right. There's other work to be done. They can be dug up later . . . maybe."

"Yeah," said Pierce. "Maybe."

He kept looking at the horizon. He did not relinquish the rifle, nor offer to aid in the digging. He was restless, moving to positions where he could see in every direction.

The station was laid out square, single-storied, with narrow embrasures and a flat roof supported by ridgepoles. There was clearing in each direction of the compass except that blanketed by corral and barn.

He decided to line up the stagecoaches and a cart which Manning used around the place into another bulwark of sorts, broadside to the road. It would interfere with a charge on horseback if nothing else. He gave instructions to Silo and Miguel.

Manning was shivering, useless, but agreed to bring in meat from the smokehouse and to pen up his livestock as best he could.

He said, "We ought to burn the outbuildings. But then we'd lose the horses. Might be we can use the horses."

"I doubt it," said Luke.

"Me, too, I doubt it. But we can't turn horses loose for the Comanches," said Pierce. "We can't give them one little thing to make 'em think we're scared. They got to believe we can fight 'em for long enough to spoil the Moon Raid."

Miguel and Silo came to help and Ben relinquished his shovel. "What does that mean?"

"The moon is full tonight," said Pierce. "Comanches, they don't like attackin' at night, but they will. They want to get down into Mexico and back with their horses before the moon wanes.''

"Moon makes night into day any old how," said Luke. "They just as soon die in moonlight, if it's bright enough."

"Apaches and Comanches, they got few superstitions," said Pierce. His eyes never stopped scanning the horizon. "They figure they can get you, they'll hop you."

"Black night, bright moon," agreed Luke. "Like you say. Maybe you better make sure of things inside, Pierce."

"Yeah. Keep your eye peeled?"

"Right."

Pierce moved toward the station like a wild animal, all his senses keyed high. The trench was dug, so Ben helped Miguel and Silo and Callahan roll the bodies into it. They covered them with tarpaulin from the stable and then began shoveling back the dirt.

The little girl looked peaceful. She had been hit by a bullet. Her mother, or whoever it was, had died of an arrow wound, which was harder, Ben thought. It was always nasty when there were women and kids.

The last shovelful of dirt made its mournful, thucking sound, and then Manning turned and faced them. His features were lined and drawn, his eyes were furtive. He spoke in a low, trembling voice.

"Listen. . . . Listen to me."

Hump leaned on the handle of the spade. Luke was wary, frowning a little. Callahan had already gone but Miguel and Silo were at hand, drawn a little apart.

"You . . . Luke Post. You can do it."

"I can? Like what can I do?"

"Pierce." The voice paused, breathless, then rattled on. "It's him. They want him. The Comanches. He's White Eye. You heard of White Eye? That's him. Pierce."

Luke said, "Sure, they want him. Want us, too. Want the horses, a few scalps, the women."

"You could do it. I seen you. I know you're a gunslinger. You could take Pierce any day. Take him and turn him over to the Indians. They'd leave us alone if you did that. They'd go away into Mexico."

Miguel breathed deeply, making a sucking noise, then

tip-toed in the direction of the barn. After a moment, Silo, his black eyes hooded, followed.

Manning chattered, "You and this big fella, you could grab him and make palaver with the Comanches. They'll do anything to get their hands on Pierce."

Ben felt shock to the core of his soul. "Are you crazy, Manning? You got to be crazy."

"It's him or all of us. We can't fight the whole damn Comanche nation. You don't know what they'll do to us. I got a wife in there. I seen what they done to women. They torture men, but what they do to women, it ain't speakable."

Luke said, "Get holt of yourself, Manning. You never saw anything, much. If rape is unspeakable to you, well, O.K. What the Injuns do to women ain't no worse than what they do to men. They aim to hurt, that's their nature. Women don't hurt no worse'n men, even if their parts is different. Main thing is, you're scared of what might happen to you, not your wife, not nobody else."

Ben said, "Turn a man over to save your own skin? Why, you low-lived——"

Luke interrupted him. "Oh, it might work. Pierce is what they're here for. I don't fault Manning for tryin'."

"But Luke, you can't do a thing like that."

"People can do anything to save their skins," said Luke. "I don't rate Pierce very much. Special when it comes to somebody like me. Now me, I rate me real high."

"You can do it," urged Manning. "They'll deal with you for Pierce. I know they will."

"Thing is," said Luke. "I don't rate myself *that* high. No, Manning. You want to turn Pierce in, you do it. Only you'll have to fight Ben, here, too. And maybe some others."

Ben said, "Ugh, this place stinks of the livin' worse than it does of the dead. Let's go."

Luke laughed as they walked toward the station. The sun threw long shadows behind them. The afternoon had run away unnoticed.

Hump stayed behind. Manning was talking to him now, Ben noted at the door to the main building.

He said, "You think anybody would listen to a proposition like that? You really believe that, Luke?"

Luke squinted in the direction of the trees. "Five'll get you ten one man is listenin' right now."

"It just don't seem possible."

"Comanches is bad medicine. You don't know about 'em. Manning, he only knows what he's heard and he's scairt to death."

Ben said, "I'd rather die any kind of death than do a thing like that. I got no special feelin' about Pierce, neither."

Luke said cheerfully, "It ain't no way a sure thing, anyhow. They might take him, then turn around and grab us, too. Comanches ain't to be trusted when there's more of them than there is of you." He winked and added, "Any more'n other folks."

They went indoors.

Chapter 9

♦ ♦ ♦

Pierce seemed to have expanded physically in a short time. Under his orders there were guns and cartridges in orderly rows athwart the windows. Every receptacle was full of water, or being filled with water by willing hands. The furniture had been rearranged to provide shelter against arrows or bullets. Gloria Vestal was tearing sheets into bandages and placing them on the largest table, ominously scrubbed and covered by a blanket and shoved to where it had most protection.

Adobe and Sligh were obeying with the others. Adobe's face was slightly rearranged and he seemed unable to fully straighten his burly frame, testimony to the power of Ben Tyler's fists.

Sligh came to Luke and Ben and said, "Reckon we yanked on the wrong string. Didn't know who you were, Luke."

"You found out."

"Nobody needed to tell us you was somebody," said Sligh dryly. "Adobe's sorry."

"Adobe better come forward," said Luke.

Sligh hesitated, then went across the room to where his partner was cleaning one of Manning's rifles.

Luke said to Ben, "You can listen, but don't believe."

"You mean they don't intend to give up, and leaves us be?"

"Their kind whistles up the breeze," Luke stated firmly. "They come late to the party and they mean harm. No way they try, they can't help it. They are posion."

Adobe lumbered up to them and said gruffly, "Reckon I was wrong. Luke Post nor his friends don't cheat at cards."

Luke said softly, "Other people do, though, don't they?"

"I didn't know who you was."

"That's a damn poor excuse for markin' a deck."

"Just wanted to run a blazer on a tenderfoot," said Adobe, turning sullen. "No call for you to ride it, Luke."

"Fun with a six gun ain't what I'd call real humorous." Luke said. "Somebody's bound to get his death. I'm servin' you with warnin', Adobe. You or your pardner come on one more time and there'll be another trench dug out yonder."

"I said I'm sorry." Adobe swiveled on his heel. Sligh looked worried; he was not the sort to move directly, he was more devious than his friend.

"Trouble," observed Luke, "comes not singly, but like bananas, in bunches."

Lamkin came staggering in under the weight of camera and tripod, brass tube on the front like a small cannon mouth, black cloth flapping at the back, the legs of the tripod swinging.

"Can't leave it in the wagon," he told them seriously. "The damage would be irreparable. There are some cases, too."

Shotgun went out with him and they returned carrying plate cases and other paraphernalia. Lamkin addressed himself to Pierce.

"Could I please place my camera at some vantage point?"

"How's that?" Pierce stared.

"Well, tomorrow, it seems, I'm finally to see Indians. I'd vastly prefer taking their pictures to shooting at them, believe me. I'm an execrable marksman. I'm afraid I close my eyes when I pull the trigger."

"Mister," Pierce said, "when the time comes, you won't have to be no sharpshooter. They'll be in so close you couldn't miss 'em if you tried."

Lamkin thought about this for a moment. "I see. Then, if it's no trouble, may I also mount the camera? Perhaps— before they got near enough—I could get a picture. Then I will do whatever you say."

"A shotgun," said Pierce. He indicated one of Manning's collection. "Take that one. Your window'll be yonder."

Ben noted that the shotgun was a double-barreled, sawed-off piece, ugly as sin. It would be loaded for bear, of course. The station might be well-defended, at that. He noted Pierce was looking to the ceiling and followed his gaze. There was a trap door.

"Manning . . . Manning, where you at?" Pierce called.

The stationmaster came from the kitchen. He was scared down to the soles of his boots, Ben recognized.

"Get the ladder that reaches to that trap."

"It's in the barn. I don't have no call to get on the roof much."

"I didn't ask where it is. Just fetch it. They'll be firing us up if they can. It's their favorite stunt. Now, the rest of you. Got your places?"

The windows were tall and narrow and faced out on three sides of the main room. The kitchen had two, the four bedrooms one each. Ben chose a window next to Luke. Callahan was on his other side, looking out toward the plains. Miguel and Silo prowled the barn and corral.

Pierce was saying, "Just as long as we present an even fire from all sides, that's the best we can do."

"Hold 'em awhile," Callahan said with assurance. "If we hold 'em awhile, the 6th will get here."

No one believed him. Lamkin was setting his tube onto the tripod. Myra was in the kitchen, as though she felt safer in this familiar place. Hump and Shotgun had been assigned to the bedroom windows.

Pierce said, "There's enough food for all the time we're likely to need it. Miz Manning'll try and have it ready when anybody's hungry."

It was quite dark now, and Ben felt the stirring of his appetite. He went toward the kitchen, listening to Pierce.

"We got an abundance of shells, seems like. Manning had a store and with what we got from the coaches and what I had, we needn't worry too much. Only don't nobody start firin' before they're within range. They'll try to make you do that but it's pure amazin' how they can estimate rifle range and stay just outside it."

Manning had returned with the ladder and was putting it in place. He said shrilly, "They haven't hit us yet! I haven't seen any Comanches. Just 'cause they got the stage and people keep talkin' about them. How do we know they're coming here? How do we know?"

Pierce took him by the arm, not urgently. "Tell you what, Manning. You go into the bedrooms and help them fellows. It's quiet-like in there and you can talk it over with them. Might take some whisky. Not too much drinkin', though. We don't want anybody gettin' too brave."

He walked with Manning, gentling him as if he were dealing with a refractory or spooked horse. He was a man for taking charge, Ben thought, never mind anything else about him.

In the kitchen Mrs. Manning was wasting no motions. She had a pot of soup on the back of the stove big enough to last ten people several days. She had a roast of beef steaming on the end of a butcher's block which Manning had somehow acquired. The smell of pork came from the oven, where a young pig was turning brown.

There were potatoes and onions and the shelves were lined with canned tomatoes and peaches. The stove was iron and had a good draft, Ben saw with his farmer's eye. They could keep it going without danger through a siege. It didn't seem likely that anyone was going to go hungry.

He cut off a slice of beef and put it between two slices of the bread on the table. He carried it outside into the main room and saw Lamkin eye it, then move to follow his example.

Gloria smiled at him and he swallowed and grinned back at her.

She moved within conversational distance and said, "Nothing interferes with your eatin' habits, I see."

"I'm a big man, I need food."

"You do run to size," she nodded. "Comes in handy with shoats like Adobe around."

"I reckon it does."

"You travelin' with Luke?"

"Sort of. I got a place left to me, northwest of El Paso. Ranch, couple hundred acres."

"Left to you? Your folks Texans?"

He had to tell her about Bob, then. Pierce returned, glanced at them, went about his preparations. Ben began to help with the bandages as they talked. It was really easy, talking to this friendly girl.

They finished all the available material fit to bind a wound. She thought she might eat and they went into the kitchen and Mrs. Manning had some soup, so he joined her. They laughed together, and it seemed as though they were old acquaintances. She spoke freely about Pierce, as if it was assured that they were to be married sometime.

The moon was rising to its full glory and it seemed natural enough that, finished with the soup, they should drift outdoors. The Comanches were, if any place in their minds, very remote. They could see Silo and Miguel, shadowy figures flitting from building to corral, flaring out, pausing, listening, going on.

She said, "If the Comanches don't come . . . But they will. They're after Pierce, you know."

"Manning said so." He didn't tell her about Manning's idea of giving up Pierce to the Indians.

They were silent for a moment. They found themselves near the fence of the corral, then heard Silo speak soothingly to the horses.

Miguel's voice came, "Son of a Comanche, are you there?"

"*Sí*," said Silo. "You be sure coyote is coyote."

"You no run to Comanche? For sure?"

"You will run first."

"I no run. I kill. I enjoy to kill."

"You see Comanche, you run."

"I see him, I shoot."

"You no shoot. You scare, you run."

There was a long wail from the plains. Miguel said, "That coyote, for sure."

"Coyote run. Like *Mexicano*."

"They run join Comanche, like breed."

Silo was silent a moment, then, "Miguel."

"*Sí*, son of Comanche?"

"*Mi madre* . . . she *Mexicana*, Miguel."

There seemed to be no answer forthcoming from Miguel. Gloria and Ben moved toward the house. The moonlight had grown sharper and there was a place between the main hall and the bedroom windows to the rear which was safe from view. It was also shadowed and dark in this spot and they stood against the wall and talked in conspiratorial whispers.

She said, "They'll come, the Indians. They'll attack us."

"You reckon?" He felt the sexuality of her. It had been a long time, not since Kansas City, and he hadn't much cared for the whores. This one, he thought, was different.

"We'll be lucky if we get through it." She sighed. They were alone and to be alone with a man like this did things to her. She began to play upon him. She could not help it any more than she could help breathing. She needed only some small justification and this was at hand. "Not that it makes much difference. I mean, where you get it, and when."

"It makes a difference to me. I don't want it to happen at all, not now, not soon."

"Oh, sure. Only, well . . . for me, what is there?" Pierce had ignored her all day. Impatience with him, anger at her uncertain relationship with him, were a handle for her driving desire for Ben. "Pierce. I keep thinkin' we'll get married. What a laugh. I just keep foolin' myself."

"Why?" He knew she wanted something. He wasn't sure, but he knew enough to play along. "Why put up with him?"

" 'Cause I'm a woman, I suppose. Pierce is around, when he ain't chasin' Comanches."

"There's other men. From what I hear and beggin' your pardon, better men."

"You don't have to excuse yourself to me. I know about Pierce. Indian hater. Bounty hunter." Then she couldn't resist the impulse to be somewhat fair about it. "Texans mostly figure if you kill an Indian, that's fine. Only you shouldn't take money for it."

"It don't set right, you know. Killin' for money."

"I've seen a man killed for ten dollars. I've seen a man stabbed over a two-bit bet on a faro layout," she blurted.

"Wherever did you see anything like that?" he was bewildered.

This farmer from the East couldn't know anything about her, of course. He saw the gray serge, which was decent enough, and her face, which was young enough, although God knows it could be better; and her hands which were soft and her eyelashes which she had fluttered at him when there was light enough to see. To him she was a lady.

"You see a lot in El Paso, places like that. You can't be blind to it," she said.

"You shouldn't have to look at things like that." His voice was decisive. "You shouldn't be going with a man like Pierce."

"It's nice of you to think that. Real nice." She moved closer to him in the darkness. She had been, for her, a very good girl since getting Pierce's message to come to Comanche Station. There were, however, certain areas in her which needed assuaging. It had always been like that. This man did not treat her as a piece of property, he met her on common ground. This gave her confidence while it added to her desire.

She could never quite clearly understand times like this. Leaving aside her real anger and resentment over Pierce, there were other depths which she tried not to explore. It had always been like this. No matter how many tales she told, and she was even now swiftly running over one to tell Ben, the pool inside her stirred to angry boiling without volition. What did Pierce always say when he had a few drinks and they were holed up in some city hotel? "You make 'em all turn around and look. They know you, what's in you, every man on the street." Fresh rage against Pierce rose in her.

She said, "You really think I could do better, Ben?"

Her upturned face was a pale oval which swam a little in his suddenly misty vision. Her message had reached him. If he wanted to quit, now was the time to play dumb. He was as honest as the next man, he didn't want to take advantage, not even of Pierce. Right now was the moment to turn her off, get back inside the station.

He couldn't do it. She was exciting, she was pretty. He said, "I sure do. I think you're makin' a big mistake."

"I made a mistake before, when I was a young girl." The fairy tale was beginning to take familiar form in her mind. "I—I couldn't afford another one."

"Lots of people make mistakes. I was married once, and it was all wrong. It started wrong and it didn't get any better."

"Imagine us, scarcely knowin' one another, standin' here, talkin' like this!" Every word was a deliberate invitation. She moved closer to him. The contact was delicious, she prolonged it, pushing a little at his bulk, talking. He did not give way.

She told him about the preacher's son, her version. She did it well, with feeling. She began to believe it, then, to believe everything she was now imagining herself. This was when it was best, when she could manage to work herself into this state. If she believed it hard enough maybe it would be true, she thought.

She wanted it to be true. Within her durable whore's soul was the wish to make it work out right, to offer some vague compromise to life. She had tried it with Pierce and knew that it would never come true. This strong, simple farmer would be different. She knew it. She could handle him. She could handle Pierce, too, when the time came, so that he would not kill Ben. In fact, Pierce might not even make a fuss. You could never tell about him.

All the time she was thinking, she was telling her story. She finished on a tremulous note, referring back to the preacher's son who had undone her.

Ben said, "He was a skunk for not marryin' you."

"It wasn't all that simple." Now that the story was ended she could scarcely keep her hands off him.

"Nothin' should have stopped him."

"His father put a dirty name on me. I blame the father. A preacher and all." Her mind wouldn't stop, reminding her that the father had been a henpecked weakling and that the mother had recognized her for what she was and had run her out of town.

Ben was feeling the impact of her nestling against him.

He was sorry for her, he felt real emotion, a desire to protect her. Yet also he now saw her as damaged goods and this, far from repelling him, increased his desire for her. Beyond where they huddled in the shadow the moon was bright and cold.

He pulled her close in one arm and said, "I woulda married you."

"I bet you wouldn't." Her lips were soft, turned up to him.

"I would, too. A girl like you."

"I'm nothin', much." She was hot as fire. This was what Pierce meant, of course. It wasn't bad, she cried silently, it was what every woman should be. She could control it if she had a good reason.

He was finding the right spots now, with his strong hands, exploring her body. She stared around.

Silo and Miguel were patrolling, which cut off the barn from their use. Indoors was out of the question. She began to feel desperation.

Ben had a grip on her, swinging her weight to him. The serge of the dress had convenient openings. She wore little or nothing underneath and her skin was fiery hot. They swayed together, making small sounds in the night.

"You're so strong," she whispered. "I love it."

"Where can we go?"

Talk, talk, talk, she thought. She said, "You won't think anything bad of me?"

He kissed her, then. It was like drowning in a well of warm sex.

He was lonely, he was ready for it. Pictures began to form in his mind. The ranch he had never seen became a stronghold in which he could keep and defend this precious piece of womanhood. He saw small, happy children clambering on his knee.

He also felt the wiriness and toughness and the demands of the small body which knew marvelous ways of moving to him. The serge skirt was above the waist. Her back was against the wall, she was thrusting herself to him. He reached down and lifted and they were together, Gloria helping him with nimble fingers.

The moment came sharp and clear.

She leaned far back until her shoulders were solid against the wall. It had to be quick and she didn't want to display too much experience. When he discovered that she had left off her drawers, she thought, it was all right. The preacher's son had known what to do, surely this big son of the soil was better and smarter than the fumbling boy.

Chapter 10

♦♦♦

Inside the station, Pierce counted again the things necessary for defense. He went into the bedrooms and made sure Manning was contained with the bottle of whisky. He found this weak vessel slumbering. Hump and Shotgun swore they preferred it that way. Manning like to talk them to death, they said, but did not mention the subject matter of his speech.

Returning to the main room, he sought Luke Post. He asked, "You think Adobe and Sligh will give us trouble?"

"Any time they think they see a way."

"We need their guns."

"And more besides."

Callahan was telling Lamkin, as the latter fussed with his camera, "The 6th'll make it. They wouldn't never have had me report in Texas if they wasn't around some place."

Pierce said, "The sergeant beleives it."

"He's heard about how the cavalry always gets there," said Luke. "What he ain't heard is how many times the bloomin' troop is too late with too little."

Pierce said, "If the Army had enough men and horses it couldn't stop Comanche raids. Comanches can make a peace today and hit a rancheria tonight."

"I've had little to do with them," said Luke. "Ask me about the Sioux, now, and I can tell you plenty. The Sioux can't drink whisky, but otherwise he's quite a critter."

"Comanches drink tiswin, when they can get it," said Pierce. He hadn't talked to a man like Post in a long while. He seldom had much conversation anyway, but somehow he now felt expansive. Perhaps because today people had listened to him, obeyed him without question, not people like Dutch and the Kid, either. "It's an Apache booze. All Indians'll drink liquor and none I ever seen could handle it."

"When do you figure they're goin' to hit us?"

"Any time, now. The moonlight is good enough. I got to set watches." He went on carefully, "Maybe you got some ideas?"

"I'm copperin' your play," said Luke. "I'm also keepin' awake with some slight difficulty. I could use some shut-eye. Otherwise, you call your shots."

Pierce hesitated, then said in a low voice, "I reckon you know we can't hold 'em long?"

"I know."

"What'll happen in El Paso when your stage don't get in?"

"Well, not much. Somebody'll say it's too bad the Injuns got it. Some'll say shouldn't they do somethin'? Then they'll likker up. Then maybe there'll be a telegraph sent to Austin. If there is any troops around, some real smart fella might go and tell 'em about it. Along about next week if everything goes right well, they might send out a party."

"That's what I figured. I been out there around the hills for a while, and seen no sign of cavalry. Way I look at it, nobody's goin' to get here in time."

"How many you really reckon is out there?"

"Aplenty. They didn't even bother with the photographer and his wagon, or Adobe and Sligh. Just chivvied them in here, way I see it. Get us all in one grab. It ain't often they work like that."

"They mean business," agreed Luke. "When they do take a notion and follow it through, they're plain snake bite."

"Better save a bullet for each of the women," Pierce said darkly.

"Why only the women? Anybody dumb enough to fall into their laps alive deserves what he gets," said Luke. "Howsomever, we'll give 'em something to remember. This here's a sturdy place. Bar accidents, there'll be a heap of 'em come to judgment before they get us."

"I better look around and figure out the watches," Pierce said.

The man was taking his responsibility seriously, Luke thought, and he would do a good job. Callahan was all right, too. Hump and Shotgun were veterans.

He missed Ben, wondered where he was, then saw that Gloria was not present and permitted himself a small smile. He decided to postpone his nap and went into the kitchen for some coffee. Lamkin joined him there and Myra was slightly disappointed because Luke chose not to leave her alone with the photographer.

Pierce finished his rounds about that time and also missed Gloria. He had decided to take the first watch. The Comanches were too quiet. They should have shown themselves by now, and it was even Stephen they would strike early. He went outside to look around.

Silo and Miguel were on the job. They had not seen Gloria, they said. Pierce began to worry.

He cut swiftly around the edge of the building. In the darkness he saw movement, and immediately he brought up his rifle.

Gloria cried, "Don't shoot. It's only us."

Then he saw Tyler. The big man was making quick motions with his hands, which might have had to do with the arrangement of clothing. Pierce lifted the rifle again, then paused.

He had no illusions about Gloria. If there was anything going on, he believed, it couldn't be much and she would be mostly to blame. She just didn't think anything of making up to a man.

She said, "We were taking a walk. The moon is so pretty and you were busy."

"The Comanches think the moon is pretty, too. Pretty good for night attack," said Pierce. She'd been up to something, all right. Later he'd get after her. "You better go inside."

Tyler came out of the shadows then, and Pierce saw resentment in him. He couldn't use the rifle on the man, and he knew it wouldn't do to fight him here and now. Not that he was scared of Tyler's fists. He knew some Indian tricks that could make better men than Tyler holler calf rope. He said, extemporizing, "You and me got the first watch, Tyler. You better get a rifle."

"Now, just a minute—"

A wild scream cut off forever anything Ben might have had to say. Pierce snapped, "Get inside, I tell you!"

It was at the corral. They had come in without Silo or Miguel being able to detect them, which was extraordinary and meant the cream of the Comanche young braves was on this first raid.

Pierce heard Tyler lumbering behind him, unarmed and virtually useless, but it was too late to stop. The horses were already piling through bars let down on the far side of the corral. Silo's rifle sounded from somewhere near the barn. It had been Miguel who screamed. Pierce knew the Mexican's voice.

The rear guard was shooting back at Silo. Pierce caught sight of a figure in moonlight and knelt, taking careful aim. He hit dead center and the Indian flew backwards as though blown by the wind, his death cry keening on the night.

Wild shots came from the station and Pierce cursed. He was in as much danger from friends as enemies. Moonlight is bright but tricky. He moved, trying to find a spot to level off at the fleeing horses and riders.

Tyler blundered past him, stumbled and fell. Pierce then saw Miguel, doubled over on the ground. He had been knifed, to prevent sound, but had managed his last yell. Otherwise it would have been rough going. The young ones seldom were satisfied unless they successfully stole the horses, then killed someone.

Silo must have nailed one of them. As Tyler groped his way to his feet, a prone figure which had lain in shadows came up and over, arching like a leaping trout, a blade shining in his grasp.

Pierce fired again. Tyler stepped back and the Comanche barely missed him with a final sweep of the knife, then fell and was still.

Ben called, "Pierce? They got Miguel. Cut his throat."

"I know it. Get down!"

Tyler knelt, fumbling around for a weapon. He came up with a smoothbore musket, empty, discarded by one of the Indians. He clubbed it, looking for an enemy.

Silo came gliding from the barn. A shot from the house almost clipped him.

Pierce yelled at the station, "Cease firing, damn it!"

Silo said, "Miguel not know coyote from Comanche."

The horses were gone, the Comanches were gone. Miguel was gone. Pierce knew they should have killed the horses and burned the barn and the corral. He felt guilty for not insisting on it.

People were coming now, with flares. He shouted at them, "Go back. Put out those torches."

He couldn't stop them. Even Callahan was out there. Manning, shivering, expecting the worst, was nevertheless first to arrive, gawking at the two dead Indians, at Miguel. Gloria stood in the background and Pierce noted that Tyler went straight to her.

Luke Post was trying to herd them back. The young braves might foresee just such a contingency and return in a wild ride to take advantage.

Raging, Pierce pulled his knife. He took the first scalp without thinking.

Then he realized what he had done. It was one thing to bring in dried hair. It was another to strip it right in front of people to whom the sight was strange, even horrible. He felt the wave of varied emotions which came from them.

Still kneeling, he looked at each and every one of them in the moonlight. He saw Gloria's revulsion, saw her hand dig into the arm of the big farmer from Jersey. He saw Manning's moist-lipped fascination, Callahan's soldierlike disapproval.

He arose, went grimly to the other Comanche corpse. Defiantly, he took the scalp. Dangling the two gory trophies, he said, "I'll just put these with the two Miguel hung for me in the barn."

He walked away from them. The difference between him and other people had never been so blatant. It infuriated him, but it shook him in another sense also. He had not sought to be a man apart. It was no pleasure to him that they looked upon him with eyes that did not see what he saw, did not convey to the brain the things that he could not escape.

He heard Luke say, "We better haul poor Miguel over to the buryin' ground. The Injuns too, I reckon. Can't plant 'em until daylight, but it'd be better if they were over yonder."

Then he was in the barn, and he thought alone, until he saw Silo.

The breed said, "You take hair. Good!"

"You want yours?" he offered one of the scalps.

Silo shook his head. "Not take. My father was Comanche. Want to take! No take."

"I see. You'd like to, but it wouldn't be right on account of your old man was a Comanche."

"*Sí*, Señor Pierce. You take. Good!"

It was a fine point, but Pierce thought he understood. Silo was only part savage. He had never lived with his father's people. He only hated them because they had wronged his mother, left her to bear a bastard son in a land where she could not ever marry, therefore could not survive.

He hooked the scalps on his wires. He would have liked to stay with Silo for a while and compose himself, but there was work to be done. There were fools afoot and they must learn to take orders or they would be dead, and he would be dead with them.

They had all gone indoors when he approached the station. Only Tyler awaited him, a rifle at trail under his left arm. Pierce grunted, remembering that he had set the first watch for the two of them.

"You walk this way. I'll walk that route. Silo'll handle the barn. He's plenty smart, Silo."

"O.K."

They walked in opposite directions around the building.

Chapter 11

♦♦♦

Indoors there were signs of unrest. Luke wanted to sleep, knowing what was ahead. He saw Lamkin wander into the kitchen and Manning's wife sitting at the table, looking straight ahead, dazed.

He saw Adobe and Sligh, heads together, in a corner where Pierce had slung his saddlebag. They had come outside later than the others, there was about them now a bullish, conspiratorial air.

Shotgun and Hump had gone to their bedroom posts. There were pallets on the floor between main room and sleeping quarters for those who could lie down.

Callahan said to him, "The 6th'll make it. You see if I ain't right. They must have been held up some place in the hills north of here. Maybe they had to fight a detachment of this here force. They'll get through."

"Sergeant, you're a veteran," said Luke curiously. "Do you truly believe that?"

"I been infantry. I been artillery. That's where I learned to ride, light artillery. I seen Jeb Stuart ride around us when I was with McClellan. I seen Mosby ride in Virginia. I seen Sheridan's troop and Pleasanton's. Then I was with the 6th. I know what cavalry can do."

The man did believe it. Luke shook his head. "You're talkin' about a war. This ain't war. This is murder. The Comanches know where the 6th is at. They wouldn't be hittin' here, even for a prize like Pierce, if there was considerable troops around."

"They'll get here," said Callahan. "I know it in me bones."

"It better be quick," sighed Luke. "It better be real quick."

He turned toward the bedrooms. The girl was there, her back against the wall, sitting on one of the mattresses, her legs straight out. There was a candle in a wall bracket and he could see that she was excited.

He dropped to the makeshift bed next to her. "Walkin' out with Ben Tyler, wasn't you?"

She turned her head too quickly, spoke with too much emphasis. "What's it to you? You own him or something?"

"He's a hell of a man," said Luke softly. "You know Sadie Forest, in El Paso?"

"Sure, I know Sadie. Yellow hair. Works for the mayor in that restaurant of his."

"You know Cora Beesom?"

"I worked with her."

"Me and Cora, we hit it off some."

"I know about you and Cora. Wonder you wouldn't marry the girl."

Luke chuckled, settling down on the blankets. "Me, I'm like Pierce. Move around too much for marryin'."

"You're damn right. You and Pierce. Indians or cards, it don't make any difference."

"Only Cora ain't like you. She ain't smart."

"Cora's all right. She's got a big heart. When I was sick that time she took care of me."

"Until you could get back on your butt?"

She jerked convulsively, then lowered her head despairingly. "I had a good doctor. I'm cured."

"There ain't no real cure," he told her coldly. "Oh, sure, it seems like you're all right. But you know there ain't no cure for consumption of the lungs."

"There is. The Doc said so. I'm strong. I'm all right. He said so."

Luke said, "I been thinkin' about Sadie. And Ben Tyler. He's got hisself a spread. If the stock is gone down, or run off, I can see it gets replaced. He needs a woman. He's a man wants a woman."

She made a defensive gesture and then he was sure about what had happened outside. Worry nibbled at him.

He said, "Me, I like people. Always did. Never could stand ridin' the range, all alone, just the cattle. Many a night I dealt the cards to myself, learnin' my business, reckonin' the odds on poker hands, wishin' there was someone to talk to about it."

"Practicin' with your gun, too," she said harshly.

"There's all kinds of people. A dead man can't enjoy them, he can't learn much, now, can he? I aim to stay alive and improve myself some. Meantime, if I like a man I stand by him."

"And if you don't, you shoot him."

He shook his head. "That ain't true. I've taken care of them that came after me. Mainly I hated to do it. Gave lots of 'em first shot."

"Because you know they're wild," she said. "Because you're cold in a fight. I know you, Luke Post. You're always figurin'. Give 'em first shot, sure. They see you sittin' there, like you are, and it gets 'em. They think they got to fling lead fast. They always miss."

"Someday maybe a man won't miss. You got to play the odds," said Luke.

"I saw Jake Pulski killed. He fired four shots at Lindeman before Lindeman fired one. They ran around the tables in the Pioneer Saloon for hours, seemed like. Lindeman nearly emptied his gun before he got Jake." She paused, then said, "I forgot. You shot Lindeman."

"Yeah. He missed me, one time. But gettin' back to Sadie, I figure her and Ben, maybe—"

She broke in, "I got as much rights as Sadie. Or anybody else."

"You got your eye on Ben because Pierce won't marry you."

"That's my business, Luke. You got no call to butt in."

"Maybe I ain't. I got nothin' against you, much. Course I aim to see the Doc, about your lungs."

"Ben's a good man. I could be a wife to a good man. You don't know me, Luke Post. You don't know what's inside me."

He recognized the struggle, the pain, the reaching out. She had ambitions and he was not a man to go blindly against anyone who wanted to get ahead. "No, I don't know you that good."

"I want a life."

"On a ranch? Totin' water, tendin' chickens and pigs? Your hands in lye soap? Your skin dried by the sun, your back bent? You sure, Gloria?"

"If it's a life, with the right man."

She believed it. He did not. He could always recognize a block in the road.

He said quietly, "All right, Gloria."

"You mean you won't say anything to him?"

"I'm not promisin' nothin'."

"I'll show you. You'll see. Look at the other folks here. They're scared or they're tryin' to figure a way out. They're scared of dyin'. I ain't."

"You sure of that?"

"There'll be a thousand Indians out there shootin' at us tomorrow morning. You know it and I know it. Wait and see."

"Kinda foolish, us arguin' about the future," grinned Luke. "May not be any."

"You don't believe that and neither do I."

"I reckon few people can see their own death." He lay down and prepared to sleep. "Me, I always figured to get it in a barroom or on a town street. Injuns, I never figured."

"It won't happen," she said. She had not altered her position. "Some of us'll get killed. Not you, nor me."

"You got a big belief, sister." He was already half-asleep.

"And if I do get it, I won't go scared." It was a simple statement of fact. "Nothin' is worse than what I've been and the way I've lived. Why should I be scared?"

"Don't talk yourself into it," he advised sleepily.

She still sat there, her head back against the wall, as he drifted off to sleep. He had stopped thinking about her. Something was gnawing at him, about Adobe and Sligh. When he woke up he would have to keep any eye on them. . . . He drifted off.

Adobe saw Sligh listening to Manning, pondering in his slow way. He didn't care about Manning, the stationmaster was a real no-account. Getting mixed up with him could cause even more trouble.

It was true that Sligh had ridden with El Segundo along the border. That was a cutthroat bunch. Wouldn't think Sligh could make it with El Segundo's people. It was a way out, all right, if they could get down to the border.

Manning was talking it up, all right. Now Sligh came over to the corner where Adobe waited. He said, ''Manning's got the idea. The Injuns'll take him and we'll be able to get away clean.''

''How do you know that?''

''Look, the Comanches want Pierce. They don't want us.''

''They goddam well want everything. I know them bastards.''

''They'll take Pierce. Look, even if they only stop to slice him up, we can get away. El Segundo knows me. We can get down in the country there, and sell the scalps.''

''How many, again?''

''Twenty-two. Countin' those in the barn.''

Adobe totted up on his fingers, but his mind couldn't quite make it. ''I need a pencil and paper.''

''You need a new brain in your head.''

Adobe couldn't concentrate too long on any one thing. ''What about Luke?''

''He won't make no play to help Pierce.''

''Can I kill the farmer?''

''Maybe. If it works that way.''

It still didn't seem right. ''I don't like it.''

''Manning's got it figured, I tell you.''

''It don't smell right.''

Sligh altered his tone. ''You want to stick here until the cavalary maybe comes in?''

''Ain't goin' to be no cavalry.''

''You hope there ain't. We got bad enough luck lately. We ain't had any good luck since you downed that corporal.''

''I didn't go for to kill the fool. He was drunk. I only wanted his poke. He hadn't been drunk, he wouldn't of tried nothin' and he'd be alive today." Adobe felt the need to defend himself.

"We've been through all that."

"Dumb goddam horse soldier."

"He belonged to the 6th. You know the way they are."

"Goddam the 6th, too." When he was pushed, or felt wrong, Adobe became flustered and his mind wouldn't work at all.

Sligh said patiently. "All right. Here's our chance to get squared away. Manning's got it figured. We go along with him and his play against Pierce and then grab the scalps. There's got to be a time when they're palaverin' or somethin' when we can grab ponies and ride south."

Adobe was tired of arguing. "O.K. Only I don't like it."

"We won't be alone. Everybody'll be glad to get off the hook, once it's done."

"O.K., then. I'll play along."

"Manning's scared enough to be good in there."

"All right, all right!"

Sligh remained patient, going over the whole thing in his own mind, warily regarding Adobe. The big man was unpredictable. "You can kill the farmer before we leave."

"You damn right I'll kill him."

Sligh took a look around the big room. Callahan was polishing a rifle barrel. Hump, Shotgun, and Manning were in the bedrooms. Pierce and the farmer were on patrol. The girl and Luke were sleeping. In the kitchen were Mrs. Manning and Lamkin. . . .

Mrs. Manning was saying, "Miguel was a good and faithful servant. It's not right he should lay out there on the ground."

"A dead person with whom we are not closely acquainted is merely a corpse," Lamkin mused. "Tragedy lies in knowledge."

"Are you a religious man?" she asked timidly. That was what she wanted, knowledge of him.

"Not in the formal sense. I am a nature lover, of course." He had not thought about it in years. "I believe in God."

"Pa was an all-out hell-and-damnation preacher," she confessed. "I was raised on the Bible."

"If you believe in it at all, I'm sure it's quite comforting."

"It's my staff." She bowed her head. She did not want him to know how very much she needed support. She felt that it would draw pity from him. She boldly confessed to herself that pity was not what she desired.

He was a man too sensitive not to understand that more lay behind her words than she would have him know. He was worn, he was lonely, and he was unsure of himself. This excursion to the West in which he had placed not only his small funds but his waning strength and purpose could well be, within twenty-four hours, the end of him. Myra Manning looked fair to him and he spoke very softly, "This is not a place for you. Only very strong people can survive in outposts. Or very ignorant people, perhaps."

"I'm not clever." She faltered. She must be careful not to speak ill of Manning. "I would prefer town life."

"I wonder if I am not making a mistake." he went on. "Is it worth while to try to focus on history? The War, that was different. I was there, it was unavoidable. Why do I seek history in a wilderness?"

"Maybe you would be better off in a town, too. Maybe you could set up a shop." It was piercingly pleasant to plan for him.

"I'd still be alone." He shook his head. "Some people are fated to be lonely."

She wanted to tell him of another loneliness, coupled with repugnance for the person of its sharing. She wanted to spill out her soul to him because he was kindly, but most of all because he was the only person she had ever met who would understand. She did not have the words.

They sat together, each thinking the same things, each prevented from expressing innermost thoughts. There was as much communion between them in this interim among violences as though they had been legally mated.

She did not even remember, for that time, that Manning existed. . . .

*   *   *

Manning awoke with his head swollen on the inside and his tongue fuzzy and thick. He squirmed on the bed in half remembrance of a nightmare in which Indians were attacking him in droves.

When he got up, however, he could think and maneuver, for he had not taken that much whisky, it was just that he could not stand very much. He oriented himself and crept to the hall, where by the candlelight he could see Luke and Gloria sleeping.

He went back into another bedroom and said, "Hump? Shotgun?"

"Yeah."

"Where's everybody?"

"Pierce and Tyler are on patrol," said Shotgun. "The others, they're around."

Manning sat on the edge of a bed and rubbed his thinning hair, then smoothed it back as best he could. "I'm right about Pierce. You know I'm right."

"Mebbe."

"Look, we got to think about it. Them two, Adobe and Sligh. They agree. With us three, we could do it. We could."

"Mebbe."

"You wanta be killed? You wanta mebbe be captured and get your balls sliced off while you watch? You wanta be burned on the chest, staked out on the plain, them red devils laughin' at you?"

"We got no guarantee it'll work. Luke Post said it might not work."

"Indians ain't no different than nobody else. They come here for Pierce. They come out of their way for him. They aim to hit in Mexico, like always. Only they want him first. He's a bounty hunter. Nobody gives a damn about a bounty hunter. We got a right to turn him over."

"I ain't stickin' up for Pierce. I'd just a dumb sight rather have him on my side if we got to fight Comanches."

"It stands to reason. All of us against him. Why should we have to die because of him?"

"The cavalry could get here," muttered Shotgun uncertainly.

"If we did make the deal, people'd talk," said Hump.

"Let 'em talk. Just as many'd say we were right. A bounty hunter agin decent folks. His life for ours."

"I dunno."

Manning felt weakness in them kindred to his own. "Look. I got Adobe and Sligh to go along. You'll side us?"

"Well . . . mebbe."

He sensed that they wouldn't fight it. That might be enough. Adobe and Sligh were tough. Lamkin meant nothing. The women didn't count. Luke Post was asleep. Pierce was outdoors with the farmer and they could handle the big Easterner if they got the drop on him.

His mind seething with the idea, he stumbled out of the bedroom, and tiptoed past Luke and Gloria. Callahan, he thought, they could handle him too, he was a dumb one. Silo was a breed, they should shoot him, and no one the wiser. Oh, it would work all right. If only he could hold Adobe and Sligh in line.

Chapter 12

◆◆◆

Ben Tyler looked out over the countryside for a distance he could not estimate, so clear was the moon almost at full. There were shadows sharp around barn and corral in which Silo moved on his watch. It was eerie and unreal, walking up and down outside the squat, square way station.

He came face to face with Pierce. Neither man spoke. Ben about-faced and retraced his steps. It was a retreat, in a way, because he could not help feeling guilty.

Hasty as it was, the act with the girl had been consummated. He felt that between them there had passed something more than the deed itself. He could not explain it. He just felt there was in Gloria something which he had never possessed but always wanted, as if he knew the answers to unasked questions and was satisfied.

There remained the fact of Pierce. He was not prepared for Pierce as yet. He was not afraid. He simply did not know how he should proceed.

Time passed and the newness and strangeness of the moonlit night in Texas diminished and his eyes grew accustomed to the surroundings. With familiarity came a natural relaxation. When he met Pierce, he said, "It's a bright moon."

The bounty hunter grunted and turned on his heel. Pierce was thinking hard, and he was off balance and he knew why. It was the way people had looked at him when he took the scalps.

He had hitherto not minded, moving about always, keeping his own counsel, bottling up inside him the worm which ate at his gizzard. Gloria did not know. No one knew.

Now he was cornered and it could well be the end of him, as he knew better than the others, and the worm was gnawing through him. He had never felt need of justification, but this was different. He was satisfied to live without the approval of people. The thing was different, this was dying. If only one person understood, if he could spell it out for someone, maybe it would help.

He met Tyler again, and it was as if the two of them were alone on a vast plain, with no safe destination. He said abruptly, without thought, out of his inner confusion, "You got no call foolin' around Gloria."

The big farmer glowered. "I don't see no ring on her finger."

"That's none of your damn business."

"I don't see no chain around her neck."

"There's things no man can see. Stay away from her."

Tyler growled, "And what are you goin' to do about it if I don't?"

"I ain't dumb enough to kill you while you're needed," said Pierce. "Later, we'll see about it."

They separated, then came back together again. Tyler said, "It's up to Gloria, ain't it?"

"Just leave it up to her."

"What have you got for her?" persisted Tyler. "You think you got anything good for her?"

"What I got, she likes."

"Then let her decide if she wants to stick with it. And I'll be honest with you, Pierce. Any man goes around killin' people and sellin' their scalps, I got no use for."

Pierce seized on one word of the speech. "*People?* Comanches? *People?*"

"Well, they walk and talk and have babies and for all I know, they go to heaven like anybody else. Or to hell, for that matter."

The inner urge seized Pierce and shook him. Even then he did not forget the watch, he clutched Tyler's arm and they walked together. He did not let go of the big arm in his vehemence, his voice was almost pleading, "Comanches ain't people. I ought to know. I lived with 'em seven years."

"There's been people lived with Indians. I read about it back East. They learned to get along with Indians."

"You read about 'em." Pierce despaired. But he had to explain to someone, he had to tell how it really was. He could no longer prevent himself. The cork was out of the bottle and perhaps this way he could rid himself of the worm.

"The people in Washington break treaties with the Indians," Ben was saying. "All the way back to the Cherokees and the Trail of Tears, we been breakin' promises to 'em."

"And you think for one goddam minute they keep their promises? Not unless it's to murder everybody they can lay hands on. Listen, Tyler, they kept me a slave for seven years." Now he poured it out, talking as he had never talked before, as much to himself as to the farmer, as much to clarify his own mind as to convince another. "I'm alive all right. I got my strength. But it killed somethin' in me. Like the preachers say you got a soul. If that's it, that's what they kill."

"Nobody can do that."

"Mister, I bet you don't even know what you got inside you. Way down deep, where it don't show. You never had Comanches bring it out and laugh at it. You never crawled and ate shit because they told you to eat shit."

"I wouldn't."

"Ha! You wouldn't. You don't know 'em. They let the Kiowas go along with 'em, apurpose. The Kiowas, they take you apart bit by bit. They keep you alive longer'n anybody. But in the end, you die. The Comanches let you see that. Then they go to work, only they keep you alive. It may seem like that's better, and after you see the Kiowas you believe it's better, you believe anything's better. So the Comanches got you."

A coyote wailed and he broke off, swallowing, listening. It was a real coyote this time and he walked again, the farmer beside him.

"People turn their backs because I take hair for money. They say I ain't choosy what hair I take. Women, kids, just so it's Injun. Well, people are right. Women and kids. They were the goddam worst.''

"I can't see any excuse for takin' scalps from women and kids," said Ben.

Pierce wasn't listening, he was talking. He had to talk. "The squaws with them sharp sticks. They know where to poke and make it hurt. The kids throwin' stones. You get to savvy their talk and you hear what they're sayin' about you. They got one thing in their craw, just one thing. To maim or kill every white human being on earth. You seen the one came at you in the corral? He was dead and he knew it. All he wanted was to take a white man along with him.''

"Anybody'll fight." Ben was suddenly abashed. "Uh, Pierce. I reckon you saved my life.''

"I wasn't thinkin' of savin' anybody. I was killin' a damn Comanche. I took his hair, didn't I? That was for what they did to me.''

Ben said awkwardly, "Anyway, thanks.''

Pierce drew out the little sharp knife at his belt. "You see this? It was one of theirs. Seven years it took me to get hold of it. It was owned by Iron Head, then.'' His voice dropped a tone. "They come back from a raid and they had booze and was drinkin' and braggin'. Lord, how they brag! Iron Head and two of his sons fell asleep with their squaws in the big chief's tent, you couldn't tell who was sleepin' with who, that's the way they are. I had ponies staked out. I sliced their throats.''

"The squaws, too?''

"All of 'em. I wish they'd knowed who did it to 'em. I went to—'' He broke off. Even now, with this compulsion on him, it was hard to talk about Josie. "I got away.''

"Then you were free. Why couldn't you forget it? Start a new life? I mean, the way you go along now, it don't seem like it holds much." Ben tried to make himself clear. "What I mean, how long can you keep it up?''

Pierce scarcely heard him. "I got away. . . . I joined up as a scout. I took the cavalry back into the Staked Plains, right where the Comanches live. We got to 'em. We killed a whole hell of a lot of 'em. There was some good officers

then. But they always get hit or transferred, the good ones.
Now only MacKenzie'll chase 'em, keep 'em runnin'.
That's the only way to beat 'em. . . . Well, then the Mex
government couldn't handle 'em, and started offerin' the
bounty. That was good. I got money in the bank, a real
bank in Kaycee."

"I can't see that way of doin'," said Ben stubbornly. "I
can't see no good comin' out of it."

For the space of another round of the buildings, Pierce
was silent. It wasn't any use talking, nobody understood
him.

He had kept his secret well, he could let it die with him
and none the wiser. Why did he want to talk to this
stranger he did not particularly like, whom he might have
to kill if he survived the attack? Maybe that was it, maybe
if he had to get it out, better it should be a man like this.
Maybe it was because of Gloria, some strange bond which
he only faintly felt and understood. Maybe it was just a
desire to justify himself to someone who was not listening.
Maybe to Josie.

Those who had known about it in the beginning, in the
scattered ranches around his father's place, they were gone,
or had forgotten. He should let it go. It would be better to
shut up.

But he could not. He heard himself begin cautiously
enough, "You read about men livin' with Injuns. Sure,
you did. The mountainy men and the Ree squaws and Kit
Carson and his Blackfoot wives and Clyman and Williams
and them in the early days. But you never read no true
stories about the Comanches. The don't tell it, about the
Comanches and the Kiowas and the Apaches."

"You mean they're different? How do you reckon?"

"Different? They got balls. They're smart in plenty ways.
Not altogether smart. Animal smart. Animal cruel. Only
thing makes 'em laugh is somebody's sufferin'. I seen 'em
stick a cute little Mex boy full of fatty pine splinters and
set it afire. Kept him alive two days. Laughed themselves
sick over it."

"That's hard to believe Pierce."

The resistance to truth of this Easterner somehow failed

to make Pierce angry. Instead, it fanned the fires of his
desire to make the pictures clear to someone beside himself.

He took a deep breath. he said. "I had a sister."

Puzzled, Ben asked, "Is she alive?"

"Oh, yes. She's alive, all right."

"The—the Comanches got her?"

"Josie was her name. She was so pretty." Now Pierce's
voice changed again, so that Ben peered at him in the
moonlight. "My old man, he was doin' well enough, but
there wasn't much you could call pretty around the ranch.
My ma, she was fine. But Josie . . . Josie was laughin'
and playin'. She was so pretty."

"They killed her " Ben frowned. He had no desire to
sympathize with Pierce.

"It's funny how, when you're little, you got a big
sister, you think she's everything in the world."

Ben thought of his brother, Bob. Older, bigger, smarter,
Bob had been. When Ben was little, he had worshiped
Bob. They had boxed hats, wrestled, fought off the coun-
tryside gangs until everyone knew enough to leave the
Tyler brothers alone or suffer sad consequences.

Now he wondered whether Bob had not taught him as
a convenience. Now, knowing about Bob, he had no big
feeling about it, only that once his brother had been a
hero, but that life had changed things.

"Me and Josie, we was close as thieves," Pierce said.
"We was out pickin' berries. When we come home we
walked right into the Comanches."

Now Pierce's voice deepened, became harsh. He went
on, "They already had Ma and Pa. They made us watch
what they did. Then, always laughin' and laughin', they
grabbed Josie and put her on the ground. They piled on
her. Eight, nine, a dozen, one right after the other. I dunno
how many, because they banged me cold when I tried to
get at 'em."

Tyler had no words for this, although Pierce stopped
talking for a moment. He couldn't quite picture the horror,
he only could see the Frog Hollow gang jumping Bob, and
the way he had begun banging their heads together. He

could not visualize a gang of Indians repeatedly raping a girl in her teens.

The inexorable voice went on, "It was worse, though, later, in the Comanche camp. The way they do, whoever touches a captive woman first, he owns her. They gamble a lot and a white woman she brings big money. Josie . . . she was pretty, even to them. They kept winnin' and losin' her."

Ben began to see it in spite of himself.

"The squaws, they beat her because she was wanted more'n them. She was fifteen, that year. She had the first little bastard that year. Walkin' Jay. A damn half-breed boy."

Ben hadn't thought of kids as the product of rape. The picture became clearer.

Pierce said tautly, his mouth ugly in the moonlight, "When they found out how I felt about Josie, they made me watch. I couldn't learn not to show what it did to me. They got a flock of laughs outa me, that way."

"Why—why didn't she kill herself?"

"I begged her to. Then she got pregnant. She couldn't kill the baby, she said. It wasn't the baby's fault, she said. Then Bear Head got her."

"Bear Head?" Ben was annoyed with himself. The picture had become too clear, the young girl, with child, the Indians.

"Iron Head's oldest. An important one, Bear Head. He wouldn't swap her. Or gamble for her. She had his kid. Then another, by him. He beat her, he had another wife. But he kept the squaws offen her. By the time I was ready to go, she looked old and wore out, she had the kids and Bear Head protected her."

"She wouldn't go with you?" he began to see it all, now. There was no justification for scalping women and children, there was no mitigation of the crime of murder, but he began to sense the emotion which twisted Pierce. When he had tried to straighten out the trouble between Dolly and Bob, his brother had listened in apparent sympathy, then had run away, leaving Ben to hold the sack. He knew a bit about what this could do to a man.

Pierce said, "Maybe I shoulda killed her. Only I couldn't. Never mind right and wrong. Even if I'd known she would tool Bear Head away by some excuse that night I got the knife, to save him. She said she wouldn't leave on account of the brats. She looked at the little red-skinned bastards on a filthy blanket and said she wouldn't leave. She answered me in the Comanche lingo!"

"Well, it was her choice," Ben said, then wished he hadn't, although Pierce seemed not to hear him.

"She could make Bear Head listen to her. Only woman, red, black, white, or Mex I ever seen could make a Comanche listen to her. She got him away and I missed him when I got Iron Head and the others."

"Then she is still with 'em?"

"She's with 'em. She might be out there, right now. After a while, I'll find out."

"And they did come here on your trail?"

"I expect so." Now that it was out, he was weary. "You never knew Josie, like she was. It was different, then. Everything was different. I figured to get her back."

He had come to the end. The secret was out. Both men fell silent.

They were poles apart, yet for this moment they were close together. The killer and the nonkiller knew that they were in it together, the battle, the doom, whatever was to take place. Each in his way was formulating a credo to face whatever was to come, neither was certain of his exact decision.

Then Silo whistled against the moon.

There had been no coyote wail. There had been nothing but the wavering dance of moon on the countryside. Ben looked around, feeling the danger but inept, unable to adjust to the strange terrain, to the circumstance of mortal danger from other unseen people.

"Get down!" said Pierce. "Hold tight. Guard that door."

They were, Ben now perceived, close to the main entrance of the station. He watched Pierce glide through the night, not in a straight line, moving like an animal of nocturnal habits, slinking, quartering, always maneuvering toward the outbuildings which were the weak point in the defense. There was no further sound from Silo. Those within might not know.

Should he warn them? Would his least movement bring an arrow or a shot?

He had not the advantage of war experience. With Bob gone to the West, he alone could manage the farm. This too was a mark against Bob, even though the elder might have been the one expected to enlist. It would never have been Bob, he knew now, because of the selfishness. He had suffered much, within himself and outwardly on public occasions when his size rendered him an object of suspicion as a draft dodger. He had paid blood money voluntarily, three hundred dollars for a substitute, which his position did not warrant, Obie McMurtrie, who had been killed somewhere in Georgia, with Sherman's Bummers.

He thought of these things and realized dimly the paltriness of war. The fear of something he could not see griped his bowels. What he had heard from Pierce did nothing to reassure him. "Fiends in human form," he had read in Fox's paper, and if they were fiends, then he was wrong and they were not humans and Pierce was right.

Now he heard a coyote scream and an answer and then a wild yell and then shots from the direction of the barn. He started instinctively in that direction, restrained himself, knowing that he must obey Pierce, knowing that the house would now be aroused. He clutched the rifle, straining every sense.

He saw a torch flicker to life, then brighten. Beyond the corral there was a solitary figure, naked to the waist, a single feather slanted atop its head, a bow in hands. The tip of the arrow blazed and the string was drawn.

A rifle crackled and the lone, stalwart figure dropped and the blazing arrow fell and fizzled on the ground and then there were two more shots from the barn and another scream. Silo and Pierce were fighting shrewdly, it seemed. He relaxed a little, straightening, lowering the rifle.

Now there was a ragged shot or two from the house, but he heard Callahan shouting, warning them to hold the fire, that they might kill Pierce or someone else—namely Ben, he realized, and turned toward the door.

From no place, it seemed a greasy, naked, leaping form came at him. The rifle was knocked out of his grasp in the first rush. Only his reactions and strength saved him from decapitation as the Comanche sliced with a foot-long bowie.

If there were further sounds of action or if there was anything else in the world at that moment, Ben knew it not. He held onto the knife wrist, he spun. There was a greasy odor which nauseated him, there was in his hands a sinewy fighting machine which scratched and kicked and bit and twisted so that there seemed to be more than one of him.

The brave was young and slight but like a panther, clawing, writhing, trying to free the knife hand. This was a minor error of stubbornness because of Ben's muscles and because it gave a single direction to the struggle. He could use leverage and weight against this, he would swing this man by the wrist and avoid most of the tactics which might otherwise have hamstrung him and allowed the buck to prevail on the moment, through surprise and agility.

There had been barroom fights in Jersey, the Apple Mill had not been without its incidents. As his brain began to lose the numbness, he reflected upon various devices. He managed to stamp a heavy shoe upon the Indian's moccasin.

He felt the sag, although no cry of pain came from the Comanche. He kicked at a shin and brought, at last, a low moan. And then the teeth clamped down upon his left wrist.

The shock of the pain, the thought of the poison in the fangs of a wild Indian, the sudden impatience of wrestling with a smaller man, drove him to using a lifted knee; feeling it go home in the crotch, to a reverse of his shoulder, a wrestling spin and swing.

The Indian's head hit the wall of the station and the bowie dropped and still both hands dug, ripping at Ben. He drove a fist into the red throat, seized the neck in his hands and used the wall, battering, slamming, shaking the slight figure as though it were a straw dummy.

He was still worrying the sorry corpse when Pierce's voice called him to reason. "Just a few young bucks tryin' their wings. Damn fire arrows, they're bad. . . Hey, what you got there, Tyler?''

Someone opened the door and a feeble ray of light fell on the face of the Comanche as Ben dropped him like a hot coal, the adrenalin dying within him, his hands greasy and weak, sweat standing on him. "He . . . come out of nowhere.''

"Yeah. They generally do.'' Pierce was peering questioningly at Ben's face. "Got him barehanded, h'mmm?''

"I never heard anything nor saw anything. He just came at me.'' With shaking fingers he bent and picked up the bowie. It had been honed to paper-cutting edge. "With this.''

No one seemed to want to come out of the station. They huddled behind Callahan, who was looking at the Indian's face. It was a flat-cheeked, hawk-nosed young face, the mouth hard, the eyes slanted a bit, Oriental-like. The head was broken and bloodied but the features were composed.

"They die hard one way. They take it good,'' Pierce said. "They figure to die in battle. That's O.K. with them.''

Ben said, "He fought like a girl.'' He stared stupidly at his left wrist. The marks of incisors were there, but the skin had not quite been broken. "Scratchin', bitin'.''

"You wasn't so big, you'd be dead. They fight good.''

"Yeah.'' He could finally draw a normal breath. "They fight to kill. They try to kill you all over, not just in one place.''

"That's what I was tryin' to tell you. That's the way they are.''

Ben shivered and Pierce smiled thinly and asked, "Well, you got your Injun. You gonna scalp him? Or should I?''

He took from his belt the small knife he had filched from Iron Head. Ben turned and stumbled into the station.

For a moment Pierce lingered, looking out toward the plains where he knew the Comanches were gathered. They would be scheming, and if it was Bear Head he had a good idea of the way it had to work out.

He bent and spat on the ground and took the scalp. It

never had made any difference whose Indian it was, he thought. The Mex people paid and it all added up.

He headed for the barn. There was another hunk of hair to be taken there. Whole hog or none, that was the way it had to be. It was lonely and still at the barn.

He stood, staring at nothing and the reaction set in. He had finally got it off his chest about Josie and he didn't know if it was good or bad. He had the empty feeling which came after killing and scalping.

Worse, he was all mixed up. The world was in turmoil, his part of it, anyway. He didn't have his usual control. There was a worriment in him that the emptiness might never fill up.

He fought himself. He knew what he had to do. He strung the scalps and hung them in the barn and went back toward the station.

Chapter 13

♦ ♦ ♦

Ben wanted coffee. His nerve ends were raw, sleep was far away.

Luke Post seemed not to have fully awakened under the alarm and went stumbling back to bed. The girl was exhausted to the point of indifference and deep in slumber.

Pierce addressed Callahan. "You want to take the next tour?"

"Right." The sergeant had helped move the dead Indian from the door. He was a durable man, Ben thought, stolid but friendly and willing.

In the morning there would be another ugly burial. That is, he added to himself, if morning came.

Then he had to smile, for he knew morning would come whether or not anyone was alive. He immediately felt better for it, for remembering it. Cowardice lies partly in the belief that with one's own death the sun will not rise, his Uncle Tiger had told him years ago.

Pierce was saying, "Mr. Lamkin, you mind joinin' the sergeant?"

"I've stood a few watches in the War. Not with a gun, with a camera."

Pierce broke the double-barreled shotgun and saw that it was charged with buckshot. "This'll do it."

Lamkin accepted the gun, calm under Callahan's amused regard. "I'm not a proper Southerner, you see. I don't shoot. I don't ride very well, either. And I never learned to hate a Yankee."

"Well," said Callahan, "hatin' the other fella never win no battle."

"Our people believed in what they were doing. They

felt they were invaded, that their rights were taken from them. I don't yet know the truth, frankly.''

"I was in the Regulars. You're under orders, you do what you're told to do.'' Callahan grinned. "The bloody volunteers, that was different. They hated everybody. Even their officers, they hated.''

"Our entire army was volunteer,'' sighed Lamkin.

"You take the Army, it usually knows what it's doin'. Slow and all that. But it knows.'' Callahan raised a thick, hairy hand. "I swear to ginney, the 6th knows about them Comanches. The 6th'll be here.''

The big soldier and the small photographer went out and Pierce followed to set them on the right paths.

Adobe growled, "The 6th wouldn't go against that crowd nohow.''

"Too damn many Injuns for a troop of blue shirts,'' said Sligh. "Just too damn many Injuns.''

They moved to the bar, where Manning served them. Ben wondered why the three of them didn't sleep, wished he could lie down and rest himself. In the kitchen Myra Manning swung away from the window, flushing. She poured coffee redolent with chicory and said, "It—it must have been awful. That Indian jumping on you.''

"It wasn't nice,'' said Ben. His insides had stopped churning. He went on slowly, "I ain't used to that kinda fighting. Don't know as I ever could get used to it.''

She nodded. "Some of us don't. Nor lots of other things in this country. All the years, I never got used to things.''

He realized that he was looking at her for the first time, really looking at her. There was a light in her that had not been there before, he thought, but he could not be sure. Her hair was caught back, she looked alive. She went to the window, then came across the room, her shoulders held back, smiling a woman's smile, inscrutable.

She said, "You'll see what I mean if you stay in Texas. It's more than just a big sky and miles of country. It's the people, the way they think, the things they do. Like they never care. They want different things.''

"You from the East?''

"Ohio. Cincinnati. Then we moved here. But we were

Southerners first. Left there when I was a child. My pa was a preacher. A Georgia-born preacher. My ma was a hill girl, but she had schoolin' in Savannah before she married pa." Thinking of Lamkin, she was particular about mentioning the schooling. "She taught me. Most poor folks in Georgia can't read or write. They learn the Bible by heart, some of 'em. Never learn to read print."

"We didn't have but a one-room country school," said Ben. "They used to tell us west of the Mississippi was a vast wilderness. That's what they called it. A vast wilderness."

She nodded vigorously. "And you know what? They were purely right!"

The mousy woman had come alive. She was pink-cheeked, younger looking. He smiled at her.

"Lots of people comin' this way to fill it up."

"The worse it'll be for them."

"The War shook up the country. Farms back East ain't what you'd call excitin' to an ex-soldier. The Southerners, they want out of carpetbaggin' and such. They head west."

She gestured toward the window. "To fight Indians?"

"That's excitin', too."

'They think so? Maybe they'll like the sandstorms and the drought and sun beatin' you down till you drop. No, Mr. Tyler, if they knew the truth, they'd stay at home."

"That they wouldn't. Everybody figures he's the one can whip anything. No ma'am, there's a restlessness in 'em. They got their eyes on the settin' sun."

"It'll set on a plenty of them untimely."

"Some'll dig in. There's all this land, all the open space, everything new. They'll settle in."

She sighed. "Reckon you're right, at that. They'll multiply and inherit the earth. And they can have it."

There seemed nothing more to be said. She went back to the window. Ben put down the coffee mug, conscious of weariness. He should join Luke and get some rest. He went into the main room.

Manning was still behind the bar but he wasn't at the bottle. Adobe and Sligh were spaced against the far wall. Ben yawned and said, "Reckon we all oughta sleep a bit."

Then he saw the revolver in Manning's hand. He shook himself fully to the moment, looked at Adobe and Sligh.

"Just take it easy, Tyler," said Sligh.

"We don't want no trouble with you," said Adobe.

Gloria appeared, then Luke. They were rubbing cobwebs from their eyes. Behind them were Hump and Shotgun, not quite sure of themselves, but holding cocked rifles.

"Over there," said Adobe, motioning to the bar.

Luke went to the end of the wooden counter and leaned negligently against it. Gloria slid behind him.

Ben said, "Where's Pierce?"

"Tackin' up more scalps in the barn," said Sligh. "Where else would he be?"

"It's against nature," Manning cried, his voice shaking. "I won't die because of him and his scalpin' and murderin'."

Luke said calmly, "You got that a bit backwards, Manning. He kills 'em first. Then he scalps 'em."

"I don't care. I won't risk everybody's life just for him. It ain't reasonable."

Ben started to speak and Adobe butted in, "Don't holler at us. It won't do no good."

'I was just about to say that you'll have to kill him to turn him in," Ben said. "You'll never take Pierce alive."

"That's all right with me. They'll take his carcass. Save them some trouble. They wanta get on with the Moon Raid."

Luke said, "The moon's got you, all of you."

"Shut up!"

The door opened and Pierce walked in, trailing his rifle. Adobe and Sligh both turned revolvers on him.

He closed the door and leaned against it. His eyes, now again reflecting the light in that peculiar fashion, went around the room. He nodded, accepting the odds, noting those who were not inimical, estimating, Ben knew, every element.

"Put down that rifle," said Adobe.

He hesitated, then carefully leaned the gun against the wall. "Showdown, huh?"

Manning yelled, "They'll take you and quit. You know they will. They only want you."

The revolver shook in Manning's grasp, but Shotgun and Hump were steady and there was no question of the saddle tramps on the other side of the room. Manning was likely to shoot anyone, once he started, Ben thought, like the time Rufe Maddox went crazy back in Bernardsville and killed the constable and two innocent farmers.

Luke observed, "This is the damnedest fool thing I ever seen since the pigs ate my little brother. You're gonna trade with Comanches? When they got their dead to get hunk for? When you got women?"

Adobe looked at Sligh, who said, "We're gonna make a try at it. They can't do no worse than what they'll do anyhow."

There was a slight noise in the room where no one moved nor breathed normally and Ben saw Mrs. Manning, in the doorway to the kitchen, uncertain, wiping her hands on her apron, staring about.

"What—what's going on?"

"Get back in there," her husband said. His voice was loud, unnatural. "It's none of your affair, woman. Get back in the kitchen where you belong."

"Yeah," said Luke. "Stay out of it, Miz Manning. Your husband and a couple others gone loco, is all."

"We're gonna save your life. All our lives," Manning intoned. He was sweating and he stank of stale whisky fumes. "We're gonna turn in this renegade to the Comanches. White Eye! Lookit him! White Eye!"

Pierce was careful not to move. His blank gaze went around the room, skipped carefully over Gloria, who was fully behind the bar, now. His mouth was a tight, straight line.

Ben began to see things with more clarity. He saw that Shotgun held Luke's revolver in one hand. He knew that this would have started a fire in the gambler which he was carefully concealing. Luke was mighty particular about that revolver.

Gloria's hair was disarranged, but her color was good. He thought that she was debating something in her mind. He could sense the excitement, the lack of fear in her. She was poised and she looked prettier than ever.

Mrs. Manning said, "But you can't do that. It ain't Christian."

"Get out of here!" Manning waved the revolver at her. "Damn fool woman, you don't know nothin'."

"It's against the Lord," she said, moving into the room. "Turn a white man over to savages? No."

Manning stepped from behind the bar. He struck at her with his fist. "You wanta spoil everything? Get in the kitchen."

The blow caught her on the side of the head. She went down to her knees and Ben made a start, but Adobe swung the revolver muzzle on him and he saw that it would be a pleasure to the big man if he had the chance to shoot. Mrs. Manning struggled, got to her feet. She was drained of color. She leaned against the jamb of the door for support and said, "The Lord will take his vengeance if you do this thing. The Lord is looking down on you."

Luke said, "Reckon He is, at that. Reckon He's lookin' inside folks." He turned to Hump and Shotgun. "Looks to me like you'd have more sense than this."

Hump said, "We agreed. We agreed it's a chance to save the rest of us. Nothin' against you, Luke. Only they want Pierce, they don't want us."

"All this time you been around and you can't see through this blazer?"

Shotgun said, "I dunno what you mean, Luke."

The little gambler moved forward, away from the bar. Without his hardhat he seemed very small indeed. He faced Sligh and Adobe and said, "That saddlebag. I seen you checkin' it from time to time. Several thousand Mex in there, ain't it?"

Sligh said sharply. "Watch out what you're sayin', Luke."

"You see what they're doin'?" Luke addressed Hump and Shotgun. "They turn over Pierce, grab his scalps, and head for the border. Wouldn't surprise me a bit they done some ridin' with El Segundo in the past."

Adobe said, "By Gawd, you can't talk to us like that."

It was a strange thing, thought Ben. They could shoot Luke down. They could shoot Pierce just as easily, and offer his body to the Comanches. Why didn't they do it?

Was it because they knew they were on dangerous ground and that they were afraid of alienating Hump and Shotgun and maybe of the two men outdoors patrolling, Callahan and Lamkin? Why should they have fears or doubts? Why didn't they open fire and be done with it?

Sligh said, "Now, just a minute. We're tryin' to help everybody. Pierce ain't even a white man, hardly. He's part Injun, he lived with them so long."

Manning joined in. "They'll go away if they get him. We never been hurt by Indians. They'll go into Mexico."

"To kill and murder and burn down there," said Mrs. Manning. Her hand was against her face, she did not move, but her voice was strong, beating at them. "Are Mexicans not people? Miguel was a man. Miguel died out there for all of us."

"Shut up, woman," Manning shrieked. "Shut up!"

Luke said, "You damn fools. You'd never get through with them scalps. You dumb, no-account slobs."

He was baiting them, Ben thought with alarm. He was unarmed and there were five against him and he was trying to make them act. He couldn't hope to live through it.

Gloria moved behind Luke and Ben altered his position slightly. Manning had gone beyond the far end of the bar to get at his wife. He now crouched, the revolver unsteady, glaring at Luke.

Sligh said in strained accents. "You're askin' for it, Luke. I told you, we don't want trouble with you. Why are you askin' for it?"

"Because if you take Pierce, you're takin' me, too. Now go ahead, make your play."

Gloria's hand was on a whisky bottle. She pulled it toward her. She looked at Ben, but she was not thinking about the two of them, he sensed, nor about anything which had to do with other than the immediate present. There was an issue here and she knew which side she was on. If she had in her mind the idea of breaking with Pierce, she certainly had no wish to see him sacrificed. He moved slightly to get out of her way. She held the bottle tight, deciding which way to use it to best advantage.

Adobe said, 'Nobody can talk to me like that."

He aimed the revolver at Luke.

Gloria made her move. Even in that instant Ben admired the way she threw the bottle, like a man, overhand, following through.

He saw that, then his reflexes took over and he was driving across the space between him and Adobe. When Gloria's bottle hit the man's elbow he was close enough to grab hold. The bullet exploded and the ball went into the floor and then he had Adobe in his hands.

Luke moved at the same instant, rolling behind the bar. Mrs. Manning had seized her husband and was hampering him. Luke took the revolver away from him, carefully chose the exact spot on his face where Manning had struck his wife and laid the gun barrel against it with considerable force.

Ben took Adobe down to the floor, holding onto the gun hand, rolling with blows hammered at him by Adobe's left fist. At any moment he expected to be drilled by a bullet. His ears strained for the sound of gunfire.

None came.

Sligh had hesitated and was lost. Pierce, catlike, had his rifle.

Shotgun and Hump had never been deeply enough involved to kill in cold blood. Both put down their guns and raised their hands. Pierce, covering Sligh, moved on light feet toward the struggle between Ben and Adobe.

Luke asked lightly, "Why not let 'em go?"

Pierce's grim expression relaxed. He nodded, motioning Sligh to disarm himself, watching the struggle. Gloria came from behind the bar with another bottle in her hand, a full beer bottle, this time. Mrs. Manning, supporting herself on the end of the bar, shook her head at Lamkin as he and Callahan pelted onto the scene.

Pierce said, "Better stay outside and keep watch. This here is under control."

All this Ben dimly sensed and heard. Adobe was powerful at close grips. He bent himself to the task of maneuvering the pistol hand.

Adobe jabbed pronged fingers at his eyes. He closed them in time, but the sting roused him. He bowed his wide shoulders, twisting the wrist, slowly, inexorably upward. The breath came hard from Adobe, he cursed in a loud voice.

Ben angled his leverage. His shirt was torn, he was bleeding a little from surface scratches. He felt Adobe turn and grab for the knife at his belt.

He clamped hard on the pistol hand and squeezed. There was a muffled report. Adobe fell limply away from him.

Mrs. Manning's voice was very clear. "The Lord's judgment is on him."

Ben unkinked his muscles, stretching, as he arose. He sure would need a change of clothing. Where his garments weren't torn they were bloodied.

He looked at Adobe. There wasn't much left of the man's head. The bullet had gone up under his chin and through the top of his skull.

Pierce said, "It ain't a pretty sight. Let's haul him outa here." He paused and looked at Sligh. "There's a good hangin' limb on one of them cottonwoods. It'd be convenient to the buryin' ground."

"You won't get no more trouble from me," said Sligh. His face was pasty. "I don't wanta stretch no rope. You can depend on me when the fight comes."

Luke said cheerfully, "We'll need him, Pierce. I'll guarantee to keep an eye on him."

"He's so chicken-livered," Pierce complained. "He coulda had me afore I got my gun."

"He'll fight Injuns," said Luke. "He's gotta. Even a yellabelly will fight Injuns."

After a moment, Pierce nodded. "O.K. We'll let you bury Adobe. Get to it."

Sligh licked his lips. Then he approached his partner and gingerly took hold of his heels.

"Hell," said Pierce. "I can't stand to see even him drug out like that. Hump, Shotgun—give him a hand."

Gloria's nails dug into Ben's arm. "I don't want to see any more," she whispered. "Please. . . ."

She tugged at him. His blood still hot, oblivious to everything else, he caught her glance and followed. They crossed the room toward the bedrooms.

Pierce turned away from the door as the three former recalcitrants carried out Adobe. He looked at Luke, then at the empty passage through which Gloria and Ben had gone, his woman and the man he had told his story to. The old bitterness rose in him. His grip on the rifle tightened, he took a quick step.

Luke said gently, "I just saved Sligh for future use. I wouldn't want to lose a better man than he'll ever be."

Pierce said, "The goddam farmer, he's got no right."

"Could be," Luke admitted. "Tell you this much: I'm on your side to a certain point."

"I oughta blow out her goddam brains."

"We'll need her, too. There's bandages to roll and she can help patch up those of us what need it."

"Goddam bitch."

"She's your bitch," Luke said reasonably. "Now what tarnation difference does it make with who she bitches? Why don't you look at it thataway?"

Pierce relaxed his grip on the rifle. "I reckon I got to. For now."

"You don't have to like Ben. Just get along with him till this fracas is over. Then, if you live, things'll level off."

"If any of us live," muttered Pierce. He looked at Mrs. Manning. Her face was flaming. He pointed to her husband. "What we goin' to do about that worm?"

"See to it that he turns." Luke grinned. "There's ways of directin' a man's fear. When we get through remonstratin' with this lil ole wife beater, could be he'll be more scared of us than anything else."

They moved toward the recumbent Manning. He sputtered, opened his eyes, wildly waved his arms. He saw Luke and Pierce coming at him and promptly fainted.

Pierce said, "See what you mean."

"You can work out some of your pizen on him," Luke said shrewdly. "It'll do you good . . . and he deserves it."

Chapter 14

♦♦♦

There was no passion between them as they sat in the bedroom. Gloria had barred the door, but Ben could only feel the reaction of having killed.

"Two men inside one evenin'. I never killed anybody before. I never figured to kill a man."

She was wise enough not to make love to him. She held his hand and said, "Shh! It wasn't your doin's."

"It's no good to kill. That's Pierce's trouble, too much killin'." On both sides, he could have added, but he chose not to repeat anything Pierce had said to him. Pierce had been sinned against before he began his sinning. Values were becoming more confused every hour.

"Don't think about it, Ben."

"I can't help seein' their faces." There had been little left of Adobe's face.

She demanded, "What could you do? What else?"

"Nothin'. A man should be able to do something, though."

She said, "Let's talk about us. It's better to talk about what we're going to do."

He put his arms around her, then, but it was for comfort and reassurance. She murmured to him and after a while he could shake it off and think straight again. He told her how much it meant to him to have her there.

He said, "If we ever get out of this, we'll work the ranch and grow things and stay out of trouble. At night we can look at the sky and feel free and safe."

"And Saturday nights we can go to town. And I can buy things."

"We'll have dogs and cats and chickens and pigs," she said. "They're company for folks that understand."

"A kitten. I'll have a kitten and tie a big bow around her neck. I had a kitten, once." She broke off. Cactus Horner, who had too much money and power to argue with, Cactus had shot her kitten in a drunken moment. Then she had to go to bed with him, on account of his money and the men who rode with him and who would shoot up a town if anyone crossed Cactus Horner.

"Whatever kind of place it is, I'll fix it up. I'm handy with tools. All our family is handy with hammer and saw." Bob, too, Bob had been a good carpenter. Pa had taught them, painstakingly, in the old-fashioned way. You went to be a carpenter in Jersey, they gave you a shovel and a wheelbarrow and started you digging a foundation. When you topped off the last wooden shingle on the roof, you had learned the trade.

"I can make curtains. Real fancy. A lady taught me." It was the preacher's cousin and she was a lady, all right, but she had never married and she had peculiar habits. Worse than the preacher's son. That had been some home town she had grown up in. Or maybe it was the way she was built, the bubbling inside her that people always saw, she had thought of that, too. "I can sew good."

"I'll gentle a horse for you right away. Then we can take rides."

"I can ride. I enjoy to ride." Handsome young Billy Endelman had taught her. She had repaid him on hillsides, in her early days in the West, before she found that she could have charged him a good price because Billy was an easy-going young rancher. He got killed in a card game because he was too easy, too good-natured to suspect a tinhorn of possessing a hide-out gun.

"It'll be clean and pretty. We won't bother with none of those hard cases that settle in Texas." He said with vigor, "I won't have this killin'. I wasn't raised with killin'."

"It don't mean so much in this country." She soothed him. "Sudden country, they call it. Don't fret about it, Ben. Tell me more about the ranch and about us."

After a moment he said, "I got money, you know. I

wouldn't want you to think we'll starve on the ranch until soemthin' grows.''

"That's nice," she sighed. "It's nice to have money. I got a couple hundred my own self."

"I got almost a thousand,' he said proudly.

"That's wonderful, honey," Pierce now had the makings of four-five thousand. Pierce knew how to put it together if he had a mind to. She shivered a little, thinking of Pierce, and was grateful for the brawny arms which closed in on her.

"Somebody walkin' over your grave. . . . That's what they used to say in Jersey when a body shivered like that." He was immediately abashed. "I didn't mean nothin' by that, honest."

"Don't fret," she said. "You and Luke and me. We'll get out of this. I know it. Injuns ain't goin' to kill you nor Luke nor me. We ain't Injun bait."

"You're plumb positive, ain't you?"

She nodded, snuggling close to him. It couldn't happen to her, not after all she had been through. She had this big, strong farmer, and if she got the chance she could be a rancher's wife. She could wear decent clothes and leave off her corsets unless she was going to town, or to a party, and live like other people, safe and secure. How could she die within twenty-four hours, a healthy, strong girl, alive with plans?

He said, "I been talkin' to Luke. He don't know much about farmin', but he knows about cattle. He'd like to invest in some cattle. He knows how to buy and when to sell and all that. He was a cowhand when he was young. I put a heap of trust in Luke."

"Luke's a square shooter," she said sleepily.

After a moment he said, "I expect we'll have trouble with Pierce."

"Oh, sure. But we can handle him."

"I wouldn't want to kill Pierce."

"You won't have to."

"He's got somethin' on his side."

"He's loco."

"No, he ain't crazy. Only on one subject. Outside the

way he feels about Indians, he's as sane as anybody else. Maybe saner."

"You only need to be crazy on one subject," she said positively. "That's trouble enough. I know Pierce. He's all right in plenty of ways. But he's loco."

"Man's got a reason," muttered Ben.

"Pierce can't forget." She herself could not forget too many things. She knew what it did to a person to have such memories. Maybe she could lose them living with a simple man like Ben. She could control herself, she averred silently. She could keep that driving need bottled inside her until it had evaporated forever. A new start, that was all she needed.

She fell asleep on the instant. Ben made himself comfortable, looking at her. Then his mind wandered away.

He thought about Pierce and about the story, which kept coming back to him as he remembered Pierce's voice, the way Pierce had shivered when he spoke of the Comanches and of Josie. The truth, his grandfather always said, lay somewhere in the middle of things. Maybe no one would ever be able to know the real truth about Pierce.

He turned back to the girl. She was mysterious and very pretty, lying there in the moonlight which crept between the slats of the shutters. He wondered if Pierce had ever looked at her this way, making plans for the future.

It was better not to think of that. He put his head down and resolutely sought sleep.

Manning, a miserable wreck, was trying to get coffee into his queasy stomach. His eye kept going to Pierce, who slept on a pallet in the main room, next to Luke.

Across the kitchen table from him Myra looked out of the window, catching a glimpse now and then of the lumbering form of Callahan or the neat, small figure of Lamkin, both of whom were still on patrol.

Adobe was dead out there some place, she knew. Violence had finally come home, to where she had seen it, experienced it. It had left her only partly numb. She was able to look at Manning and despise him and to let him see it in her eyes.

Manning quavered, "I was right. It would've worked."

"You were never right in your life," said Myra.

He tried to glare at her, saw the bruise on the side of her face and dropped his eyes. "I meant to save us. They didn't have to talk to me like they did."

"You try and turn a man over to Indians. You play Judas and expect them to be nice to you?"

"That Luke Post, he's a common gambler. He's got no right to curse me out."

"He had a good right."

He was confused by her attitude. He had never struck her before, maybe that was it. He said tentatively, "I didn't go for to hit you, Myra. It was just I was scared you'd get in the way."

"You were drunk and makin' a fool of yourself. Pierce told you the way you are. You and those others, fools. Puttin' in to help Adobe and Sligh steal Pierce's scalp bag."

"We never. They was goin' to save us."

"If the Lord wills, we'll be saved. Although why He should bother is more than I'll ever fathom."

"We'll never be saved. There's too many Comanches out there. They want Pierce and they'll get him and all of us."

"Maybe the Lord looks down on Comanches, too."

Manning snorted into his coffee. He was trying desperately to regain some self-respect. Luke and Pierce had scared him to the point of distraction. He had groveled at their feet in protestations of good behavior. The calm disinterest of his wife was not helping him get back on his feet.

"Maybe you know more'n I do."

She smiled. "Manning, the little children at play know more than you do."

"I won't have that kinda talk from you."

"I've been talking to you like that ever since you sat down there," she said. "There's goin' to be a fight. All your whining and squirmin' can't stop it. There's goin' to be a big battle and people are goin' to die right in this kitchen, maybe, and in the other room and in the bedrooms. Out yonder Indians are goin' to die. You think I care anything about what you say or think now, Manning?''

He tried to fire hot words back at her and found himself choking on the coffee. He wanted to shout and scream and wail his protest to the world, and there was no one to listen. The clutch of fear sent paroxysms through his body. He could not sit at the table, he arose and moved about, going from the kitchen into the main room, then back into the kitchen.

He could not understand about Myra. She sat there and was as calm as he had ever known her. He had always been dimly aware that she was a quiet woman, maybe a bit queer in her ways, but she had always deferred to him in bed and that was enough to satisfy him. Now she didn't seem to be afraid and this was incomprehensible. She had been scared of stray blanket Indians, or tarantulas and field mice and the rats in the stable. Why wasn't she fearful of a pack of warring Comanches?

They would burn and maim and torture everyone. Why didn't everyone feel as he did? Parched, shaking, he went into the bedroom off the kitchen and lay down on the bed and shook in every bone and muscle. He heard Pierce arise and go into the kitchen. Didn't the man need more than cat naps? It was time to change the watch. In a few hours the moon would be full and sometime before dawn there would be battle. Maybe Pierce was right. Why waste your few remaining hours in sleep?

If there was only someone he could talk to. Even Myra. But he could not tell her anything. Myra was removed from his ken. He was alone and he was scared clear down to his meager soul, where he found no surcease. He tried to pray but could only babble.

Callahan came in off patrol and his heavy voice was sullen. "No sign of the 6th yet."

"No sign of Indians, either," said Lamkin.

"They sleep good before a battle," Pierce told them. "They're out there watchin'. They got us surrounded, so they sleep fine."

Callahan said, "Funny thing about the cavalry. You can always know they're comin'."

"Maybe you can," said Pierce. "I was with the 6th for a while. I was never sure we were goin' to make it, not against Comanches."

"Oh, I didn't mean that. I mean the bugle."

"Yeah. The bugle."

"Nothin' carries like a bugle. I been in battles where the cannons had you deef. But you could always hear the bugles. From miles away you could hear 'em."

"Now that's plumb funny," said Pierce.

Lamkin observed, "He's right about the carrying power of brass."

"May be," said Pierce. "Truth is, I musta heard 'em. But danged if I can recollect it."

"A man often hears what he wants to hear," said Lamkin.

"Reckon I was listenin' for bullets or arrows. Or maybe for their yells. You can sometimes peg the bunch by their yellin'. Reckon I was listenin' for a voice I'd know."

"When the bugles sound, you hear 'em," said Callahan.

"If they was to sound now, I'd hear 'em," said Pierce. "Yep, I'd hear 'em good. If they was to sound."

Manning pounded on the straw mattress with an ineffectual fist. Why couldn't Pierce let them have the 6th, even if it wasn't coming?

Chapter 15

♦♦♦

The burial detail was composed of Hump, Shotgun, and Sligh. They went glumly about their task in the early hour before dawn. The plains lay flat and shimmering so that it seemed they could see for miles, but they could not.

Silo and his rifle were between barn and corral. Off beyond vision the Indians were making their preparations, but nothing could be done about them. It was necessary to keep cleaned up as smartly as possible, it was always necessary to bury the dead.

"Pierce don't trust us none," grumbled Sligh. "That breed would shoot us in a minute."

"Pierce is right," said Hump. "He's got to watch out." He toed Adobe's blanket-wrapped body into the ditch. "You wanta say a prayer for your side-kick?"

"The hell with him," said Sligh. "He didn't have a lick of sense."

Shotgun shoveled dirt onto the dead man. "I got to admit you was right, Hump."

"Me! I ain't been right since I quit wranglin' and picked up the ribbons on my first stage."

"About the Comanches."

"Oh, them." Hump leaned on his shovel handle. "I know Comanches all right. But I don't know a patch compared to that Pierce."

"Why we ever let this lunkhead and Manning talk us into that rangdoodle agin him, I'll never understand," complained Shotgun.

"Because we was plumb scared," said Hump. "A man gets panicky. Never did think about Sligh and Adobe wantin' those scalps."

"Now looky here," Sligh protested.

"Aw, shut up," said Hump. "Pierce was right. Don't try and lie out of it. And don't try no more funny business, 'cause we're all watchin' you, now."

"Where the hell would I get if I did somethin'?" demanded Sligh. "Where would a man go?"

"He's right," Shotgun nodded. "We're in it now, all together. No place to go."

"The Injuns might of taken Pierce, at that," Sligh said. "It was the only chance we had."

"They might of," said Hump. "Odds are they'd of taken him, then they'd of taken us, like Luke says. We're buryin' one of the reasons, right now." He threw dirt on the naked Indian killed by Ben Tyler.

"I don't see why we got to bury an Injun."

"That's easy. Pierce knows. It hurts 'em when they can't recover one of their corpuses. Furthermore, it does 'em good when they can momick up one of ours. Otherwise we wouldn't be plantin' your pardner."

Sligh said, "Adobe wasn't a real pardner of mine. We just was prospectin' together."

"On the dodge."

"That's none of your affair."

"Hell, no," said Hump cheerfully. "Saint or sinner, nobody's gonna look any different to the Comanches. One'll be as dead as t'other."

"You're talkin' mighty brave for a man as scared as you admits to bein'."

Hump considered this, then said, "Tell you, Sligh. A man can only get so scared for so long a time. Then, if he is any kind of a man, he figures to hell with it."

"Yeah," said Shotgun gloomily. "What the hell has anybody got comin' to him outside six feet of ground?"

"Which the Comanches won't even give a man."

Pierce wakened automatically and squinted at the sky and came up, reaching for his rifle. He was in the barn. He had caught another nap here for various reasons. He thought once of Gloria and Ben, shook off depression.

Silo eased in, gestured toward the trees where the sound

of shovels came faintly on the still air. "They are Christians now, I think."

"Yeah."

"No more trouble from them." Silo spoke soft, easy-flowing Spanish.

"No. No more trouble." Pierce answered in kind. "Only from Bear Head."

"We burn the barn, señor?"

"I'd like to. However, if the wind should rise, there could be bad trouble."

"No wind. Only Comanches."

There were still the horses from the stages and some hay and straw and the harness and gear and tools. The barn would provide a certain amount of shelter for dismounted Comanches, but on the other hand it would give no help to a horseback raid, in fact could split a wild-riding open charge.

Pierce said, "They will fight their way. I think we will not fire the barn."

"But in the end, señor?"

"Yes. When they come afoot, we may fire the barn."

They walked outside. The lamps were lit within the station and through the narrow windows he could see shapes moving. Were they up, Gloria and Ben?

He looked out and the haze was lifting and he could see the Indians on the hills and stretched across the southern plain. They would be on either side of the road and no one would get through their patrols. What he could not see he could visualize from his experience of seven years in bondage.

They formed in a circle, but they never remained still. He could see the round, tufted shields, the lances now picking up the first of the rays of the sun. Bear Head would be in charge, he imagined. Walking Horse had been the big chief of war parties, but command shifted according to the whim of the Council and Bear Head had been growing in importance for years. It was a disgrace that his white wife's brother should be taking many scalps and Bear Head would be for wiping it off and this was his chance.

They had ponies enough. They always thought they needed more, but the tough, wiry little animals who cavorted in the distance would carry them on the charge. He thought of scouting out alone and making a try at stampeding the herd but discarded the idea at once. Bear Head would be ready for such an attempt by Pierce.

The Comanches understood the whites. They had no notion that this was an easy task, to take the way station. The Moon Raid was an easy way to get loot, they would rather have gone on down into Mexico. But they wanted Pierce and they would give up something to get him.

Not everything, they would not risk everything, he thought. They did not want to get killed any more than did the defenders. They would plan carefully, make their runs, try and hold down casualties in their own peculiar way. They were wolf-brave.

Now, as light grew stronger, he could see more of them, riding back and forth, exercising their ponies and building up their desire to fight. He could close his eyes and know how they looked, their copper skin, their flat noses, their black, greasy hair. They were supple and horse-wise and they could carry hot lead and still fight; they could be spooked and panic and run away. He knew all about them.

They were hell on wheels when they outnumbered the enemy. That was the trouble. He stared until his eyes ached, turning slowly to all points of the compass. They were everywhere. It was almost the entire nation, on the annual Moon Raid, and it was a sight to see, but not to enjoy.

He lingered, turning over in his mind the exact chances of defense. He could picture part of it, he could see how to beat off horseback attack on a building as solid as the way station. It was when they got over the stubbornness and stupidity of such methods, when their losses mounted and they came in afoot for the kill, that he could not see it. There would be a lot of killing, but how long could the defenders hold out?

Silo asked, "The cavalry, señor? It will come, as the sergeant says?"

"No, the cavalry will not come as the sergeant says."

That simply did not make sense. The 6th was coping with Cochise and the Kiowas and orders from Washington and green personnel and the distances between places. The 6th had its own troubles without worrying over a lousy little stage station with its few occupants.

Silo said, "Then we die here, Señor Pierce?"

"Some have already died."

"Miguel died. He was not a very good hombre, you know. He was one to talk with the mouth. He did not listen well."

"Miguel got caught by the slick young ones," said Pierce. "Make sure you are not also caught by them."

"When they come, I will be ready."

"When you spot them, fire a shot and run to the house. You understand?"

"*Sí*, señor. I understand."

"Possibly they will themselves fire the barn. This we cannot prevent. This may be good or bad."

"*Sí*. Good or bad. I think we will kill many Comanches."

"Oh, we'll kill plenty," said Pierce in English. "Trouble is we can't kill enough."

"To kill them is good," said Silo. "Let us not look, at this moment, further into it."

"You got the right idea there, boy." He went toward the station. He had to face it sooner or later. He had to speak with Gloria.

He saw a small form trudging, laden with paraphernalia, from the odd, covered wagon to the house. He overtook Lamkin at the door.

The photographer explained, "I thought I would bring in all my gear."

"You still think you're goin' to take pictures of Comanches?"

"There have been some quite interesting shots caught by chance. I'll expose my plates until they are close enough for me to feel able to hit them. Then I'll fire the shotgun."

Pierce said. "Well, I'll be damned."

"We'll all be damned," corrected Lamkin, twinkling. "You are amazed."

"Yeah."

"If they fail to smash all the plates, someone might find them, later. Then there would be a small record of what happened here."

"Hell, Lamkin, what good'll that do?"

"No good to us. It's merely something I like to think of. Let us say, a small joke."

"You got a strange notion of what's funny, Lamkin."

Nevertheless, he went to the wagon and helped bring in the rest of the equipment, more of the heavy little boxes of plates, the ill-smelling containers. He felt an odd need of communication with fellow men; he was also reluctant to speak with Gloria. They set up a dark room in Manning's bedroom.

He noted Myra Manning's protective attitude toward Lamkin, her open contempt of her husband. It was perplexing, it was something else to think about when he got the time.

He had a cup of coffee with Luke Post.

The gambler said, "Who you got outside?"

"Silo. And the burial detail."

"Silo's enough, I reckon. They won't sneak in next time."

"No, they won't. They'll put on their show."

"You think it'll be exactly full moon?"

"They ain't much on that stuff, but it just might be they're makin' medicine." Bear Head would use the medicine man to his own advantage, not because he believed in him. Bear Head had got his name when as a boy, while escaping a wounded puma, he had run full tilt into a tree without suffering any damage, but inside his skull was plenty of common sense. Pierce went on diffidently, "Uh— meant to say somethin' about the way you sided me."

Luke looked surprised. "Just plain, everyday thinkin'. How else can a man go?"

"Every which way," Pierce told him. "Specially when it comes to a fight."

"It's accordin' to how many fights a man has been in, the way I reckon," said Luke.

"And who's been in 'em with him?"

"That, too. Take a fella like Ben Tyler, now, he ain't used to all this. He'll do to take along, though." He watched Pierce's reaction, was sorry he spoke when the frown deepened on the round, tough face.

"He'll fight."

"Hell, everybody'll fight."

"You think so?"

"When a man sees his end right close, he lashes out like a buckin' bronc. The bronc may know in his heart he can't win, but it don't keep him from sunfishin'."

"A coyote won't fight. He'll dog it till he's run down and howl while he's dyin'."

"I seen men do that. Maybe we got one or two with us. I wouldn't lay odds on Manning. Mainly, though, a man'll cling to life until somethin' gets more important."

"More important? Like what?"

Luke considered. "Seems like some people got a steam engine inside 'em. Keeps drivin' 'em along a track. Long as they're on the rails, they go fine. Comes a washout and they get derailed. They can go haywire, then."

Pierce felt vaguely uncomfortable. "Reckon I been out too long. I don't altogether savvy you."

"Hell, me neither," grinned Luke.

"You been around more people than me. All kinds of folks. You got a higher regard for 'em."

"When I was ridin' range there used to be books around. Nothin' else to do, so I read 'em. Found out you can learn a heap from books. Hell, that's how I got a yearnin' for good clothes, readin' the mail-order catalogues." He stroked the lapel of his brightly checkered jacket. "They was some other readin' matter, little old things you could send for, nickel apiece. Right interestin'. Fella name of Shakespeare, wrote funny lingo, but it made sense if you studied. Used to read him a lot. Can't remember how he said things, but it sure hit home sometimes."

"I never did learn to read good," confessed Pierce.

"Like this fella in a thing called *Macbeth*, he says life is a story told by a idiot, full of sound and fury, somethin' like that. And he says 'signifyin' nothin'.' "

Lamkin, coming from the improvised dark room, paused and smiled at Luke. "You find that comforting?"

"It gives you somethin' to ponder."

"You agree that life signifies nothing?"

"If I was Mac . . . you know, the king, and in the fix he was in, his wife dead and all the killin's and that, mebbe so. Now, if I was me, and hereabouts, and all them Injuns out there, it ain't quite the same."

"No quotation is valid out of context," said Lamkin.

"I dunno what that means, but it sounds like you're on the trail," said Luke. "Maybe my life signifies nothin' so far as anybody else is concerned. It ain't precisely the way I see it."

Lamkin looked at Pierce. "That's why I'm setting up my camera, you see?"

"Because you want to signify." This was simple, this satisfied Pierce. He found his mind a little clearer. This talking with people, there was something in it.

Lamkin said, "Some small gesture toward the fates."

"He talks like a book," said Luke, admiringly.

They had chosen a window easy to defend. Lamkin struggled with the heavy equipment and Luke went to help him. Myra hovered nearby. Pierce watched them a moment, as they set up the camera.

Here was death at hand, and here were people going about an ordinary task which under the circumstances was somewhat ridiculous, yet he felt no desire to laugh or expostulate. This wasn't Dutch and the Kid, this was people.

He found it easier to go into the main room. Ben Tyler was not in sight, but Gloria was working at the largest table, which had been placed against the wall where it might have some protection from outside, and was covered with blankets. She was rolling more bandages from clean white sheets and stacking them on the table.

In the lamplight she looked younger and perversely more attractive than he could remember. He did not understand this, nor why it should be true, and it made him angry. He went across the room and stood staring at her.

She met his gaze with serenity. It was quite easy for her

to transfer all blame to Pierce. He had evaded her desire to be married, he had treated her like a whore. Ben Tyler had offered to wed her and treated her like a whore. There was, to her, a vast difference.

He said, "You bitch."

Her lips curled away from extraordinarily good, even teeth. "Your mother, you bastard."

"I ought to kill you."

"Try it."

He made a gesture toward the knife at his belt. His eyes went pale. "You think I won't?"

"I know you won't, you damned Indian."

In that instant she was afraid she had gone a bit too far. The knife came half out of its scabbard.

She said quickly. "You got no call to holler at me."

"You slept with that goddam farmer."

She drew herself up, looking down her nose. "For your information, Ben and me are goin' to get married."

The knife slid back into place. He was confused. "You and him. . . . You believe that?"

"I damn well know it. We're goin' to his ranch and live like folks. We're goin' to have pigs and chickens and—and a kitten."

"A kitten?" He could not visualize a kitten. "You gone completely loco?"

"The doctor said I'm cured." It was the only flaw she could see in herself. She was honest about it, and she meant to have another checkup. "I got a right."

"Cured of what?" The shock was wearing off, he could sneer at her now. "Cured of bitchin'?"

"You better not call me that."

"Hell, what are you? What have you ever been?"

"All right." She made a swift alteration in terrain. "If that's what I am, leave me alone."

"I never minded. I know what you are. I know how you're made, Gloria."

"Then don't bother me. Go away. Leave me alone, if I'm what you say." She could not resist adding, "You got such wonderful friends and all."

He said, "I got you and you got me and we deserve what we got."

"You ain't got me, Pierce. Put that in your pipe and smoke it."

"I got you." His head had completely cleared. He laughed. "You'll see. If we live through this, you'll see. Nobody's goin' to marry you."

Now she was so enraged she could have taken the knife from his belt and slaughtered him. "*You* sure as hell wasn't. You acted like you would. You never said you wouldn't. But you didn't have no idea of marryin' me."

"That's right. Why should I buy a cow when milk's so cheap?"

"You dirty, bounty-huntin', goddam—Indian!"

He reached for her, still laughing, his good nature restored, trying to drag her to him. She leaned away and slapped him hard alongside the cheek.

He drew back a clenched fist. His wrist was taken in a grip which was numbing in its power. He turned and shoved against the wall.

He brought up a knee to the crotch of Ben Tyler and the big man fell away, then came back. Pierce reached for the knife. A sharp blow at his arm prevented completion of the move and then Ben hit him on the jaw and he saw black for a moment.

He shook his head, aware vaguely that he was on one knee and unable to roll with it if Ben kicked him. He heard Luke's voice and tried to banish the stars which kept exploding inside his aching head.

Luke's dry voice came through to him, "You two are actin' like tomcats on a back fence."

"It was all Pierce's fault," said Gloria.

"The hell it was," said Luke.

"He was goin' to hit her," Ben said.

Luke said, "She's been hit before. Goddam it, the Comanches will be on us any minute now and you people are squabblin' over what amounts to nothin'."

"We're goin' to be married, Ben and me," she wailed.

"That ain't nothin' and you can't make it nothin'."

"Not today you ain't goin' to be married. Nor tomorrow, neither. So the hell with it."

Pierce found he could see again. He stood up and was able to speak quietly, looking hard at Ben.

"Luke's right. To tell with it."

"You keep your hands off her," said Ben.

"Yeah. I'll do that."

"He said he'd kill me," Gloria protested.

"The goddam Injuns will kill us all, most likely," snapped Luke.

Pierce sighed. "Yeah. O.K., Luke. O.K."

He went to where his rifle stood against the wall. He picked it up and opened the door and went into the dawning. Better he should think about Bear Head and Josie. Why worry about a whore just because he'd known her sometime and because she happened to look good by lamplight? He knew the way she looked. He knew all there was to know about her.

All right, she was a bitch. She'd been his bitch, that was the thing of it.

He looked at the moon in its full brilliance. He heard Silo's whistle, then a shot.

He moved to where he could see the plain. There they were, the red bastards.

They were drawn up in their battle array, a circle which seemed thin, but contained two waves. The young ones would come in and then the older, wiser heads would follow. They wore paint, he knew, although he could not see at this distance, they wore everything it was their custom to wear when they fought, and in which they had no fear of dying.

Silo came, looking back over his shoulder, trailing his rifle. "They ride soon, now, señor?"

"Any minute, now."

"So many I have never seen."

"They are very many."

"Perhaps there are some of yours, those who did wrong to you?"

"Most damn likely," said Pierce, in English.

"It will be a pleasure to kill some of those."

He nodded, thinking again about the barn. It could not be properly defended with so small a force. If he tried that, some of them might be cut off there and quick disaster would follow.

He said, "Into the house, Silo," and watched the breed move to obey, toeing in like an Indian, but swaggering a little, too, which showed he had other blood. It must be rough to be a breed, he thought, worse than being White Eye. If he lived to go out again maybe he could take Silo along. Give him something. Like what Luke had said, a steam engine inside him to keep him driving.

There was some riding back and forth by the Indians. They were in a hurry and they needed that moon for the raid below the border. It was funny how they figured, making up their minds to come in, yet slightly uneasy. Their superstitions were few, their religion was stealing and cruelty, but they worried a lot about their souls in afterlife. Their spirit, they called it, and they couldn't bear to think of it wandering forever in darkness.

About the sun, that was odd, too. They would lie around in it for hours. They soaked it up, luxuriated in it. Yet they didn't exactly worship the sun, not the Comanches.

The red bastards mostly worshiped themselves and their ability to rape and murder. That was their steam engine. They'd been hanging onto it for generations, so far back no man knew when they'd started, before the Spaniards brought the horse to make things easier for them.

He shook his rifle at them and addressed them in their own guttural tongue. "Come and die, you sons of whores. Come and meet White Eye and die."

Then he went back into the station.

Chapter 16

♦♦♦

Hump and Shotgun were back at their places in the bedrooms, Lamkin peered through his camera viewer and prayed for proper lighting, Silo, Luke, and Pierce stood at the narrow windows they were to defend, Manning lingered in the hall where it was safe, Gloria and Mrs. Manning moved quietly about from kitchen to the rude dressing table where the bandages lay ominously piled and ready. Ben Tyler leaned on the sill of the window to which he had been assigned and stared out at the brilliant hour between dawn and sunrise.

The Comanches had moved closer. The line of them curved to his eye, surrounding the house, yet Pierce had said they would not come across the road from the south because of danger of collision and crossfire. They were not that dumb, Pierce told everybody. They would come in on the half-moon and strike and wheel and then come back again.

Ben could see horses and small figures aboard the animals and vaguely he could detect some waving feathers and once he thought he saw a lance brandished. They would have muskets, a few rifles, tomahawks, knives, and the lethal bow and arrow, which in this fight was their best weapon, Pierce said. They were bad rifle shots, but they had the nerve to ride close and fire point-blank. With the bow and arrow they were superb shots and could stand off and make everyone take cover, but they had lost confidence in their traditional weapon years ago when the mountain men demonstrated their great skill with the rifle at so much longer range.

Ben murmured to Luke, "Pierce talks a whole hell of a lot. Acts like he's nervous."

"He's a fightin' fool," said Luke. "He's talkin' because he wants everybody to keep his nerve and hold his fire and not waste ammunition. Pierce'd 've been a hiyu Army officer. He's got the savvy and don't you forget it."

"Well, he sounds nervous."

"You're thinkin' of that—of Gloria," said Luke, as near to anger at Ben as he could get. "Never mind her. Think about them red bastards out there and listen to Pierce."

Well, he deserved that, Ben thought. He had been thinking of Gloria and of last night and how they had slept snuggled together and how warm and soft she was and how it had seemed good.

And he had been thinking of stories he'd read about strong and silent heroes and redmen killed by the hundreds and never a trapper or hunter or cowboy or cavalryman more than "creased" or slightly stuck with an arrow, so that they wore rakish bandages in the florid illustrations of the dime weeklies and were nurtured by brave, sweet, good women. None of it matched this situation in which he found himself floundering.

He was not simple enough to believe that Gloria was a good woman in the churchgoing or storybook meaning of the word. Not many people really care about that, he thought. They talk about it a lot, but when they're grown up they don't really care very much. It was nicer, maybe, if it was true, but the hell with it.

He couldn't even be jealous of Pierce, maybe because Pierce was the past just as though he was dead, instead of moving around here, giving advice, going from one window to the other, watching the Indians.

"If Bear Head's in charge, it'll be worse. He can't stop them from puttin' on the show. They got to make that first charge to get their blood up. Seems like the damn fools got to get a few of 'em killed before they really begin to fight," Pierce was saying. "Bear Head'll let 'em go just so far. Maybe they'll make a couple runs. Then he'll dismount and deploy, then we got real trouble."

Bear Head? It rang a bell, and then Ben remembered about Josie Pierce and her Comanche husband.

He thought then of Manning and his accusation that all of this was because of Pierce. Most likely Manning was right and Bear Head was here because of his dead father and brothers, and all the other Comanches whom Pierce had scalped, and because of Josie and her children, his children also.

It didn't make any difference whether Manning was right, but it was kind of funny that everyone despised and detested Manning and all the time he was correct. "It's not enough to be right." Ben thought, "you have to adjust to situations, physical and moral." He looked across the room and saw Sligh, whom he had momentarily forgotten.

Sligh was lounging at a window facing the enemy. He had two rifles at hand and a row of cartridges on an upturned crate. His close-set eyes were calm, he looked like a man without a care in the world.

Sligh had adjusted. Manning had not. That was the difference. The battle hadn't started and suddenly it occurred to Ben that there would be other deviations in character and for a horrified instant he wondered about himself.

Until now he had, like Gloria, possibly because of her reiterations, excluded Luke and himself and the girl from the possibility of death. The others swam in and out of his thoughts, he began looking more closely at them, wondering what they felt, if they were dubious.

He had been scared plenty of times, as everyone is momentarily panicked by a real or fancied danger. Other times, as in Kaycee against the River Gang, he had been exalted and strong and felt the desire to fight. He certainly had not feared Adobe, nor Sligh, Manning, Hump, and Shotgun when they joined forces. This was different.

There were, Ben estimated, around a thousand Indians out there, nearly the entire Comanche nation. They were brave, useful fighters. They were determined to exterminate this garrison.

A thousand was ten hundred. He wondered if there were a thousand shots in the locker of the defenders, supposing every one counted, which was ridiculous. A thousand Red Indians, all bent on killing, it was too many, he realized.

Then he became aware that his left hand was quivering.

He lifted it, looked at it. He tried very hard to will it to stop. It shook like palsy.

Uncle Tiger had once said, "A scared man is a critter. You can't never tell which way he's goin' to jump. I remember the time the lion got loose from the circus and the town coward, Timothy Futch, took an ordinary broom and chased it clean over into Sussex County. Timothy was too busy to run away for fear the lion might ketch him."

Ben didn't feel like running. He just wished he was some place else and that the hole he now noticed in his stomach was filled with something besides fear of death.

The sun will rise, he told himself. If you see it, well and good. Meantime, here is this Comanche moon and those redskins.

Pierce said, "Listen!"

He heard a wave of sound. To his amazement it was not very frightening. The voices were high, almost feminine. They sounded more like kids playing Indians than like Comanches loaded to kill. He forgot about his shaking hand and the emptiness in his middle, staring out through his narrow window at the oncoming wild wave of the first charge.

The dawn threw weird shadows as ponies picked up speed and riders yelled, waving arms. The ponies were disproportionately small, he thought. They scuttled over the plain like an army of bugs.

There was little color to the scene. It was gray and black with touches of silver. It was all fluid motion, a show of riding skill, it had an air of unreality.

Pierce's voice grew hard and sharp. "Don't nobody shoot until I say."

They took a long while to come close enough for Ben to pick out individuals. There was no question of choosing a target, as there were so many of them, possibly a quarter of the entire band within his range of vision. He realized that he was leaning too far out the window and drew back.

He checked his rifle, and his hand was steady enough as he cocked the hammer. He laid the barrel carefully along the window sill and waited, his breath coming quickly, his eyes straining to keep the approaching riders in focus. The light was uncertain, particularly where the barn threw its shadow.

Then he heard the first shot. He did not detect the course of the bullet because he never heard it strike and he thought it strange, for surely the way station was a big enough target.

Pierce said, "They ain't tryin' to hit us. They're tryin' to draw our fire. They don't know how much powder and shot we got."

There were more shots, then and more yells. Ben watched for them to come in past the barn. Then it would be all right to turn loose. They were riding harder and harder. There were so many of them that it seemed they could ride right through the buildings, sweeping everything away.

He began to be very angry about this. All those Indians and only a few inside to fight them; it wasn't fair. He began to wish they'd come within range of his rifle. He had forgotten nearly all the fear. There was just one little place deep inside him which kept repeating that it did not want to die. He found he could ignore it.

"Don't shoot," Pierce said again, pleading. He was watching over Ben's shoulder, now. "It makes the bastards real happy if they can draw fire."

They came almost to the barn, within Ben's range of vision. On the other sides of the station the ranks kept fairly even, diminishing the space to the station. No one loosed a shot at them. They came on and on.

Then, as Ben raised the rifle and it seemed that they would be into the yard part the barn, they swerved. They were well drilled at this. Yelling, firing at the building, brandishing lances, they showed superb horsemanship as they circled, riding clockwise around the way station, just out of pistol range, within rifle range but making uncertain, bobbing, weaving targets in the moonlight.

"Let 'em ride," said Pierce. "Its a show the young ones got to put on." He went to the central window he had chosen for himself. His rifle seemed a part of him as he peered out at the wild, sound-filled scene. "They figure if anybody's goin' to be scared to death, this is the time. They believe they can scare people to death. They believe that."

Ben was aware of discomfort from straining forward. He pulled back to relax his muscles, looking about the room. There was only one lamp burning, on the table against the wall, in such a manner that it did not illuminate the windows. Gloria was carefully rerolling a bandage by its glow. She smiled at him. She was a bit pale, but her smile was steady.

Myra Manning had her Bible and was reading it just inside the kitchen door. Manning had not appeared.

Lamkin had the shotgun in his hands and was leaning against the wall near his camera. He glanced at Myra, who was bending near to a shadowed candle in the kitchen, her lips moving over the printed words and his eyes were soft with sympathy.

Luke had refused a rifle. He had found a long-barreled Colt's among the armament and with this and his own revolver he waited at one of the front windows, smoking a cheroot, dispassionate, calm.

Callahan was scowling, shaking his bull head. "Damn monkey tricks. That ain't no real cavalry charge. When the 6th gets here, you'll see a cavalry charge."

Pierce said harshly, "You're lookin' at the best goddam cavalry the world has ever seen, Sergeant. The Cheyenne, the Sioux, and the Comanches, and I'll take the goddam Comanches."

"They can ride," admitted Callahan. "But they waste ammunition and they're too fancy. The 6th'd cut right through 'em."

"And come out on the other side dead," Pierce told him. "I been on both sides, Sergeant. Only one trouble with the Injun. He's got a way of wantin' to live to fight again. He won't fight blue uniforms when he can massacree farmers."

"Or citizens in a way station," said Luke dryly. "They ain't serious this time, Pierce."

It was true, Ben saw. They had circled away. They were cantering in a slow circle and behind them the main body was sitting motionless just over the horizon. A small cloud slid over the moon and was gone.

Chapter 17

♦ ♦ ♦

Lamkin inhaled the smoke from his cigar, blew it out. He looked past his camera's barrel at the Comanches and thought that they were the most dramatic beings in the world. They must rehearse before the battle, they must make their show before the enemy for the satisfaction of . . . of what? Their composite ego? For tradition? Strategy? Or was it their art, the art of making war?

He must remember to ask Pierce about their art. . . . Pierce was moving about, missing no details of the defense to come. He was an active man, a man of intelligence, thought Lamkin. If his urge were in another direction he would be a good citizen, perhaps. Ruthless, possibly too strong and impulsive, but basically useful.

They were all moving restlessly, unconscious of their gestures. It was not a time for repose. In the dim, reflected light their shadows were sometimes huge, sometimes misshapen, as if to portend what might come to each.

Lamkin had wanted to be an artist, a painter, when he was young. It had been decided, not by him, but by the family, that it could not be afforded. Perhaps he would have been no good at it anyway. Desire alone cannot make for talent, he said, half-aloud.

Myra Manning looked up and smiled at him. Curious how she had preserved something out of the morass of her existence. Her body was good in all its proportions. Her breasts were high and firm, her hips had not spread, her ankles were trim.

He had not so dissected a women for a long time, except for the purposes of his profession. He had been dry and brittle and without life since the last affair, in New York, with Cynthia Van Owen. He could scarcely remember her features now, the deceptive Cynthia, who had seemed so warm and proved only tepid and cowardly besides. The lack was in himself, that he should have allowed such a woman to dry up his life force.

He had been fashionable in New York after the War. He had protested in vain that he was a noncombatant, everyone with the South in his mouth was a living embodiment of the Gallant Lost Cause. His studio had been swamped by simpering women and some not so wishy-washy, some with guts and willingness and loneliness because of men dead in combat. And then there was Cynthia.

The Van Owens had not always been rich. They had profited mightily in shabby uniforms and blankets and papier-mâché shoes which even the Confederates had disdained as loot. The family was old, however, and the noses high and the blood thin. They had posed for frozen, ugly photographic portraits and Cynthia had returned for a cabinet study and the damage was begun. It had ended when the rich rejected the humble cameraman and Cynthia had refused to elope.

He saw now how silly it was of him to expect her to show courage. He had invested her with qualities which she lacked. The fault lay not in her, but in his own romanticism. It had taken him a long time to figure this out. Too long, he added, for look at him now, warmly observing a married woman in a doomed outpost of civilization.

All his love affairs had ended in such trailings off. The world he lived in was inhabited only by himself and some few odd creatures who entered, then vanished like the smoke rings he was now trying to blow from the cigar that was dwindling in his fingers.

Yet he had been often amused, always diverted. Nothing is lost in the eye of God, someone had said. Statesmen and generals and painters and writers, all ended in the common grave, and what lived on of them or their works no one could know for a hundred years, perhaps more. He had seen some things truly through his camera and his experience had taught him other small truths, he believed. He had little regret at making an end of it, if he must.

He would have liked trying a life with this woman, because she needed him, because she reached out to him and there were things he might teach her of love and kindliness and understanding. She was plain of feature, humble in origin, the exact antithesis of Cynthia, and she was what he needed, as she needed someone like him. The brute, the cowardly Manning, did not matter, he was a circumstance which could be somehow avoided when necessity demanded.

He put out the butt of his cheroot. If he lived, he decided suddenly, he would do something about this woman. He would leave it up to that, the fact of his survival. At least it might give his remaining span of life an objective. He went over to her.

"Have you found an appropriate passage for this morning?"

"It's a comfort just to read the Word."

"Yes. However, we are not yet dead."

"I'm not reading the litany." She surprised him with the frankness of her smile. "I guess I'm looking for hope."

He lowered his voice. "Would you leave here? With me?"

"Tomorrow," she said. "Tonight, if we could get away."

"You know what it would mean?"

"We'd go north, among the friendly Indians." She had been thinking about it, then. "After a while, in another part of the country, what would it matter? Maybe I could get a divorce sometime and it would be all right."

She would soon forget whether it was all right, he knew. He could see the eagerness in her, in every lineament as she strained toward him.

"Then we will go," he said. "When this is over, we will get into the wagon and go."

"Will we? You truly mean it?"

"I swear it."

She lowered her eyes. "All right, then." She put the Bible carefully away on a shelf. She remained standing, looking at him with all of her in her eyes. "All right, then. I can go on, then."

It was putting away an old life and donning a new one, he realized. His responsibility choked him for an instant. Then he faced it and touched her hand and said, "You are a woman to be loved, Myra. I will do my best."

Her grip was quick and cool, then she moved toward Gloria and the bandages and the table for the wounded. Instinctive, he thought, going to the soiled dove. Knowing that she herself would freely sin made the whore cleaner in her eyes.

So, Cynthia, he said to a shadow he could not clearly define, but which for this last time hovered a moment, so there is an ending and a beginning and you were a fool and I was a fool. Are you happy, Cynthia, with your tradesman husband and his muttonchop whiskers? As happy as you can ever be, I fear, or would ever had been with me. Love and marriage are two different things, Cynthia, and, when you examine it, we were not very good at being lovers.

The shadow went away and he knew he would never see it again and had no regrets. He turned his attention to Pierce, from whom all action seemed to flow.

Pierce was talking with Luke, gesturing toward the distant Indians. "This here is a powwow goin' on. They're thinkin' and that's bad."

"I figure it's the barn," said Luke. "We might of made a mistake there."

"I thought on it. Fire is risky."

Luke said. "Supposin' they're plannin' to throw some of their best shots into it?"

"Bear Head might think of it," Pierce nodded.

Lamkin went toward them, interested.

Luke said, "We could still burn it down."

"They'd come in behind the smoke and flames and if the wind shifted, it'd be all hell to pay."

Lamkin said, "Do you think it should be destroyed?"

"I'm afraid so," said Luke. "Have to shoot the horses."

"Yeah. Can't let them have the horses."

Everyone was listening now and Lamkin debated with himself for a moment. Then he said slowly, "I have some dynamite."

Pierce's strange eyes fixed upon him. "It could still start a fire."

"I was thinking if they did put some men in there."

"You got a detonator?" asked Luke.

"I bought some odd lot junk from a prospector. I'm not sure what is in the box."

Sligh moved from his window. "I got what it takes and a couple extra sticks of dynamite, too. It's in my pack."

Pierce said, "If we move fast it might work. They hate big noises. Cannons scare 'em silly. It just might work."

Callahan said, "What are we waitin' for?"

"Who's the best shots? Tyler? Luke? Get Silo out here. You'll have to cover us. The rest stay indoors in case anything goes wrong." Pierce was going to the door.

Luke said, "Pierce, you're the best shot of all. Let Lamkin and Sligh handle the stuff."

Pierce stopped, then nodded. Luke was right.

Callahan said, "I got experience. Blew up a few bridges. I'll go with 'em."

Lamkin could see Myra's eyes across the room, glowing like a cat's eyes in the night. He motioned to her and smiled. Then he followed the others out into the open.

It was bright as day. The Comanches could see them coming from the station. They would indubitably make a charge. Lamkin was shaking a little, as he had always shivered under fire, but he could think clearly enough. He ran to his wagon and took hold of the box. It was too heavy for him. Callahan lifted it with ease and threw it open.

Inside the barn there were repeated shots, a few whinnies, and a pig grunted as the slaughter went on. Then Callahan had the sticks of dynamite out and was binding them together with wire and moving toward the barn and Sligh was joining him, uncoiling a thin wire.

Pierce gripped his arm and said, "At the corner of the barn. Set it under the sills. They might think we was only killin' the stock. Here they come. Work fast."

Lamkin joined Callahan and Sligh, not knowing exactly what was required of him, but with swift hands, taking orders from the two who worked at placing the dynamite where it would wreck the structure in one blast.

The sound of the hoofs of the Indian ponies was like rain approaching across the roofs of Savannah during a thundershower, growing louder every instant. They would never get finished with the job in time.

Lamkin was nearby, flat on the ground behind a dead sow. There were others deployed to cover the barn, he knew. He heard the wild, keening yells and now the Indians did not seem a brave band of showmen, they were deadly instruments bent on destruction.

Yet as always his senses remained clear and he found the end of a wire when both the others cursed, fumbling for it, and they gave him the coil and Callahan said, "Slow and easy does it. Won't do no damn good if it breaks, y' know."

He began uncoiling the wire, backing toward the house, making sure it was flat on the earth so that no one might not trip it when retreating to safety. The first spatter of shots sounded and Pierce roared. "Take the leaders. Pile 'em up."

Then the firing became steady and this was the first of the real battle, Lamkin realized, with the dawn throwing its tricky light and Tyler out there kneeling and shooting with calm steadiness and Luke Post and now Callahan, who joined him to stand guard over the wire and let off his rifle.

Noises buzzed about his ears and he saw one brave break through with a lance and saw Pierce kill him with a head shot and the horse ran through but miraculously escaped the wire. Then they were at a window and inside Myra was holding out her hand and he was pressing the coil of wire into it.

Now he had to make for the door. He was aware of

Callahan as a bulk which shielded him. He heard Pierce
give sharp orders, heard the shrieks of Indians, wondered
if any of the defenders had been hit, wondered if he would
make it, stumbling, regaining his balance, skidding on the
hard ground as he came to the corner of the building.

Then something hit him and drove him down and he
thought it was an Indian and lashed out, but immediately
knew he was wrong. It was Callahan lurching into him and
the butt of the rifle knocked out his breath but he hung onto
the big sergeant and staggered for the door.

A rider came through and aimed a lance at them, racing
across the yard, a feathered man who yipped like a prairie
dog, urging his horse, bent on impaling the two oddly
coupled men in one thrust. Lamkin lifted the rifle and
managed to get a finger on the trigger and pull.

The horse lost stride and the rider came running to earth
graceful as a skimming swallow and did not stop, continuing at his target afoot, the lance poised to throw. Lamkin
fired again, realizing that Callahan was a cushion between
him and the lance, holding steady on the trigger.

The bullets went into the Comanche but he came on running. The gun was empty and time stood still for a second,
and then Lamkin tried to drag the bulk of the sergeant out
of the path of the lance and found he could barely move
the man.

There it was, then, death at the end of a nastily infec-
tious spear point in the hands of a crazed savage. He let go
of Callahan and tried to take some action, any action to
prevent the helpless man from suffering a further wound.

As if struck by a bolt from the sky, the Indian fell. The
lance stuck in the ground and quivered, giving off a small,
slithering sound. Without conscious thought, Lamkin seized
it, yanked it free and ran at the prone Indian.

Ben Tyler grasped his elbow, spinning him around and
said, "You already killed him once. Let's get Callahan
inside."

Pierce and the others formed a knot which blazed fire
as the enemy rode a circle around them. From the far end
of the station Hump and Shotgun were taking toll. There

were some excited Indian cries and then the door was open.

An arrow drove into its wood, humming, and Tyler heaved Callahan indoors and Lamkin found himself still clutching the lance even as he helped Tyler swing the heavy form up and stretch it out.

Gloria said, "Get his tunic off. Cut it away if you have to, but get it off. The dye will get into the wound."

"Is he—is he alive?" Myra had a basin of warm water.

"That's what we got to find out." Gloria's voice was cool and steady and Lamkin went weakly to the window where his camera was mounted and leaned against it. He wanted to vomit but could not. His eyes watered and his mouth twisted so that he put both hands to his face and set himself to regain control.

Tyler was saying bluffly, "If Callahan's alive he can thank the little rooster, there."

They were all inside. Sligh had a scratch from an arrow on his chest, but was laughing about it. There are many kinds of courage, Lamkin thought dimly.

Tyler went on, "Lamkin brought him in. Killed an Indian doin' it. I never did see anything like these damn Indians since the gypsy brought the fightin' cocks to Peapack. Fight you till you're dead and then some after."

Gloria said, "It's a bullet wound. It's on the right side, but it might have got the lung."

"Shut up," said Pierce. "We know you worked with a doc, you don't have to tell Callahan everything."

Lamkin saw Ben Tyler scowl and take a step toward Pierce. Luke interposed, saying smoothingly, "Lucky we got someone knows about them things."

"Damn little she knows," Pierce said harshly.

From the window, Sligh said excitedly, "They in the barn, all right. A whole shootin' mess of 'em."

An arrow whirred into the room through one of the windows. Sligh was attaching the end of the coil of wire to a detonator. Pierce turned to him, forgetting Gloria and Ben for the moment.

Lamkin slid down to a sitting position on the floor. He

felt as thought he had run a hundred miles uphill. He had to laugh a little, soundlessly, thinking of Pierce and his whore and Ben Tyler. Violence and death all around, yet they squabbled as thought it was all a theatrical production.

Lamkin couldn't have argued for Myra, for anything not in that moment. Now he had looked straight into the face of extinction and had survived, now he had seen it up close and not faltered, he should feel better perhaps.

He did not. He had not liked the look of death, nor the feel of it in his soul.

Chapter 18

♦♦♦

Gloria finished the bandaging, tying off neatly, angry at Pierce, sore at everyone for the moment, remembering the business with Doc. Sure, she had hung around his office, helping with the gunshot wounds which were a daily occurrance. She wanted to make sure about her lungs didn't she? Doc was a whisky-head, you had to stick around Doc a lot to find out the truth.

And she was well, no matter what Pierce said. Doc had finally convinced her. She'd been scared enough. She'd seen the girls from the houses die of the consumption and she had to know she was well and healthy.

So she had learned things and now they should be damned glad, because she knew enough to be cleanly and to tend a wound like Callahan's and lots of other tricks. She had learned hanging around Doc, and if they didn't like it they were ungrateful bastards, all of them.

It was seldom that she felt that she had a grievance. This was one of the times and she gave Ben Tyler a dirty glance in the bargain and said to Myra Manning, "Thanks for helping so good, dearie. I think we better throw out the dirty water and make sure we got some more hot."

She followed Myra into the kitchen and said, "He got it in the lung, all right. I can tell by his breathin'."

"Shouldn't it be taken out? The bullet, I mean?"

"Only a real doc could do that. Anybody else'd kill him."

"Will—will he die, anyway?"

Gloria said gloomily. "I expect he will. He'll get a fever. If we could get out of this and get him to a doc, he'd have a chance."

Myra said, "If we ever do get out of this. Any of us.'

"I will. I swear I will!" Maybe if worse came to worse the Indians wouldn't kill her. Maybe she could survive whatever they did to her. God knows she had survived plenty. She wouldn't die, she fiercely rejected death.

Myra said, "I believe they're goin' to blow up the barn."

Pierce and Sligh were working together at the end of the thin wire. The others were watching. Gloria was suddenly aware of the sounds from outside. She had been so occupied with Callahan and her own anger that she hadn't noticed until now. The Indians were shooting fast and furious.

She started to take a look and Ben Tyler caught her arm and said, "You want to get killed?"

Then she saw another arrow come through a window and stick into the wall.

She said, "How come they're shootin' that good?"

"They're in the barn."

"Oh, I see." She watched them at the detonator. It was amazing the things a girl picked up knocking around. She had known miners, too. "What'll we do if it won't go off?"

"It'll go off."

"Plenty of times it don't."

"It'll work," said Ben. "Sligh's an expert."

"Look at 'em, Sligh and Pierce," she said. "A little while ago Sligh was goin' to turn him in. Then Pierce was ready to hang Sligh."

"Circumstances alter cases, my Uncle Tiger always said."

She looked at him. He was hurt by the way she had glared at him, she realized. "Look, I didn't mean anything. I could see Callahan was bad hurt and that damn Pierce made me mad."

"I'll attend to Pierce," he told her flatly. "You leave him to me. You think about us."

"I'm thinkin' about us. I'm thinkin' Pierce'll have somethin' to say about you takin' care of him. He's like those Indians he lived with so long. He's poison."

"I'm not scared of Pierce."

She felt relaxed with Ben glowering, insisting that he would take care of her. "You're sweet, you know that?"

"Just don't you fret about Pierce."

She rubbed against him, letting him feel the thrust of her breast, smiling up at him. "I'm frettin' about you. That's all I'm frettin' about."

"I'll be all right."

She said thoughtfully, "You're not scared, but Luke could handle him. If he wanted to."

"I'll take him apart with my bare hands."

"Pierce don't fight that way. He uses that knife like Doc used a scalpel." Careful, she warned herself, not too much about Doc in front of Ben. If Pierce shoots off his bad mouth I can handle it, because Ben'll be sore at Pierce. But no man wants damaged goods, not that kind of damaged. She said quickly, "Luke is gun-quick. There ain't a more dangerous gun in the country than Luke Post."

"You leave Luke out of this."

She looked at him with fond scorn. "Luke wouldn't lift his finger for me. He's your friend, he'll look out for you. He won't let Pierce get you from behind, that's all I want."

In the other room, Pierce said, "O.K. Get ready."

Sligh said, "Everybody down on the floor."

"What about Callahan? Will he be all right where he is?"

"Stand the table clean against the wall," said Pierce. "This here is goin' to shake things considerable."

Lamkin had come into the kitchen. He looked mighty puny, Gloria thought. Myra gave him some coffee and for the first time Gloria noted the exchange between them.

She almost exclaimed aloud. She saw Myra force the little photographer down to the floor against the partition to the bedroom and lie alongside him and then she knew for sure. Well, she thought, you never can tell where a blister will raise. She eased herself down and Ben lay alongside her, partly covering her with his big body against possible falling debris. She was chuckling to herself.

Women have got guts, she thought. Just give them a

chance, that's all. Myra's been living with that no-good wonder, that dirty, whining husband of hers, and putting up with anything he dished out. There wasn't anything else for her to do. Who'd look at her, with no clothes, nothing to take care of herself?

But let a mild little man, a gentleman at that, take one peek, and it was Katy bar the door. Now wasn't that something? That was a thing and a half, that was. It made Gloria feel warm and happy. She listened to the men at the detonator. Bullets entered the room, knocking Myra's Bible from its shelf.

Pierce said, "You ready, Sligh?"

"Better warn them in the back rooms."

Pierce called, "Silo."

The breed came in, ducking low, graceful and lithe and darkly handsome, and Gloria thought that he moved a lot like Pierce and that, too, was the Indian of it. Pierce gave him orders in Spanish and Silo slithered back to the passageway.

Sligh asked, "How many you think are in there?"

"Not enough. Not damn near enough."

Ben moved a little and she snuggled closer. She saw Pierce's eyes, white again, watching her.

Pierce growled, "Tyler, you get in here and cover Callahan. You can brace the table."

Ben hesitated, then left her. She felt naked under Pierce's glare. She mouthed at him silently, "You sonofabitch." She crawled along the floor past Sligh and the detonator, staring Pierce down. Ben had put his shoulder against a leg of the sturdy table. She crept under the table and grinned at Ben, then turned and deliberately stuck out her tongue at Pierce.

Pierce said, "All right. Let her rip."

Sligh worked the plunger. The explosion was a conglomeration of noise and physical sensation. Gloria felt the floor shake beneath her and then for an instant she was deafened. The entire station shook and quivered.

She could not refrain from getting to a window. She looked over the shoulder of Luke Post at the barn. It had settled down on itself like a house built of cards. There was dust and licking little flames coming from it, but not a large blaze. There were bits and pieces of things here and there and as she watched an Indian rolled free of the wreckage and stood up. One of his arms was gone. After a moment he fell down.

Other figures moved and Luke fired his revolver. Pierce's rifle crackled and near the broken-down corral one of the Comanches coughed and died. There was already a stench rising from the yard and Gloria put a handkerchief to her nose. She saw part of an Indian torso across a broken musket and half of a horse strangely intermingled with the remnants of another Comanche.

Far in the distance she could see the main body of the Indians. It was in full flight for the hills.

"They're gone," she cried. "They're running away."

"Yeah, they're scared of noise," Pierce repeated.

"We can get out of here!"

Luke laughed a little. "Afoot? How far could we get?"

She had forgotten about the horses. She said, "Why couldn't we have saved some of them to pull a stage?"

Pierce snorted. "Comanches are scared of noise but they don't stay that way. They'll be back."

"You know they'll be back." Luke yawned. "Sure could use some more shut-eye in the meantime."

"It blowed real good," Sligh was saying. "It sure went good. I swan, I never see a prettier blow."

Gloria whispered to Luke, "You better not sleep too good. You better keep an eye on Pierce."

The gambler regarded her coolly. "Scared?"

"Not for me. He won't do no more'n bat me around some."

"For Ben?"

"You know it as good as I do."

"It's a hell of a note," said Luke. "I got to protect him for you. It's a hell of a rotten note."

"I know what you think of me. Just so you don't let him do the Injun on Ben."

"Well, I'll tell you. In the first place he won't, not till this is over. In the second place, I misdoubt he gets away with it, even if the time comes. Meantime, you can quit worryin'.''

"I know you ain't doin' anything for me. But thanks anyway," she said. "Thanks a whole heap."

He batted his eyes, unwilling to give her an inch. He went into the hallway.

In a moment he was back. He had Manning by the shirt at the small of his back and was shoving him into the dim light. "This galoot was under my mattress. Somebody do somethin' about him. Pierce?"

He let go of the man, who promptly fell on his knees. Pierce went over to him, looking down.

"I thought you were at a back window."

"I—I couldn't."

Pierce said, "You couldn't shoot off a gun?"

"They were comin' in so fast. I couldn't aim." The man's voice was a hoarse whisper. His lips moved but no further sound came from them.

Gloria started for the kitchen. Myra was already in the doorway, staring at her husband. Gloria said, "You better not watch this. I know Pierce."

Myra said. "I don't want to watch. I just had to see him, the way he is."

Gloria blocked her vision, gently turning her back to where Lamkin sat at the table over the coffee mug. "Shut the door. It'll be better that way."

She stayed on guard, not thinking of herself, holding the door against Myra. Pierce had Manning by the hair and was lifting him. She said sharply, "Watch out for Callahan. Take him away from that table."

Pierce dragged and Manning shrieked once, scrabbling to go where he was directed. Pierce lifted him and slammed him against the wall. Manning stuck there as though plastered to it; he seemed to have no more substance than wallpaper.

Ben started forward, saying, "Now, just a minute, Pierce . . ." and Sligh moved to intercept him.

Gloria sat across the room. "Pierce is right, Ben."

The big man stopped, his head on one side. Pierce held

Manning up with one hand, saying over his shoulder, "Nothing personal in this, Tyler."

"Well . . . all right. I reckon it has to be."

"It damn well has got to be done," Pierce said.

Ben looked at Gloria, shrugged, then went into the hall. Pierce turned his attention back to Manning.

"I could do your wife a favor and turn you aloose out there," he said, gesturing toward the door. He yanked Manning's head around so that he could see out the window. "Take a look at how things are, out there."

Manning sobbed, "I wanted to fight 'em. I tried to. Ask Hump. Ask Shotgun."

Hump and Shotgun came into the room as their names were uttered, heading for the kitchen. When they saw what was going on they paused and Hump said, "That chile needs coaxin', sure enough. He's got the collywobbles."

Gloria let them pass her, closed the door again. She could have left now, she knew, but she didn't want to. She was beginning to be a part of it, and she had to see and know all that was necessary.

Pierce said, "I thought we had you worse scared of us than the Injuns. That's what I thought."

"I'll do anything. I try. I always try."

"You tried to turn me over to 'em," Pierce reminded him dispassionately. "That was your one big try. After that, you give up. Sligh didn't give up. Nor Hump, nor Shotgun. They seen the light."

"I only wanted to save everybody."

Pierce took out his little knife. It was wickedly sharp. The reflected light caught it and the gleam hit Manning's rolling eyeballs.

Pierce said, "We talked to you, Luke and me. We tried to get it through your head. There's only a certain number of windows and they got to be covered. A man's got to stand at 'em and shoot. That's all. It ain't much."

"Don't cut me, Pierce. Don't! I'll do anything you say. Only don't cut me."

Pierce's hand was quick as light. He took off an ear lobe with one slice. The blood ran freely down Manning's neck. Propping him against the wall, Pierce showed him the bloody edge of the blade. "You thought we wouldn't hurt you. You didn't believe us. You was scared of Injuns. You ain't seen nothin', yet, Manning."

Gloria's ears rang with the man's shrieks. She could not take her eyes from the scene if she tried, now. All the things men had done to her crystallized in her mind. She exulted to see a man weep and beg. She was proud of Pierce in that moment for showing how a man could be, a bullying, loud-mouthed man.

Pierce said in his calm voice, "You coulda done that to yourself shavin' after a hard night. It's nothing court plaster won't fix up in a jiffy. It's just a start, Manning. If you don't get in there and man one of those windows, I'm goin' to really do it to you. I'm goin' to show you what the Comanches will do when we turn you out for them to grab. I'm goin' to keep you just barely alive and then I'm goin' to give you to them to finish. You understand, Manning?"

Manning put his hand to his neck, then looked at it, at the blood on it. For a moment Gloria thought he was going to faint. Then he wiped the hand on his shirt front and stared at Pierce and it seemed his eyes came to life in that moment.

"Someday I'll kill you for that."

Pierce nodded, stepped back. Manning stood against the wall, his shoulders straightening. "Yeah. O.K.," said Pierce.

"I swear to God, I'll kill you."

"After this rangdoodle is over," said Pierce cheerfully.

"Any time I get the chance." Tears welled from Manning's eyes. "Any time, Pierce."

"I heard you the first time. Now get in the back, there. Take a rifle."

Nerved up to where he could mop at his ear, Manning walked, stiff-legged but erect, into the passageway. The knife in his hand, Pierce turned and looked at Gloria.

She said, "It don't scare me, you know."

"I ain't aimin' to scare you."

"Don't ever figure on it."

He wiped the knife and returned it to its place. "I don't

need to. You won't ever marry that farmer. He ain't for you."

"All your talk don't make it so," she said, and opened the door and went into the kitchen.

He was a tough man, he could make them come to him, she thought. He could handle them, the brave ones and the cowards. In his own way, he was all hell.

For that matter, so was Ben Tyler. If they didn't think so, Luke would hold them off while Ben proved it.

A small shiver ran up and down her spine. Two strong men fighting over her? Over Gloria Spriggs, who called herself Gloria Vestal?

Chapter 19

♦ ♦ ♦

Silo was dragging the many carcasses, man and beast, to the remnants of the smoldering fire. Pierce joined him, took hold of a scalplock, stripped it. He went methodically among the Indians, taking the hair, dropping the bloody pieces into an old bucket.

Silo said, "We kill plenty. The driver and the Shotgun, they fight good, Señor Pierce."

"Everybody fights good today."

This would be one of those fights people talked about in saloons and lone army posts and maybe even there would be a piece in the Kaycee newspapers about it. Nobody survived, but it made a story and those who were known to be in it would be heroes every one.

Manning too, he thought. If he lived, or if he died, Manning would go down as a hero. He could remember the fight at Silver, in New Mexico, when half the company wanted to quit and one coward killed himself rather than continue. There was a real big story told about Silver, how Andy Dane had gone out under fire and tried to bring in Sergeant Bowdoin, who was wounded. They told how the Comanches had fired fifty shots before they killed both men.

The truth was that Sergeant Bowdoin and Dane had tried to get away from the fight and break through to safety. They had believed it hopeless on the hilltop. Several shots had been fired at them, all right, but by their own company. An old buffalo hunter had downed Bowdoin, then the Comanches had closed in and of course Dane put up a fight. He knew he'd be staked out in view of the men he had deserted, and he knew they'd laugh at the sight of a bonfire on his coward's belly.

The others had stuck on the hilltop because they were experienced, practical men who knew a strong position when they held it and because there was a hell of a lieutenant in command and the buffalo hunters were smart and the best shots in the country. Pierce had known the Comanches wouldn't waste too much time fighting entrenched men and the lietuenant had agreed, and after a while the Indians went away.

This could hold true in the present fight, excepting for his own presence, he thought. He looked carefully at the few indentifiable dead, seeking a clue to Bear Head's presence.

It was then he heard Silo grunt.

He leaped across a charred, fallen roof beam and saw the breed bent over, trying to lift his rifle, unable to manage it. He saw an arrow sticking in Silo's belly, saw the blood.

He hit the ground with scant cover, estimating the spot from which the arrow could have come, cursing himself for not having been more careful. It seemed impossible that anyone could have lived through the holocaust, but he of all people should have realized that a Comanche can survive where no other man or beast would have the chance of a tissue-paper cat in hell.

The barn had collapsed on the side nearest the house, the explosion under the sill having directed its force outward. Therefore the far side was tumbled every which way into a rubble heap.

There was a jumble of beams and broken planks to his right. He looked at the spot of ground where Silo silently writhed out his life. The angle was right and it was also one from which it might be difficult for the Indian to loose another arrow in the direction of Pierce.

He began to crawl, very slowly, to his left. He used his elbows, managing the rifle with the skill of long practice. The Comanches had taught him this. He could move silent as a snake. He dragged himself across bits and pieces of horror without consciousness of anything but the hiding place of his quarry.

He knew how long a wounded Indian could lie without

sound or without exposing himself. He wished he could yell, alarm the station, get help for Silo. He wished these things, but there was in him no impulse to do so. To leave the Comanche where he lay would be to expose someone else to the fate suffered by Silo. He had to take care of this quickly and neatly, alone.

He made his circle and came beyond any shelter to where the stagecoaches stood side by side. For one instant he thought that the Comanche might possibly have gained one of the stages and was holed up waiting for him.

When no arrow came he knew he had been right in the first place. He continued on the arc he had designed in his mind. It took him farther and farther from the station. If a Comanche party returned to pick up their dead or to reconnoiter, he was doomed.

He lay for long moments, ever fearful that someone from within the station would expose himself and receive a tufted message from the Comanche. He could detect no movement among the rubble. There was nothing at which to shoot and there was no cover under which he could charge.

He got up very slowly, to his knees, to his feet. He had to make sure the Comanche could not see him. He moved forward, bent at the middle, loping.

He was almost to the spot he had selected when he saw the motion of a dim figure, hasty, as though his surprise had been completed, as though this was a desperate last chance, a motion he knew well. He threw himself down and fired.

An arrow whizzed nearby. Then Pierce was up and running, his gun abandoned, the knife ready in his grasp.

The Comanche was propped against a jangle of harness and broken boxes. He did not move as Pierce came in, merely stared.

Pierce dropped to one knee. Their eyes met. There was a bullet hole in the Comanche's chest and the position of his left leg left no doubt that he had been crushed in the wreckage of the barn. Pierce's bullet had done for him. There was barely breath left in him, yet he managed to spit.

The spray was faint on Pierce's face. He brushed it away. He said, "Walking Jay?"

The Comanche was a boy no more than fifteen. Pierce need not have asked his name. The eyes were not right for a full-blooded Indian. There were flecks of gray in them.

He said, in Comanche lingo, "I am sorry, Walking Jay."

The boy tried hard to spit again, failed. His head dropped, his jaw slackened.

Pierce sat back on his haunches. There were voices coming from the station, everyone wanted to know about the shot he had fired. They discovered the body of Silo and raised an outcry and he heard his name repeated.

He called out, "O.K. I'm O.K. Be right in."

Now he knew that Josie and Bear Head were out there. Now he knew they would never quit until they got him.

He had just done for Josie's oldest boy, the product of her rape.

He tried to examine the past, to evaluate it against the present. A link had been broken in the chain which forged by the attack upon his father's ranch, had extended on through his captivity, his escape, and his continuing war upon the Comanches. He had to look at it, understand it.

He had to make clear to himself the difference between Josie warm and radiant and young, his big sister whom he had adored, and the Josie of today. He had to admit he wanted her back as she had been, that hidden inside him there had always been the dream of the old Josie.

He was accustomed to introspection, because he had lived alone for so long a time, but he was not used to complete dredging of his inner impulse and intentions. Had he envisioned a Josie restored, perhaps married to a white man, happy, carefree? He stared at the dead Walking Jay.

. Here was the truth, a fifteen-year-old son sent to kill Josie's brother. Here was evidence of what she was now, the wife of a Comanche chieftain, upon whom he had not laid eyes for eight years. She dressed, ate, lived, like an Indian. She had chosen to remain an Indian.

All right, she had remained with them because she loved her children. She had cherished them far more than her brother. He saw himself, a wild youth, half-clad, half-starved, desperate, a bit crazed, begging her to escape with him. He remembered her refusal, abrupt, decisive.

She had not betrayed him then. Now it was different. Now she would see him killed without turning a hair.

He had killed some hundred Comanches and sold their scalps and piled the money in a bank. Had he done this in a dream of restoring a Josie who could never be restored? The thought numbed him. His sister hated him. There was nothing left of the girl he had loved. The knowledge shook him as though a giant had him by the nape of his neck.

He forced himself to stand, walk back to where he had left his rifle. He saw people coming toward him and said harshly, "There was a young buck got Silo. I had to scout him out and kill him."

No use to say more, no use of anything. A part of him had been damaged. He felt exhausted. It had been a hard time, the long chase after Dutch and the Kid were taken, the business here, the lack of sleep for more than a few moments at a stretch, the strain on his emotions.

He had been able to endure the side glances and slurring remarks of people only because he had never thought of himself as an ordinary bounty hunter, that was it. He could see it, now. He had been thinking like a young puke, dreaming of Josie restored, of a Josie who had once lived but was now a Comanche.

His sister was a squaw. It diminished him.

He had suffered captivity among them, he knew what it meant to be an Indian woman. He knew the filth, the degeneration of all that was dear to white women.

He was stunned by the knowledge of his dream, of its complete futility. He had to adjust to the fact that Josie was his mortal enemy. His mind and his body suffered, he never remembered having felt like this.

Hump and Shotgun were examining Walking Jay's body. "It's only a button."

"Them's the worst. Them and squaws."

"This one here's got a breed look about him."

"Them's worse'n kids and squaws, even."

"He done for Silo."

"A breed kills a breed. Each on t'other side. Now that's a circumstance."

"Silo was a good breed."

"His Mex momma was good folks."

"You knew her?"

"She was around some. Years back. Had a hard way to go. Silo was a bright young 'un. She raised him good."

"You think we got to bury Silo?"

"Sure. Got to burn or bury everything we can, afore they get back onto us."

"We better look for shovels. If there's a shovel left around."

"Ain't that a hell of a note?"

"What?"

"Things are gettin' so rough around here you can't find a spade to bury the corpuses."

Pierce went to the pump. It was still working, by some small miracle and the clever disposition of the dynamite by Callahan, Lamkin, and Sligh. He washed himself as best he could, removing his shirt, letting down his pants. He felt dirty all over.

The sun poked a red finger into the eastern horizon. He looked at it and knew the Comanches would be back soon and why they would come. They were unstable in battle, charging and retreating and holding parleys, but this time they would return for a reason. His brother-in-law wanted his scalp.

The knot in his belly would dissolve in time, he thought. He'd go on, doing the things which had to be done, he hoped. If he survived, life would be about the same. If he had not learned that lesson, long ago, he would never have been able to exist among the Comanches.

He went into the station carrying his rifle and the torn shirt. Gloria was leaning over Callahan and he had to pass her to get to the saddlebags, but somehow he didn't care to pause, nor even to look at her. He pulled a clean shirt over his head.

Myra Manning was offering him a platter containing a

sandwich of meat and bread. He couldn't find words, so deep had he plunged into thought. She peered at him, withdrew the offering and said, "Mayhap you'd like a drink of whisky."

"Thank you, ma'am. I ain't much for whisky." He managed to add, "I could do with some coffee."

He tried to force himself back to thoughts of the siege. Bear Head wouldn't quit so long as he had Pierce trapped. If need be, he would skip the Moon Raid into Mexico. He was tough enough and strong enough to control the tribe, to make them believe that getting White Eye was more important than raiding below the border.

Myra Manning had sensed something, it appeared. She led him firmly into the kitchen. Lamkin looked up with interest, his eyes narrowing as he noted Pierce's gaunt withdrawal. The sandwich on a plate before the photographer and he was hacking at it with a dull table knife.

Pierce took the little, curved scalping blade from his belt, and without thinking, reached over and sliced the meat and bread in two.

Lamkin hesitated, then smiled. He picked up half of the sandwich and said, "It doesn't matter, does it?"

Pierce reached for the coffee. It was as if he was bound with chains and powerless to do anything about it. He had seldom known weakness, but his guts were empty for this time. He couldn't get rid of his new knowledge of how Josie must look today, how she must feel, of her hatred for him.

Now that he knew of his dream and its utter futility, he was half-ashamed, half-defiant. In time maybe he would understand, but he was drained and helpless in the face of conglomerate emotions to which he was in no way accustomed.

Chapter 20

♦ ♦ ♦

Callahan was conscious when Ben and Gloria, who had been bathing his brow, looked down at him. The sergeant's eyes were too bright, his voice a husky monotone. Luke came and stood by, exchanging a worried glance with the other two.

Callahan droned, "Comes a time when you get in wrong. Bad wrong. Nothin' to do but join up. No money, no way to go. Join up, they say."

"You oughta try and sleep," said Gloria.

"I know, I know." His light blue eyes went to Ben and Luke. A small smile lit the florid features. "I got it good. I know it. Inside me, that's how it feels. All gone."

"You'll be all right," said Luke.

"If the 6th don't make it, I'll be as good as anybody else." The fever seemed to have lessened. His voice picked up strength. "'They'll make it. An Army doc could help me. I seen one at Gettysburg, he was takin' off arms and legs like a butcher cuttin' lamb chops. Never turned a hair, neither. Took a Minié ball outa my shoulder. . . . You seen the scar?"

Gloria said, "I saw it. Please don't talk."

"Man don't talk enough, ordinary," said Callahan stubbornly. "Don't get it out of him. Like about Five Points, the way it was. Nobody got enough to eat, enough to wear, enough of anything whatsoever."

"Five Points, that's New York," said Ben. "The city."

"Fight, steal and lie, or you starve." Callahan closed his eyes, opened them again. "Where's the Indians?"

"Gone, but not forgotten," said Luke. "They'll be back."

"The 6th'll make it. You'll hear that bugle."

"It'll be sweet music."

Gloria repeated, "You should try to sleep."

Callahan's voice altered, ruminating, "I seen the elephant. I seen it before Gettysburg. First Bull Run, right at the beginnin'. Regular Army, I was. A dumb war, all them volunteer regiments, them dumb officers."

Luke said to Ben, "He's got to talk, I reckon."

Callahan rambled on, "If somebody could take that bullet outa me . . . That doc at Gettysburg . . . I wisht I was back in Pennsylvania."

"You don't like Pennsylvania, remember?"

Color rose in Callahan's face. "She was a Dutch gal, name of Katzie. Cook? Keep a clean house? You never seen anything like it. All right, she wasn't smart or quick with the talk. Her and me, we understood without talk. We coulda made it good. The Irish and the Dutch . . . You might beat the Irish but you can't beat the Dutch."

"A woman," sighed Luke. "Always it's a woman."

Ben stared at Gloria, admiring her as she adjusted another wet cloth on the fevered brow of the wounded man. She was frowning, but she looked pretty and efficient. It was close to dawn and the light in the room was changing to a rosy glow.

Callahan rambled on. "Five Points is dirty and the people is dirty. In Pennsylvania it's green and there's hills, all green, and fruit and vegetables and cows and pigs. They eat good. Fat they are, even the strong boys is fatty. But they got respectability."

"There's all kinds of respectability," Ben said, thinking of Gloria. She gave him a grateful look.

"In the Army, you're a bummer. Only Katzie didn't think so. She didn't know different. She thought I was good enough. It was her folks. To them I was a bummer."

"Take it easy, Sergeant," Gloria pleaded.

Luke shrugged and went back to watching for the Comanches. Ben lingered, both because of Gloria and because of his sympathy for Callahan. He knew about farmers and their limited view, their preoccupation with crops and the weather, always the weather. They seldom saw beyond their narrow horizons. He could imagine the Dutch farmers looking askance at Callahan.

Pierce came in from the kitchen. He said flatly, "They're back with us."

Everyone rushed to the windows. The color of the early morning was rose gold. It bathed even the bitter shambles of the barn, where Walking Jay lay dead. In the distance the Comanches came slowly, in a crescent formation, their ranks solid on the east, north, and west.

"Bear Head's got his reasons for this raid," said Pierce. His voice sounded dull even to himself.

"Bear Head?" asked Luke. "He the big chief of this caboodle?"

"He's it."

"Then they will be hard to discourage."

"This time it'll be a fast hit and run." Pierce tried to regain his poise. He was not succeeding, he knew.

Luke lowered his voice, "The second time'll do it."

Pierce nodded. "When they come afoot, that'll do it."

"Might be Bear Head'll wait for night. I've heard about that Injun." Luke considered, then said, "If the woman can shoot some, we got ten good guns. That's countin' Manning."

"Better the women should reload for us when they get close."

Luke frowned at Pierce's listlessness. "What's the matter? You don't feel too pretty good?"

"I'm O.K." He straightened his shoulders. It was an effort. He was tired all the way through.

"You ain't caught enough shut-eye. Maybe a shot of what Manning calls whisky?"

"Had some coffee." He looked out of the window. He would have to fight it off, he thought without caring. "I'm all right."

Luke prowled, dissatisfied with Pierce's responses, worried about Callahan. They needed Pierce's leadership and they needed Callahan for the fight. He looked into the kitchen where Myra Manning and Lamkin were talking as they watched for the charge of the Comanches.

Lamkin said, "The sun is fine. I can expose some plates."

Luke shook his head, turning away, going back to where Ben and Gloria listened to Callahan. Pierce was outdoors, he noted, leaning against the wall, staring at the Indians. There was something wrong with the bounty hunter, all right.

Callahan was wandering, his voice rising and falling. "Five Points was dirty. You jined the Dead Rabbits or got beat to death."

Ben said, "The Dead Rabbits is a New York gang. They used to fight all the time. Fought the Bowery Boys a lot. I remember about 'em, before the War."

Gloria sounded her warming, "Talkin' ain't good for you, Sergeant."

"If the 6th don't come soon, I'll be quiet long enough," he answered. "Mickey Callahan, thirty-eight years old, dead on a table in Texas, a place he never hoped to see, nor wanted to, for the matter of it."

And calling for the Army to get him out of it, Luke thought, the Army he had damned since the day he joined up, like every proper veteran.

"We went down to Delancey, the Dead Rabbits," Callahan said. "It was a fight, like all of 'em. Only Corrigan was Tweed's man and he had a big stick. I took it from him, I did. I beat him over the head with it. Could I help it the man had a soft skull?"

Ben said, "They were always fightin' over the fire companies, over anything at all. I remember about them."

"Corrigan was no good, but he was Tweed's man and mind you, Tweed was comin' up then. So it was into the bleedin' Army and good-by to Five Points," Callahan said. He was now talking to himself. "It could all have turned out good, if only Katzie's folks had not been so pigheaded."

"If man could do without woman," said Luke, "it would be a heap easier on him."

"Why should it be easier on a man?" demanded Gloria. "You got a nerve, Luke Post. You wouldn't be here, wasn't for a woman."

"I never knew her," Luke said blandly. "I wish her luck, wherever she is."

Callahan said. "The way they did it, that was the worst part, y'know. Me, with never a black mark on me record. So I was a wee bit overstayed on the leave. Nobody would've cared a hoot, me with the wound and the medal and all. But they made a smell with the provost marshal and I was picked up like a common deserter, and with Katzie lookin' on. Taken away like a criminal, what could she think of me? Who can call her wrong to marry the farmer from Lancaster? T'wasn't Katzie, it was the old folks, the way they did me."

Gloria said, "Certainly it wasn't her fault. What could she do? A woman needs a husband."

"She does, she does." Callahan was silent.

Thinking of Ben, Luke said, "A woman's got to earn a husband."

"That's your idea. That's what you believe." She tried to control her anger. She might need Luke, she realized. She lowered her voice, "We better leave Callahan alone, maybe he'll drift off to sleep."

The three of them walked to the window and Luke saw Ben pat Gloria's hand and shook his head in disapproval. The Indians were spreading out now, coming toward the station. Pierce had said they had a purpose beyond winning the battle. Pierce should know, thought Luke.

Bear Head . . . He tried to remember what he had been told about that Indian. Quite a lot, he thought.

Pierce came in, then, and said, "Pretty soon now."

Luke asked, "You got any ideas?"

"Kill 'em," said Pierce. "What the hell else?"

Gloria saw to the weapons with quick hands. She moved well, Luke thought, reluctantly admiring her sureness. Under other circumstances, and if she was different in her guts, she wouldn't be so bad. He knew too much about her, from El Paso days.

Ben was a tenderfoot in more ways than one. He was woman-conscious, that had been plain in Kaycee.

He said to Pierce, "I mind somethin' about Bear Head. It'll come to me."

"You don't mind anything good about him," Pierce muttered. He was feeling low, he wasn't even keyed up for a fight. He never remembered when he couldn't get high for a fight. Killing Comanches had been pretty nearly all of his existence, it was true. It was bothering him, now. They had hurt him plenty, they had taken everything from him, but he had never truly admitted that his vengeance was for itself alone, for what they had done to him. He had always made Josie a part of it.

Now he admitted it, and the result was bad. It left him low. He shouldn't be low. Hell, anyone would admit he had a reason, if they knew all that had happened to him while he was among the Indians.

Of course, nobody could really know. The things of the body they could understand, but the things of the spirit were another matter. That was what was now jabbing him, he decided, the things he could never make clear to anyone.

He looked at Callahan. Maybe it would be better if he lay there in the sergeant's place, drowning in his own lung fluid. Maybe it would have been better if Manning, after all, had turned him over. . . .

He struggled to banish the gloom which enveloped him. Why couldn't he be like Callahan and believe the bugle would sound and they they could all begin life over again?

Callahan was dreaming of the bugle. And he was thinking of the end, if the bugle did not sound. What would be the end?

The priests had words for it.

The cloud of the Church formed about his head and suddenly Mickey Callahan wanted a priest. Not since he was a boy had he thought about the Church, except maybe occasionally when he was scared under fire or when he had his wound that July of '64. Now his big muscles were of no use and he felt the gurgling in his lungs and the imminence of death. Now he wanted a priest.

The fever buzzed in his head. Luke came and put a square revolver beside him and he could not close his fingers around it, not even to raise it to his own head.

The last rites, he thought, am I not to have the sacrament? What will happen to my immortal soul?

The 6th, he thought, they got to get here. They'll have a chaplain, perhaps, of the Faith. The bugle will sound like the trumpet of Gabriel and a priest will come to me.

He let the fever have him, then, and his mind drifted on clouds and nothing mattered.

Chapter 21

♦♦♦

The Comanches were coming in mainly from the west, which put the sun in their eyes. Ben heard Myra Manning say behind him, "I can shoot a rifle," and then Luke answered, "Just you keep reloadin', ma'am," and there was kindly respect in Luke's voice.

Gloria came and went with cartridges and water for Callahan and word that Manning was in one of the back rooms between Hump and Shotgun and had his rifle ready. Sligh was on the south side of the building but could alternate at a west window.

Pierce no longer gave advice nor explained. He was silent, at the center window, staring out at the approaching Indians. There was something wrong with him, all right. Ben scowled, wondering if it had to do with Gloria.

It was strange, the way he felt about that. Sooner or later he would have it out with the bounty hunter. What bothered him was that it did not now seem important. He couldn't care, one way or the other.

In the beginning he would have rather welcomed a fight. His disgust for the hair-hunter had been deep. Then when Pierce had unaccountably poured out his story, and after the other happenings, there seemed to have occurred an armistice, broken only occasionally by Pierce's fierce attitude.

If the fight ended in massacre, than nothing mattered so far as he and Gloria and Pierce were concerned. Corpses couldn't quarrel, nor love, nor do other than molder.

He saw Lamkin take the brass cap from the snout of the camera and peer out at the Indians, holding the cap aloft as though invoking the sun and the clouds; then he replaced the cap and extracted the wet plate and hustled through the kitchen to his dark room. Here was a man who had something to do and who stuck to it, and he was curious about Lamkin.

When the photographer came back, Ben was examining the tube of the camera.

"I expect you think I'm crazy as a loon."

"No," said Ben. "I was just thinkin' that to have something you're so taken with is good for a man."

"It postpones the inevitable," smiled Lamkin. "I'm frightened, you know. Underneath, down deep, I'm scared."

"Who ain't?"

Lamkin looked around the room. "One way or another, we're all afraid, I reckon. Some conceal it well. Sligh, for instance. Amazing how well he behaves."

"What about Manning?"

"That was bad. But . . . he's at his post now. The shock, perhaps. Sight of his own blood, hatred of Pierce— who knows?"

"Pierce had to do it, I guess."

Lamkin said, "Luke is not conscious of fear, I believe."

"You'll never know. That poker face of his goes all the way through."

"We'd all like to be as Luke. If there is a heroic mold, he fits it. He is calm, he has good judgment. If something inside him whimpers, we are all better off because it doesn't show itself."

"He's probably figurin' the odds," Ben said. "Maybe we all are. Lookin' for that tiny chance. Like Callahan and his cavalry."

"Human beings must have hope. We'd not live long in the world without hope."

"Live in hope, die in despair, my Uncle Tiger used to say."

Lamkin nodded. "The women take it very well."

"They can't see themselves stripped naked, savages slicin' at them. So they just plain don't believe it."

"Your Uncle Tiger taught you a lot, didn't he?" Lamkin smiled.

"All farmers ain't dumb. A lot of them are, but not all."

"I didn't mean—"

"A man's given a mind. He can use it or not. There's long winter nights when a farmer can read, if he wants to."

"Still nothing prepares you for this. Bloodshed, sudden death, it's always shocking. The War couldn't prime me for it. Nothing ever could."

"I never figured to bury so many people in a lifetime as we've already planted out yonder," said Ben solemnly.

"I've taken some pictures of the dead." Lamkin pointed to the scene in the foreground. "The living and the dead. It's like a bad dream."

"I just can't see myself a corpse." Ben held up his hand and looked at it, at the muscles and tendons.

"And the Indians? How do they feel about it, about the imminence of extinction?"

"I got no time to think of them. They're probably like us. The other one might die, but not you."

The Comanches were closer. One of them raised his hand. He wore a bonnet of feathers, bright in the sun. All were silent, staring out the windows at him.

"Bear Head," Pierce muttered. "He's in the open, now."

Luke said, "It's him, for sure."

The Indians came with more deliberation this time, Ben saw. He returned to his place and looked at the rifle in his hands. Gloria brought another, a Henry, and some shells.

She said, "Callahan's sleepin'."

"The fever any better?"

"I'm not sure, but I think it's worse."

"How are you makin' it, Gloria?"

There was a flicker in her eyes, then she swallowed and said flatly, "You and me and Luke. I still feel it."

"And Pierce?"

"Have you noticed him? He's different since Silo was killed out there."

"Everybody notices. I thought maybe it was us, you and me."

"He didn't even give me a look."

"Somethin' eatin' at him, all right."

"If it is you and me, he'll be awful rough, Ben."

"I'm keepin' an eye on him."

"He's kind of crazy, you know."

Ben looked at the man. His elbows were on the window sill. His face was ever turned toward the Comanches but it lacked expression. It was as if the color had been washed from him. "Maybe he was crazy. He don't look that kind of crazy now."

She said, "No. You're right. He looks . . . different."

Myra Manning called from the kitchen that the water was hot. Gloria managed a smile and patted Ben's arm and moved on. He watched her walk and for a moment was happy with the swing of her hips.

Then Sligh yelled, "Now they're comin' for sure."

Ben thought he detected a new note in their yelling, more ominous, as though the first charge, in the dawning, had been sport, or fun; now it meant more, it was deeper, portending the end. There were so many of them, they could finish it in a few moments, he thought, swallowing hard.

They were superb riders and in the sunlight he could see the brilliance of them, their feathers, lances fluttering with ribbons, their bronze skin. As they rode their cries hit a basic rhythm and the ponies moved eccentrically, making each individual Comanche a difficult, moving target.

Pierce still crouched at his window, his hands steady on the rifle, but silent. He gave no command, made no suggestion. It was Luke who said, "Hold everything until they're close."

The first wave came within range but no one fired. Ben was for the moment fascinated at the sight of death riding beribboned and befeathered and bright in the fresh light of the morning. The chief with the headdress, Bear Head, was behind the first wave, possibly out of range. There was some method, some reason, in this charge, Ben felt.

Sligh said, "I make 'em on this side."

"Check," said Pierce.

Sligh fired, then Pierce. Two of the toy horsemen toppled.

Ben waited, looking past the wreck of the barn, frowning, then estimated his distance and shot a bit high, then ejected the shell and went low and saw a pony go down, and quickly altered his sights and shot the Indian, who had leaped free and was trying to mount behind a friend. Then he hit the friend with an offhand shot. They were coming as he remembered a storm marching across a wheat field and it was like shooting at slanting raindrops.

From the back rooms there was the drum of steady fire as the crescent of red-skinned riders swept on its mission. They were aiming at something, all right, Ben thought. Gaps in the line filled promptly, as though on orders. They came very close and Luke began his fanfarade with the pistols, taking careful aim on each shot. He was very good with the short guns and his quickness split them and they went past the station yipping and yelling, a great number of them firing wildly as they went.

Then, when it seemed they would pause and re-form, many of them detached themselves and began that circling tactic again, shooting their firearms at the windows. They were very poor shots, Ben realized, or else their weapons were faulty. Still a certain number of bullets came in through the windows by law of averages and it seemed impossible that no one was killed or injured.

He was firing with care, trying not to waste ammunition, and he was aware that he was ducking in the face of the return fire, and once that he was narrowly missed by a musket ball. He was counting his share of them. The squirrels in New Jersey had been more difficult targets by far.

They could kill Indians from inside the stout station by the hour, he thought, but how many could they not kill?

He was leaning back away from the window, reaching for the Henry, trying to relax for a moment as the fierceness of the first charge seemed to have died when Sligh yelled, "They dropped some of them by the barn. Look!"

That was the strategy, then. They had come in sailing and shooting and under cover of that, they had dropped off a few to the comparative safety of the rubble. He saw the chief on his white horse and drew a bead on him, but Bear

Head vanished. He saw, though, that the chief's skull was outsize and that he had a tough, intelligent face. He had slipped behind the wreckage at the point where Pierce had killed Silo's murderer last night.

Now the others rode and whooped and fired volleys, to provide cover for their men at the barn. They apparently rode helter-skelter, but Ben could see their purpose.

Sligh said, "We can't leave 'em there. They'll burn us out."

Nobody answered, they all fired at targets they could see. Ben watched the pile of rubble with care but no Indian showed himself. Once in a while an arrow came whizzing too close for comfort, which meant they had to get down to sensible fundamentals and their sharpshooters were covering the chief as were the horsemen.

Pierce said in his new, colorless voice, "Damn it, Gloria, my guns are empty."

She was running from one to another with boxes of shells. Her face was smudged with powder and her hair was loose and hanging down her back, caught with a bit of string, and Ben thought she looked younger that way and even more attractive, but Pierce stood solid at his window and took cartridges without comment.

Luke said, "Sligh's right. That's their dodge, fire."

They were close enough to send arrows into the room in a stream. Everyone had his head down and Ben worried about Callahan, except that he was at an angle which protected him from direct hits and anyway Callahan was now, of all times, sleeping. Steady firing from the bedrooms showed that the Comanches still thrust at that angle.

Sligh said, "I can't stand bein' burned."

"It ain't good for you," said Luke.

Still Pierce stayed at the window, refusing to take part, refusing to do anything but shoot Comanches. This he did very well, this seemed his only mission. Ben moved out of the path of an arrow, wondering what to do, missing Pierce's leadership.

A first flaming arrow arched upward into the sky. He could not see the blaze against the brass of the bowl which the sun had made, but he could see the trail of smoke.

Two more brands followed. The roof couldn't stand much of this.

Sligh shouted, "I ain't holdin' still for no fires."

He went out the door and Luke was with him. It was insanely reckless, but Ben followed. They ducked right and left and were among the riders, and Ben shot one and Luke with his revolvers spun and took two, which gave them time. Sligh was heading over the route Pierce had taken last night, where he could get at the concealed redskins who shot the fire arrows.

A little knot of warriors were concentrating on the roof. They were dismounted and intent on their job and the chief in the headdress was among them. Ben instinctively knelt to get his aim. Sligh, a little in advance, fired offhand, like a hunter after partridge. Luke, his hard hat cocked to one side, stood straddle-legged in his checkered suit and whirled the revolvers with incredible speed.

The Indians went down like tenpins but there were riders swooping in to cover those behind the rubble. Ben fired his last shot, made it count and was preparing to run for it when he saw a strange sight.

Bear Head was carrying a slight form in his arms, going to his white horse. Luke fired at him and missed. Sligh aimed with more care as the chief draped the body over the horse's back, was ready to pull the trigger.

An arrow struck Sligh in the throat. As he fell, Ben grabbed him, then his rifle. Out of the corner of his eye he saw the chief make it aboard the pony and ride off, the body swaying before him, saw the remaining Indians screening him as they retreated.

Then he was running for it as more Comanches came in and from inside the station a rataplan of shots covered them. Ben had Sligh on his shoulders and Luke had taken the precious rifle and when they got to the door they saw that Myra and Gloria were shooting past them and Pierce was still at the window.

Then the door was closed and Sligh was dying on the floor. The arrow had severed his vocal cords and there was nothing to do but stand over him and try to stanch the blood, knowing you could not and that he was finished.

Before he died, Luke said to him, "When it comes to a fight, you're a good man, Sligh. You was right there with us. Ahead of us, even."

Sligh nodded a little and then died.

Luke said, "You never know till the chips are down. This man here fought as good as anybody I ever did see."

"The roof," said Ben, remembering suddenly. "That's why we went out there. Start the water comin'."

Then he saw Pierce, already on the ladder, lifting the scuttle cover, thrusting himself through. Lamkin brought the first pail and Ben went after Pierce. Luke handed up the pail and it was difficult getting it to Pierce without spilling it. Ben went on through the hole and onto the roof, which slanted only slightly to its eaves. There was a fire burning on the corner and Pierce was clearly exposed to the attack of the Comanches as he sloshed at it.

Ben said, "Wait, maybe I can kick it out."

He wore heavy boots and he knew about fires from living in the country. Pierce came past him for more water as he went to the spot and began kicking at the small flame. It was smoldering, but he kicked loose most of it.

Then Pierce was back and they soaked the place with care, and below there was more hammering and the Comanches who came close enough could not take good aim because Myra and Gloria and Lamkin and those in the back room were slamming lead at a furious rate. It was an exultant moment for Ben and he waited while Pierce brought one more pail of water.

The Comanches were really yowling now, and he saw them form in a large body and wave their arms and then they came like a wave and he remembered that they knew Pierce and that they wanted him above all else.

He said, "Get back. Go down. I've got it licked."

He shoved Pierce and for a moment thought the man would fight him back. Then the Comanches were coming and the firing below increased and he knew Luke was back at it.

"Damn it, get down there," he roared.

Pierce looked at the Indians, then at Ben. In his eyes was little expression. He nodded, however. He turned and walked without haste to the scuttle hole. He let himself down to the ladder and disappeared.

Ben felt a missile tear at his shirt. He dropped to the rooftop and crawled all the way to the hole. He almost fell headlong to the floor. The exaltation was gone, he was scared clear through his bowels, he admitted.

Pierce was already at his window. Ben drew a deep breath, following his gaze, leaning against the wall, exhausted.

Far out on the plain Bear Head got down from the white horse. He lifted the slight body from his horse and held it a moment. Another figure joined him, and this could be a woman, Ben realized. The two of them went out of sight with the body.

Pierce dropped his head between his arms. He was, Ben thought, seeing something long ago and far away. All of Pierce's story came back to Ben and he knew what had happened.

"That was Josie?" he whispered.

Pierce's head nodded once.

"The body? It's the one you killed last night?"

Again the nod.

Ben reflected a moment. "One of her sons," he said, then. "That's bad luck, Pierce. Damn bad luck."

"The hell with it," Pierce's voice rasped. But he did not lift his head. "The hell with it all."

Chapter 22

♦♦♦

They wrapped Sligh's body in a blanket and stowed it away in a bedroom. No one had anything more to say about Sligh. He had been a man suspect and he had died bravely and that was an end to it. Pierce had no thoughts about him, except that he was another gun for defense which was gone.

Pierce could not talk to anyone, that was the trouble. Ben had offered him an outlet, but he could not talk again with the farmer. He knew they were all puzzled because he was no longer the leader, because he had withdrawn behind a barrier. He lacked a bridge to get back to where he had been.

Myra Manning came to him and said, "Are you hungry? Everyone has eaten something but you."

He could see that she was different, too, that she looked better and had a more definite personality, and he remembered how she had taken a gun, a Bible-reading woman, and had fought while the others were outdoors. What he could not do was convey anything to her. "No thanks, ma'am."

Gloria came by, cloth in hand. "Callahan's able to talk now. The fever's down a bit since he slept. You think we should put him in a bedroom?"

"He wouldn't like that."

"You ought to eat something," she said. Her voice was strained and unnatural and he looked at her, too, with new eyes and saw that she was weary but still not scared.

He said, "Yeah. I guess so." He felt far away from her.

Luke fired one of the revolvers out the window and said, "There. I been watchin' that little feller. Playin'

games, he was. Sneakin' closer every time he went around.
Got him right in the belly.''

Well, he never had been any good with people, Pierce
reflected. Hadn't had much chance to be around them,
anyway. He couldn't expect it to be any different now, just
because he had a hollow in his middle. The little Indian
had a bullet in his belly which Luke had fed him, but
Pierce had emptiness.

He went uncertainly into the kitchen. He poured himself
a cup of coffee and it was boiling hot. He sat down at the
table, nursing it. Myra Manning was looking through a
box which he recognized as one he had carried in for
Lamkin.

  She showed him a piece of cardboard on which a picture
was mounted, asking, ''Wouldn't think that was him,
would you?''

The face was young and lean, the mustache virile.
Lamkin wore gray broadcloth, not a uniform, the clothing
of a Southern gentleman. The likeness was recognizable
although the sinewy body and bright eyes were not the
same. Everybody changed, thought Pierce, that was the
thing, a man had to change.

''We all get older.''

''Weary is the road.'' She nodded, then said, ''Take
some of this soup I heated. You need it.''

''Maybe I will, at that.'' The woman was thoughtful
and kind and it touched him. He had a moment's memory
of Josie as a young girl, so good to him; then he shut it
off. He must think of Josie as she was with Bear Head, a
squaw.

He made himself eat bread and soup. Then he got up
and went into the other room. Ben and Luke were still at
the windows. Young braves were riding in and out, showing off. Lamkin was at the corner window with his camera.

''I think I caught one of them sitting still, staring at
us,'' he told Pierce. ''It might make a clear picture. They'll
try again to burn the building, won't they?''

''That's their style.''

''I found a root closet. Dirt floor, you know? I can dig a
hole and bury the plate box.''

"Sure, you could bury it."

"Someone might find it, someday. It would be a record. It would be nice if someone found the plates and developed them."

"Yeah. That's right."

He moved away from Lamkin. If he could only straighten out the difference between the old Josie and the new, it would be better, he thought. Maybe it was because he was so unaccountably tired that he was so sluggish.

Today was no different from yesterday, he told himself. There never had been a chance from the start. Callahan and his bugles, Gloria and her notions, it was all crazy. If he could get back to the time before he had killed Walking Jay, then everything would be clear and simple again.

Maybe his trouble was that he, like Gloria and Callahan, had not been ready to face the fact that the end was here, in this place. Maybe he had not believed it, any more than he had faced the fact that Josie was with Bear Head and against him, against all white people. He made a fist and pounded himself on the skull.

It didn't do any good. His mind was fuzzy. Over and over he told himself that Josie and Bear Head had together made up their minds that he must be caught, must be prevented from killing more of their tribe. It wouldn't come sharp and clear as it should.

He found himself beside Callahan. The sergeant said, "If I could get on me feet, it'd be better."

"Just stay where you are. Nothin's goin' to make much difference." He was as wrong as Callahan. His head ached horribly.

"You don't believe the 6th'll make it?"

"I wouldn't know." The 6th were in Arizona or New Mexico, having plenty of trouble with Cochise.

"They'll make it."

"If you say so."

"Could there be the whole Comanche shootin' match out there and the cavalry not know it? No! You'll hear the bugle yet."

"It'd be sweet music."

No use to say any more about it. Callahan didn't have a

chance, anyway. Pierce went into the back of the station, wandering, aimless. In separate rooms Shotgun and Hump were taking potshots at the young riders. Manning was in the middle room.

Hump said, "Pierce, I never did see so many damn Injuns to oncet."

"The Moon Raid is always a big one."

Shotgun said, "No matter how many we make come to Jesus, they got a dozen takes their place."

"The hell with it," said Hump. "Ain't nothin' can be done about it. Why talk about it?"

They were all getting nervy, Pierce thought. He looked into Manning's room and saw that the station keeper had moved a chest of drawers into position so that he could take shelter behind it. Not that the flimsy wood would stop a bullet. Manning was just more comfortable out of sight. He was firing once in a while. He paused to give Pierce a stare of hatred.

Another picture came to Pierce out of the past. He saw Walking Jay, a baby, the living evidence of Josie's shame. He saw Josie push aside a dirty squaw and reach for the tiny, squalling thing.

He had wanted to kill the baby then, but Josie would not allow him. He should have seen it then, how she would be. How she was now, how he must accept her.

Funny that he should have killed Walking Jay, after all.

Not that it mattered, one way or the other. It was only that he might have killed the baby and maybe Josie would have never had another, and he could have got her away. . . . But this was dreaming again.

Two hundred Mex, he told himself, what the hell? With careful trading it added up, and in Kaycee at the bank they never asked where the money came from. They entered it to his account and said, "Yes, sir, Mr. Pierce."

He liked going into the bank with his deposit because they bowed and said "sir" to him. This he had and this he took from the Comanches, from their goddam hair.

This was enough. Why couldn't he let it go at that? Why was he so dead-beat, without desires?

He knew about money, what other people did to get it.

He had learned, in Kaycee, on his vacations there. Some of the ways they had. It was a marvel they wasn't arrested. Bounty-hunting was no worse, rightly considered.

He rubbed a hand over his eyes.

He kept seeing the rape of the ranch and how they had done his mother and his father and he could hear their laughter, the goddam Comanche laughter, high and child-like as they tortured and violated and burned and cut living flesh. Even dogs for stew, or a pony for a feast, they had to bathe in the blood. Nothing was funny except violence done to others. He could not banish the sound of their hideous cackling.

He had to get everything straightened out inside his head. He had to see clear that the money in Kaycee was enough, that he could quit taking scalps, risking his life. He had to see it plain and believe it.

Then suddenly blind rage seared him. He would never stop killing the bastards, never. They needed killing and he was the one to do it. He went quickly into the big room and grabbed his rifle.

Luke said, "They're like a swarm of bees."

Pierce looked out of a window. The young ones were having a big party. They were trying to outdo one another in daring, riding into range, then speeding out as they lay on the far side of the mustangs, only a heel showing. They could not do any damage from this position, in fact few of them could let off any sort of weapon. It merely made them feel big and strong. It would provide fodder for long-winded stories told later around a campfire.

He waited until one of them got too frisky. Then he slapped a bullet into the pony's head, levered his gun and held down as the young buck rolled loose and leaped, skipping gaily, trying to mount behind another of his band.

Pierce let him get a foot up. Then he shot him through the neck, so that the bullet sped through and wounded the second young Comanche. His third shot took care of the wounded one and he watched them go down like a loving couple, their limbs entwined as they kicked out their lives.

Luke said, "That's hiyu shootin', Pierce,"

Lamkin cried, "I got them. I know I've got them." He

was holding the cap as the two Indians ceased struggling and one of the ponies unconcernedly grazed nearby.

"We shoot 'em, he takes their picture," said Luke. "It's funny the way life goes, sometimes."

Pierce did not speak, he was intent upon the two dead Indians. He wished they would move, either of them, so that he could put another piece of lead into their flesh. He wished he could get a bead on Bear Head.

It wasn't any use. He turned away. He knew Luke was watching, but it didn't matter. He went into the kitchen and saw Gloria talking to Ben, who was at the window with his rifle. Suddenly he was concerned about Gloria.

She'd been right with him, according to her lights. She was far superior in morals to the Comanches, who thought nothing of swapping wives over a throw of the bones. He knew the hard way it had been for her and he found himself admitting that she had shown courage and brains in maintaining herself as well as she had managed.

About the farmer, it was different. That had happened when he, Pierce, was on the grounds. That was something to be settled at some future date, if there was a future. All this was basic and simple and easy to understand. It had more to do with Tyler than with Gloria, because he could settle her hash quickly after he had disposed of the Easterner. A good whopping would fix her and bring her to taw.

He grunted, "Gloria."

She turned and looked at him. Her thoughts were far from him, he sensed. "Yes?"

"Callahan is talkin' to himself in there."

"He can't help that. He'll be out of his mind until . . . until something happens."

"You mean until the 6th gets here?" He made his voice harsh and jeering. "You fall for that bunk. You and Tyler."

Ben removed the rifle from the window sill and stepped out of range of danger from without. "You must be feelin' better, Pierce. Little while ago you had some manners."

"You don't scare me with no rifle." There was no sense in jumping Tyler now, it was the mixed emotions he

did not understand which drove him. "Any time I get
ready, I'll take care of you."

"Not while I'm lookin'," said Ben.

"Not while I'm lookin', neither," said Gloria hotly.
"Why don't you get back to your place and shoot Indians?
That's what you do best."

That was what he got for being concerned about Gloria,
he thought. He said, "I'll be killin' them when you're all
six feet under," and knew that he lied, and went back to
where Luke lounged smoking a cigar, cooling his revolvers, squinting out at the circling young men on their
ponies.

Luke said, "The day's wearin' on."

"Bear Head'll be comin' when he's ready." They would
be burying Walking Jay, and Josie would be weeping.
No—she wouldn't. The new Josie didn't cry and howl.
She just sat and hated her own people, hated her brother.
She might not know that her brother shot her eldest son
with his own hands, but that would make no difference.
He was with the party who were responsible for the death.
She would hate him, all right, there was no getting around
that.

Luke said, "I wasn't honin' for Bear Head nor anybody
like him."

"Prob'ly come at dark or thereabouts."

"Sure, he will. He don't worry about dark when there's
a moon to light his way."

Pierce said, "You know some about him."

"I remembered some. Smart and rugged," said Luke
cheerfully. "One Injun that don't hit the snake-eye too
awful much. Got himself a white squaw. Way I hear it,
she keeps him in line."

Shocked, Pierce said, "You heard about her?"

"Not many know, I reckon. Fella told me was a scout
with MacKenzie of the 4th. You know MacKenzie?"

"I know him. He counts high."

"Ranald MacKenzie's the Injun fighter Custer thinks *he*
is," said Luke. "Nearly got Quannah Parker out on the
Staked Plains in '71."

Pierce stirred uneasily. Parker was the son of a girl

captured in Texas years ago, Cynthia Parker. He wondered for a moment if Tyler had spilled everything to Luke. Why had he unbuttoned to the farmer from the East? He could not understand himself these past hours. He was uncomfortable in his own skin.

"This scout was a Seminole, part Negro. Rode into Mexico with MacKenzie just over a year ago. Bear Head was down there. The 4th woulda got the whole kit and caboodle of 'em, wasn't for Bear Head. This scout, his name was Sanchez, he talked a lot to one of the Comanche prisoners."

"I heard about that Mexican raid. MacKenzie took a chance. Coulda been big trouble."

"Sheridan was behind him. The Mexicans can't handle Indians, so they got to let the cavalry in once or twice. MacKenzie kept 'em runnin'. He knows how to rankle 'em."

"They don't like to be chased," Pierce agreed. "Put 'em on the run and they worry. They like to choose their own time to hustle or fight or anything else."

The conversation was getting safely away from Josie. He thought suddenly that he had more than one reason for killing Tyler. He wanted no one to be aware that Josie was his sister. If he could have rescued her, all would have been different. Now, knowing her hatred of him, knowing that she would always be a squaw, he must keep himself ever apart from her.

"Sanchez said Bear Head takes the white woman's advice even in a fight. Won't go anywhere without her. It kept him from bein' head chief for a while," Luke went on.

Pierce heard himself asking, "Did this here Sanchez ever see the woman?"

"Only from 'way off, ridin' with Bear Head. They were skedaddlin' pretty fast over a mountain. The Comanche prisoner said she wasn't young no more. Been with Bear Head a long time. Like Cynthia Parker, I reckon. No accountin' for a thing like that."

"That's right. No accountin' for it," mumbled Pierce.

A paint-bedaubed young buck rode too close and Luke

swung his Colt's around and fired. He missed and the Indian yowled with glee. Luke said, "Keep laughin', boy. You're goin' to laugh yourself right to the Happy Huntin' Grounds."

Pierce thrust his rifle through Luke's window and aimed at the spot he knew the Indian would hit as the pony swerved westward, leading his target, tumbling the young brave to earth.

Luke said, "Shucks, Pierce, he was mine."

"No accountin' for it," a voice repeated inside Pierce's head. "No accountin' for it, no way."

Chapter 23

◆◆◆

Hump called through the open door of the back bedroom, "Shotgun."

"Still here."

Manning was in the next room. He hadn't spoken more than a monosyllable since morning. Rage and hatred had sustained him for some hours, then Myra had brought him food and drink and he had sulkily accepted. Now he was suspended between outrage and the creeping, gnawing fear of extinction. He listened to the two voices, unable to comprehend the dry tones of the driver and the messenger.

Hump said, "I'm plumb surprised. Anybody don't know an Apache from a Comanche."

"I know enough to shoot an Injun when I see him."

They were silent for a moment. Manning wondered what was wrong with Myra. Even when she carried in the food she had not been thinking of him. She took some to Hump and Shotgun at the same time. She had looked at him as though he was a stranger. Didn't say anything about his ear or Pierce or anything. He couldn't make out what was the difference in her.

Hump said, "Say, Shotgun, how old are you goin' on, anyway?"

"What difference does it make? None of us is goin' to be much older."

Hump laughed. "Seems to me you was always around, is all. I don't remember a time I didn't see you around."

"Me neither. Only you was always lookin' down on me. I was just a button when I first seen your ugly phiz."

A shot sounded and Hump said, "Missed the bastard. . . . Say, it's gettin' on to sundown, you know it?"

"I kin measure a shadow."

"Luke says that's Bear Head out there. If so, he'll be sneakin' in pretty soon."

"Been playin' Apache on us," said Shotgun. "Figures on lettin' us get bleary-eyed and weary, then spring the trap."

"You do augur by them Apaches. Is it true you oncet lived with 'em?"

"I never lived with nobody but my ole woman and you dang well know it."

"How is the ole gal, anyways?"

"She don't like El Paso, much. Wants to go back to ranchin'. You know, the chillun all growed up and all. She craves that ranch."

Hump said, "Whyn't you let her go back?"

"It's played out. Land's no good. Never was much. It just about did get Charlie through the school and Maybelle married off. Hadn't been my ridin' the stages we never woulda made it."

Again Hump's gun sounded. "Winged him that time. . . . What you hear from Charlie?"

"He'll do all right. He's got his maw's brains."

"Hope you're right there. Long's he's got my balls, I'm happy for him."

"Maybelle's kids O.K.?"

"Goin' to pop another one. Good thing she married a storekeeper, the mouths they got to feed."

The Comanches made a small sortie to attempt revenge for Humps's shot and both men were busy for a few minutes. Manning shot off a magazine full of cartridges but could not tell if he hit anything because of a distressing habit of shutting his eyes at the moment of pulling the trigger.

Hump said, "How you for shells, Shotgun?"

"Aplenty. Manning, you sure had a stock. You expect the Comanches to come acallin'?"

Hump said, "Manning ain't talkin'. He's got a lil ear trouble."

Manning raged into the hall, shaking in every limb. "You was willin' to take Pierce and turn him over. You agreed. You went out there with Adobe and Sligh and me.''

"We sure did.''

"You got no right to say nothin'. You was in it. He might have done the same to you as he did to me. I'd like to see you do anything back to him.''

Hump said, "Manning, anybody can make a mistake. Pierce knows that. It's what happens after.''

"If the gal hadn't thrown the bottle, mebbe we'd have turned him over,'' said Shotgun. "Little things like that, they count a heap.''

"Big galoot like Tyler and that Luke Post, they make some difference, too,'' added Hump mockingly. "You run us into somethin', Manning. We ought to be kinda mad on you.''

"If it hadn't been a fight, Luke mighta ventilated several of us, specially you. Come to think of it, Manning, you're kinda lucky.''

Manning stared at first one door, then the other. Then he ran back into the room where he had been stationed and grabbed the rifle. The shadows were lengthening and there wasn't much time left. He knew it as well as anyone. Should he go in and kill the two who were tormenting him with their mocking voices, or let them kill him? What kind of end he made depended on him and he should not care one way or the other, he knew that, too.

He also knew that he would not attack Shotgun nor Hump, nor Pierce. He would have to face them without a barrier between him and their guns. It was better to shoot out a window past the chest of drawers at moving Comanches.

In his loose vest he felt the solidity of the tiny derringer. At the very end he would not allow them to catch him and torture him. He had that single bullet for himself. . . .

Hump called suddenly, "I remember.''

"You remember what?'' muttered Shotgun sourly.

"You was with Lieutenant Yeaton in '69.''

After a silence, Shotgun said, "I knew young Yeaton good. I knew Cushing good, too.''

The raillery was gone from Hump's voice. "Cushing never got over Yeaton's bein' kilt thataway."

"It's two years since Cochise got Cushing," said Shotgun.

"Goin' on three. . . . No, past three years," Hump corrected him. "John Mott pulled some of 'em out. It was up in the Whetstones. That was 3rd Cavalry."

"Yeaton was a friend," said Shotgun. "Cushing, he was a fighter. But Cochise got Cushing. Tell me about Apaches. You hadda get up early to trap Cushing."

"What was you doin' with Yeaton, anyway?"

"I got stranded. Hoss broke a leg. The 3rd picked me up. Then we run into the ambush and got away. I scouted some for the lieutenant. He was a friend."

Hump accepted this. "You was lucky to get away."

"I run," said Shotgun bluntly. "I had a good hoss. The lieutenant give him to me."

"Hootin' nanny!" said Hump. "Gimme a good hoss and an hour's start right now and I'd run, too. Much less Cochise on my trail. That devil kilt more soldiers than the Comanches kilt women and kids."

"And that's a heap a killin'," said Shotgun morosely.

They were silent and then Manning missed their voices and wished they would talk some more. The shadows were lengthening by leaps and bounds. . . .

In the large room, Luke said, "Maybe we ought to hold a powwow. Not that it'll do any good."

"What's to talk about?" asked Pierce.

"It might be better to go outside, when they start them fire arrows again."

"When it's time, we'll all go outside."

"Yeah. Reckon you're right, at that."

"We might decide about the women."

Luke said, "Reckon that'll take care of itself, too."

"Yeah." He looked at Gloria. She was trying to feed soup to Callahan, who seemed to rally for brief periods of lucidity, then lapsed into feverish ravings, laden with calls for a priest, a bugle, and the 6th Cavalry. "It'll take care of itself."

Across the room, Lamkin was polishing the barrel of the

camera with a soft cloth. The sun was gone and he could expose no more plates. There were bits of soil clinging to his knees. He had buried his accumulation of the day and his face was serene.

Myra Manning called him from the kitchen, "Is this your sister?" She was still leafing over the pictures from his box. Lamkin saw that it was Cynthia Van Owen.

"Yes." The parted hair, the coldly arranged smiling features, the narrow waist and the enormous skirt which covered a half-dozen petticoats looked ridiculous to him. No use to try to explain to Myra.

"Your family was so nice." She was looking at a likeness of his bearded, mustachioed father and plain, dumpy mother.

"They were just people, like anyone else."

They were dreadful people. They ate fried food for breakfast and even heavier at noon and slept or sat somnolent in the heat, drawling constant gossip with each other or with anyone who stopped to listen. They had no conversation about anything but the business of their acquaintances and the evil of the Republican party and the Yankees. Only they called anyone not a Democrat an "Abolitionist." Their opinions had been formed for them by their parents and the usage of Savannah. Black slaves worked the plantation in the dampness of the river, the overseer kept the books, they never saw the rice that made them comfortably well off.

He would never have known the difference if he hadn't gone North, he thought. Others didn't. Others fought and died for the South of their romantic conception, a South which existed only in their mind's eyes. Classmates at Princeton had rushed to the colors, few had survived.

By some chance he had been born with a detachment which enabled him to look on, to record without becoming involved. The camera had provided him with a stage prop. He had learned something of his fellow man; not enough, but something. For himself he had asked little and little had been granted.

Now, in this almost defeated woman, he had found a spark from which a small flame might be ignited to make a glow in his world; no raging fire of passion, more like a campfire at which comfort might be taken. In the other people of this company he saw various things, none of them completely ignoble, many of them gratifyingly heroic.

He had, he realized, sought heroism and found self-seeking in those he had observed at war. He had looked for nobility among gentlemen in private life and found ill-masked greed. Everyone had an ax to grind and would use any means to sharpen the blade.

In this place they were now fighting merely for survival. It made a difference. There were no flags flying, Callahan's bugle did not blow. They would die, one by one or several together, at the hands of savages without a written language to record their deaths.

What was the moral? Where was the lesson?

There was none, and he knew it. He could smile encouragingly at Myra Manning, bury his plates in the root closet, hold a shotgun at the window against close attack, drink the black, thick coffee from the pot, eat the foot cut by the blood-maculated knife of the scalp hunter, and in the end die like the others, but he sought a reason.

He did not expect to find a reason. He only wished there was one, that a man need not die without purpose.

Myra screamed suddenly. "Look out!"

He jerked around, grabbing for the shotgun, finding it slippery in his grasp as sweat poured from every pore. There was a painted face at the kitchen window.

He fired and there was screaming and then two more of the war-maddened young Comanches were in his line of vision, one succeeding the brave he had shot at the window and one coming through the kitchen door.

It was an insane, suicide mission. They had ridden past the kitchen without drawing fire, they had slowly converged in sallies and sorties until they were certain that this vantage was not well defended. Lamkin knew it was his fault, that he had been daydreaming as usual, while Myra had been fondly engaged with his old photographs.

The Indian in the doorway was aiming a musket at Myra, who stood frozen with the surprise. The one in the window had shoved the barrel of an old rifle across the sill, aiming at Lamkin.

He had a clear choice and his mind ran cool and strong on the knowledge of it. He heard men coming from the next room but there was no time.

He had one charge left in the double-barreled gun. He held it hip-high and pulled the trigger.

The Comanche in the doorway seemed to disintegrate. The buckshot tore him to ribbons.

The Indian in the window fired one shot. Then Luke was in the other door and snapping his revolver and again the window was a blank and a death yell mounted to the graying skies.

Lamkin hardly felt pain, only shock as the bullet from the Comanche at the window struck him. He went down slowly, as into a pit. He clearly saw Luke run across between Myra and the door and fire rapidly at the fleeing figures. They are madly brave, those Comanches, he thought. Or they are being directed by a shrewd brain, who sends in small bands in hopes that they might get to Pierce and thus save the expensive frontal attack which is weakening them for their foray into Mexico. Or maybe it's something of both bravery and brains, coupled with a certain kind of wild savagery, he thought, sinking to the floor. Well, he had found Indians, as Brady had advised. . . .

Then Myra was tearing at his shirt and her tears were hot on his flesh and Tyler came back and picked him up as though he were a child. Pierce prowled the kitchen like a lion, from door to window, went briefly outside to make certain the Indians nearby were dead and then Lamkin was lying on the kitchen table off which he had not long ago been eating bread and meat.

Gloria bent over him and her face seemed enormous and not pretty at all, merely pores and eyes too big and swimming and a twisted mouth. He tried to speak and couldn't.

She said, "It was such a close range, I think the bullet went all the way through."

Tyler said, "Here it is. On the floor."

Myra moaned once, then brought the basin and rolled towels around his own jacket and made a pillow beneath his head. He found pain, then, racking and torturous and with it came the power of speech.

"May I see . . . the bullet?"

Tyler gravely held it out between large thumb and forefinger, a small piece of misshapen lead.

Lamkin said, "Such a little thing . . . to kill a man."

"No," said Myra. "It's a clean wound. Look, it's not even bleeding very much."

He smiled. He was able to do that for her. The imminence of his end appalled him but he could still feel sympathy for the woman who was losing her last chance to anything resembling a decent life.

Gloria said, "No, it's not bleedin'." She knew that he was hemorrhaging inside. She stepped back, giving Myra the place closest to him.

He said quietly, almost inaudibly, to Myra. "There's a bit of money. Take it . . . try and get away. . . ."

She was weeping, and he knew she would never find the courage to escape, probably not even a good enough reason. He felt impatient with her. He had chosen to save her, to let himself die that she might survive for so long as it was destined. Women sometimes were exchanged, or managed to get away from the Indians. Now he saw he could do nothing for her.

Nothing he had ever attempted had come to enough in the end, he thought. There was no use to say any more. He closed his lips tight and shut his eyes.

He was inexpressibly weary, he found. Not enough sleep, too much excitement, far too much violence. First the damned War, then all this . . . It was too much.

He heard Gloria say, "He was such a nice little man. . . ."

Then he died.

Chapter 24

♦♦♦

The Comanche Moon was rising against a sky not burdened with clouds. The cool of the evening was evident in the cleanliness of Gloria's countenance after a wash, in the cessation of Callahan's fever, in a peculiar relaxation among them all. Outdoors there was an ominous silence. The young braves had been withdrawn. The light was uncertain.

Luke said, "We didn't lose a gun, at that." He gestured.

Myra Manning had caught up her skirt between her legs with a horse blanket pin. She insisted upon using the shotgun which Lamkin had utilized in saving her life. She was in the kitchen, moving restlessly from door to window.

"I believe she wants them to come in," said Ben.

"What the hell's she got to live for?" Luke had found a third revolver in Manning's gun closet and was handling it, getting used to it. This was a Starr Army .44 with the conventional eight-inch barrel, single action. There was a box of foil cartridges which had to be rammed home, chamber by chamber, by the loading lever. "Funny how they took to each other, her and the little fellow."

Gloria said, "Why not? Manning is nothin' for any woman to tie to."

"Nobody's judgin' them," said Luke mildly. "I just remarked it was a funny circumstance."

"It ain't funny," she sulked.

Luke appeared satisfied with the Starr and put it carefully on a chair near his window. "Might come in handy when they're onto us. You got a knife, Ben?"

"Never held much with knives." There was the bowie he had taken from the dead Comanche. He touched its blade.

"Well, most likely we won't get to use none. Might get caught alive thataway," said Luke. "I ain't aimin' to make a hoorah for no Comanches. I ain't right brave about a fire at my tootsies and skull, and me without a pail of water."

"Don't anybody go shootin' me," cried Gloria. "I ain't askin' anybody to do me that favor."

Luke looked at her, grinning. "You favor them bucks? You figure to get around 'em with your pretty ways?"

"I'm against killin' myself," she said. "I don't believe in it."

"Maybe Pierce will take care of it," said Luke. "Pierce is dead set agin the Injuns gettin' hold of women."

"Where is Pierce?" Ben tried to change the subject.

"In the back rooms some place," said Gloria. "He was looking at Lamkin and Sligh for a while. Just standin' there, looking at them. Like they were kids sleeping in the same bed, or something."

"Their troubles are over. No good ponderin' over them."

Ben said, "When are the Comanches comin' at us?"

"Soon enough," Luke told him. "That Bear Head, he's workin' them up. The squaws are countin' the dead. There's bound to be some old chiefs wants to get to Mexico, to save lives. But Bear Head wants us."

"He wants Pierce, you mean."

"He wants everybody who is in the fight."

Ben did not answer. He was averse by nature to repeating tales out of school, and there was nothing to be gained for them by telling what he knew about Pierce's sister and Bear Head. He alone could guess at what was going on inside Pierce. He could not ever be friends with the man, he did not like him. He only knew Pierce must be under a terrific strain and that it showed on him.

Callahan roused from lethargy and began tonelessly singing a song, about whores and brave boys in blue and Johnny Rebs and Abe Lincoln and Jeff Davis. The lyric was atrocious and there was no tune. Gloria went to him and talked soothingly and Callahan said distinctly, "You'll hear that bugle, little lady."

"Sure, we know it," said Gloria. "You'll be all right when the doctor gets here."

"That bugle plays mighty sweet. Even taps is sweet. But they ain't goin' to play taps over us."

"Funny thing," said Luke. "He's never stopped believing the cavalry would get here and neither has she."

"Maybe I haven't, neither," confessed Ben.

"Well, it's all right. No harm in wishin' and hopin'. Only thing is, Bear Head don't believe it. He holds the aces."

The curious half-light in the room threw weird shadows. The stench of decaying flesh was plain, but they had become somewhat inured to it. Ben stared out toward the plains over which the Indians would ride and wished he could hear a bugle and see a pennon flying as blue-shirted horsemen rode.

Pierce came into the room, moving a bit uncertainly now, pausing to look at Callahan and Gloria, turning his round head toward Luke, then Ben. He did not speak, going on into the kitchen.

Luke said, "A bug's been bitin' him, all right."

"Everybody's got troubles. Right now is the time they bite hard."

"He sent enough Injuns to hell," said Luke. "A man's got to take that into account."

"I reckon," said Ben. "Reckon there's a score sheet some place, maybe."

"Inside a man." Luke leaned his elbows on the window. "The way it starts, a man's young and full of beans and he don't like what he's doin', so he does somethin' else. Always there's them that would prevent him. They'd kill him to stop him. They'd kill him because he's good at something that they ain't so good at. They'd kill him because they don't like the color of his eyes."

"Well, I dunno. . . ."

"Sure, you don't know. A man comes at you, he's armed and pistol-quick. You got one chance, outshoot him. You got to know this, believe it. You got to make up your mind."

"It ain't always that way. Not every place."

"Not with guns, maybe. But one way or another, it's that way. A man comes at you."

Ben began to see what the gambler was trying to say. "The Bible says to turn the other cheek. Not that I ever noted anybody doin' much of it. Unless he was scared."

"You can bet your bottom peso on that." Luke turned slowly, facing Ben. "I wouldn't have it any different, podner. I coulda been bucked to death by some hammerhead cayuse. I coulda got caught in a stampede and squooshed to death. I coulda been bushwhacked by some tribe like that one out yonder. Never woulda had no fun, never woulda owned nice clothes and bet across the table, win, lose, or draw in the biggest games the country's got. Sure, I had to kill a few four-flushers and maybe a good man who was drunk or on the prod. I wouldn't have it no different."

"Well, then, that's enough," said Ben slowly. "If you can say that, it's plenty. I don't know if I feel just like that. Seems to me there's a lot I didn't do and some that I'd like to do."

"Stop talkin' like crapehangers," said Gloria. "It gives me the willies."

Ben had had no communion with her for hours. The death of Lamkin had softened her for a moment, then she had retreated again behind the wall of her disbelief in disaster. More and more she stayed near Callahan, as though she wanted to hear his delusions repeated, as though Callahan could bring the sound of the bugle.

She would admit neither fear nor death, he thought. There was bulldog in her and he admired it, but he could not get through to tell her that or anything else. She had a rifle, now, which she handled with some familiarity. When the time came, she would shoot.

Men, women, and a coward, he thought, killing Indians in a lost cause. It was outlandish to his entire thinking. It was something you read about in a newspaper, maybe, a few people massacred by Indians, but it wasn't anything that happened to a Jersey farmer.

He wanted to tell this to Luke, his friend, to marvel at it, to discuss it, but the only words he found were, "You just don't know how things will turn out. A man never does know."

Gloria said, "They'll turn out. I'm not worried about it." She broke through the veil for a moment, holding his arm in a strong grip.

He tried to smile at her but the effect was thin and he looked away and Pierce was in the doorway to the kitchen with his face turned to them. Pierce wore no expression, he merely looked, and Ben felt strangely ashamed and moved away from the girl, releasing his arm.

He went into the hallway, conscious of Luke's quiet amusement. He paused at the door of the room in which Sligh and Lamkin lay still in their blankets. There was a last flicker of light across the place where their heads were outlined against pillows and he shivered and went on.

Hump and Shotgun were hunkered down, maintaining vigil. Manning was an indistinguishable lump behind his chest of drawers. Ben hesitated, and Hump drawled at him. "Better set down some place and rest yourself for the shindig."

Shotgun called, "You catch the nerves from Pierce? He's been prowlin' like a cougar."

"Just wanted to see if you were O.K.," Ben said. "Guess we're all a little restless."

"Callahan still alive?"

"He's sleepin' more."

"Lung-shot, he's bound to drift off. One time he won't wake up," said Hump.

"He's still listenin' for that bugle."

"He won't hear it this side of hell. The 6th is busy with Cochise," said Shotgun.

"You tell 'em," said Hump. "Old Shotgun, he knows about Apaches and the 6th. And all the goddam cavalry."

"Yeaton was good and Cushing was good. And Mac-Kenzie is plenty good. Don't put it all on me, about the cavalry. You holler on them as much as I do."

"Yeaton and Cushing is dead and you won't see no part of MacKenzie hereabouts."

"I wish I would see him. And a whole damn regiment."

"I wish I had a couple dozen buffalo hunters. I'll take them, with Sharps rifles and the savvy they got. You take the goddam cavalry."

"I'll take both. I'll take some friendly Arapaho. I'll take a troop of *reales*."

Ben said, "While we're wishin', I'll take one of them observation balloons the Signal Corps had in the war. We could all fly away."

They laughed. They were no happier about dying than he was, but their laughter sounded all right and it made him feel easier in his mind. He went back to the main room.

The trouble was, he thought, that he could not place himself. He felt light-headed, struggling in a world which had tightened to the point of strangulation.

The first hours at the way station had been kaleidoscopic, bright, passionate. Now everything was washed to gray. His spirit was eroded. It wasn't fear, it was unwillingness to accept extinction.

Pierce was at his post, staring out at the twilight, his lips moving, his mouth elliptical where it had been rectangular and hard. Luke was glancing at him, frowning.

Ben went past them to the camera and said, "Maybe we ought to take this down."

"What for?"

"Well, I don't know. It's a valuable camera, ain't it?"

Myra Manning said, "Leave it be."

Her hair was in disarray, she no longer looked attractive. Her eyes were burning, deep in their sockets, but her skin had lost its illusionary youthfulness. The arrangement of her skirt gave her freedom of movement but made her appear coarse, masculine.

She said, "It's no good to anyone."

"I wanted to keep it from bein' damaged," said Ben trying to smile at her.

"Let them worry about it." She gestured at the window. "They won't find his plates. I stamped down the earth on top of them and threw rags over it, careless-like. They won't find 'em."

Luke said, "I'd sort of like to see the pictures he took."

"He took one of me," she said. "In the kitchen. He swung it around when the sun was right. I put our names in with the plates. All our names. If anyone finds it, they'll know who was here. I wrote 'em on a piece of paper.''

"I'd rather live to see the pictures," grinned Luke.

"Why should you live? Or any of us. *He* was kind and good. He didn't want to shoot even the Indians."

"Why, you're right about Lamkin, ma'am," said Luke. "I didn't signify he was anything but a good man. I was speakin' personal, for me."

She was not paying attention, Ben saw. She turned to go back to the kitchen, then stopped. On the floor lay the Bible which had been knocked from the shelf by a bullet. She picked it up and looked at it as if she had never seen a Bible before. She automatically put it on the shelf, half-reached for it, wagged her head, went through the door and took up the shotgun. She moved to the window and leaned hard against the wall, staring out.

Ben felt lost inside himself. "Ain't it about time for them to attack?"

Pierce moved, slowly, without the bounce and decision he had displayed earlier. "Right about now."

"They'll make a charge. Then the young ones'll dismount," said Luke. "Then we're in trouble."

Gloria said, "I've got all the ammunition stacked. And I've loaded everything that would hold a shell."

"When the time comes, just stick somethin' out the window and fire. But wait. Wait'll they come in where aim don't count for nothin'," Luke advised.

Pierce spoke in a dull, even voice. "For what good it'll do."

"Why, this ain't a time to count," said Luke calmly. "This here is a time to keep shootin'. We all know the odds, Pierce,"

"You don't know the Comanches," said Pierce.

"I ain't exactly yearnin' to make their acquaintance," said Luke.

"Just make sure you're dead," said Pierce. "Make awful damn sure you're dead."

"If I'm that close to it, what difference?" Luke kept his voice light, but his eyes were questioning.

"They'll damn near bring you back to life, after a fight like this. To have their stinkin' fun."

"You wouldn't be tryin' to scare someone, would you Pierce?"

There was no noticeable reaction as Pierce returned his attention to outdoors, then said, "Bear Head. He'll send in some fighters. Half of 'em will drop off. They won't be the brave dummies. They'll be the smart ones. The light's just about right for them to crawl in."

"You partic'lar want Bear Head?"

Pierce turned, looked at them, shook his head. "No. . . . Just so somebody gets him if they can. They always take it hard when somebody gets the chief."

"You mean if we killed him, they might go away?" asked Gloria.

"I don't think they'll go away." He hesitated, then said, as though without violation. "I killed his adopted boy out there. The young one. That's why he made the raid when Sligh got his'n. To try and burn the place and get Walkin' Jay. That's his adopted kid, Walkin' Jay. That I killed." He talked very slowly, trying to make them understand. It seemed necessary that they fully understand all about it.

Gloria said, "Oh, his son. They'll want pay for that." It worried her. It took away some of her belief in survival.

"Too bad it wasn't one of his daughters, too," said Luke. "Too bad it wasn't a whole hell of a lot of 'em."

Ben stood apart. He could see it eating at Pierce, the curious circumstance of Josie's son dying under his aim, the unknown things which only Pierce could estimate. It was rough for Pierce, all right.

No rougher than on the rest of them, though. He took a deep breath. They all had to go the same route. He sternly banished the gnawing fear which had been upsetting him. He began to feel alive again, and alert, knowing he must make up in whatever part he could for Pierce's obvious disintegration.

Out in the half-light of the early moon, the Comanches began the final ride toward the way station.

Chapter 25

♦♦♦

The sound of the hoofs of Indian horses sent a troop of buzzards into clumsy action; some were so stuffed as to have difficulty in taking off the ground. A skull gazed eyeless at the rising moon. There was no color nor any panoply in the advance of the riders now, only screaming determination and impatience.

Luke moved lightly from behind the bar. "Reckon I found Manning's private poison." There was a gurgle. "Yeah. T'ain't bad." He extended the bottle.

Ben took it, one eye on the Indians.

"It's a time for whisky, good whisky. Not too much. Just enough so a man don't die dry," said Luke.

Ben swallowed, shook his head. "It ain't that good. You should taste Uncle Tiger's aged applejack."

Luke said, "I'll divvy with the boys in the back room," and darted out.

Gloria, rifle at her side, was attending Callahan for the moment. Ben looked at Pierce, and the bounty hunter was moving his lips without releasing sound.

Callahan said sharply, "They're ridin'. You'll see. The 6th is on its way. You'll hear 'em any minute now."

There was some delay among the Comanches. Ben found himself growing impatient. He felt absolutely nothing else in this moment, only the urge that they should be at it, that it had gone on long enough, that it should be ended.

Pierce's face worked, a muscle jumped in his cheek. He lifted a rifle, which was always so much a part of him, aimed it at nothing, then awkwardly lowered it. He tried to shake off a crawling sensation beneath his skin, but had no luck. His eyeballs smarted. Rubbing did no good.

His scalp itched. He ran his knuckles through his hair, then dug with his nails. Nothing helped.

He looked at Ben, crouched and ready and calm. The big farmer was able to handle it. Why couldn't Pierce, who had been there so many times before?

Gloria was still with Callahan.

Ben said, "The whisky's warm in the belly."

Pierce could think of nothing in reply. His belly was cold.

In the back room, Luke was saying, "Go ahead, finish it, Manning won't mind."

Hump and Shotgun were taking turns and the bottle would not last another moment. Luke said, "You boys been doin' real fine."

Hump gasped, swallowed hard. "That's good stuff. . . . They ain't been comin' at this side so hard. Now it'll be different."

"It ain't never different," said Shotgun morosely. "Only sometimes it's worse'n others."

In the other room, Manning nervously counted his weapons. He had never realized why he indefatigibly and secretly collected weapons and ammunition. Any gun that would work was always a temptation to him, yet he was not a hunter, had never intended firing on a human being . . . except in nightmares.

He now had on the bed in the room a Walker Colt, 1846 model with a nine-inch barrel; a Confederate .577 Enfield rifle; a Springfield which used the same size cartridge as the Enfield, about 70 grains of powder and a 530-grain bullet; a bowie fighting knife and an Arkansas toothpick or dagger. The smaller weapons had been cached in the chest of drawers, the others in a closet. Ready for battle he had a Remington and for all the guns he had a supply of ammunition.

He tried to tell himself that his accumulation was foresight, that he had known there would be trouble. He always tried to convince himself that he was right about everything, it was necessary for him to attempt this in order not to face the truth. He was a man with every weakness and a devouring craving always to be in the right. That his conception of right or wrong was faulty in no way deterred him.

He had spent money he could ill afford on arms and ammunition. He had concealed the purchase from Myra, not through fear of her complaint, for he had no compunctions about Myra, but to keep himself from knowing that he was afraid, always afraid, and that mere possession gave him some modicum of easement.

Now he heard the others chaffing and drinking his whisky and realized they had found the good stuff and he was irate all over again. They hadn't any right, without paying. He would make them pay up. Nobody could damn well come into his place and drink his good whisky without paying through the nose. . . .

And then he realized all over again that there could be no payment from which he would benefit. If he spoke, they would throw money in his face and laugh at him again. The knowledge sent his head down into the crook of his arm. He slavered on the dirty sleeve of his shirt, shaking as though with the ague.

What chance had he ever had? he demanded of the God he had never quite dared deny. He was just an ordinary man. He had never gone much to school. He had tried hard, with all his might, in fact, to make out in towns, safe from Indian attacks. A man can't help going to women, God knew that. It was natural. God made everything like that, He must have intended for them to go with women.

It hadn't been rape, no matter what Hortense said. "Hotsy," the boys called her, she was twelve but oh my, they said. Just his bad luck, he'd been caught with her. From then on everything had been unlucky.

Taking the money from his mother's cookie jar, that wasn't stealing, he had a right to his share, didn't he? Little Old Hotsy's father was going to kill him, he had to get away. The other fellows wouldn't testify, they laughed at him. He would have had to take all the blame and that wasn't fair.

People were always blaming him, always laughing at him. Once in a while he flared up, sure, he admitted it. Maybe he shouldn't have hit Marylin so hard. But she was mean to him and puny anyway; he hadn't known she was so puny when he married her, had he? Her father hadn't told him that she was sickly, him with his big store and fine house and spanking, matched team and carriage.

So he took the rig and drove away in the night. Since marrying Myra he'd tried, hadn't he? Everything he'd tried. He didn't do anything wrong. He was trying to save money here in this place to make another start. A hog ranch, or maybe a few cattle, or maybe a store again, where he could use what he learned clerking for Marylin's father.

What had he done that was wrong? Why did the Indians come after him?

He wept on the shoulder of his God and watched the Comanches ride through the dusk.

He had the tenacity of the weak, he knew that he had to keep firing a gun, keep the Indians from getting at close grips, prevent a breach in the defense as long as possible. Otherwise his lenient God would not save him. . . .

Callahan sat up. The exertion left him pale and shaky. He strained, listening for the notes of the bugle. He said thickly, "The 6th'll be here. Keep fightin', boys."

"My ass," murmured Luke. "He'll die believin' that."

"Let him," said Ben. "Why don't they ride faster?"

"Bear Head. That's his way," said Pierce. His mind was spinning in a way he did not understand and could not control. He wanted to keep silence but found he could not. "Bear Head thinks white, most of the time. He thinks white."

That was Josie, today's Josie. She did it, advised Bear Head. Time and again Pierce had led the cavalry close to a Comanche encampment, only to find it mysteriously gone into the trackless Staked Plains. That was Josie, outthinking him.

He tried to recapture the pictures of their youth, Josie taking him into town, dressed in white, smiling, gay, gentle. It wasn't any good. He could only see the bent-back squaw with her half-breed brats, riding with Bear Head.

He could not understand how she had managed to fathom

them, their dirt and cruelty. How could she stand that shrill laughter which cut across his memory like the lash of a blacksnake whip?

She had become one of them, cruel by association. The new Josie surely had in her a response to savagery, to be able to renounce her white blood, her childhood training, everything but love for the bastards and her red consort. It was incomprehensible and he only wanted to stop thinking about it, but his plagued mind would not obey him.

He heard his voice saying, "They'll be red devils from the pit now. You'll see how they are, now. There'll be hell to pay, and nobody with the price. You'll see how it is."

His voice rang strangely in his ears, and then Callahan cried out again and he realized that he sounded like Callahan, full of fever. He could do nothing about it.

"I mind a time I was ridin' with them. Always thought I might get away on one of the raids. We was into Mexico and Bear Head was in charge, his first time. We come, unsuspectin', on this rancheria. It was night and a moon, like always."

Luke said, "They're workin' their way into range."

"Is that Bear Head on a white horse? The light is rotten bad," said Ben.

"It'll brighten up. There's only that one cloud over the moon." Both were trying to divert Pierce from his monologue, direct his attention to the impending fight.

"The vaqueros slept in a bunkhouse, and we hit that first," said Pierce. "Some of them got to the hacienda with their guns. They killed a few of us. There was a family, father, mother, three little girls, in the hacienda. They fought real good."

Gloria was in Lamkin's window, peering past the camera, a rifle in her hand. She said hoarsely, "Shut up, Pierce."

"We don't want to hear it, Pierce," said Ben.

"Mark the barn, where they're crawlin'," said Luke. "That bush, yonder, it's within range. I wish that cloud would go the hell away."

Pierce's voice cut through the ghostly light of the room. "They was all wounded when we took 'em. Bear Head brought out the men and tended to them. They raped the women and the little gals and tied 'em together inside the house. Then they set fire to it. Just a little fire, so it would take time to ketch. That was Bear Head. He wanted the woman and kids to know what was comin'. That's the way he thinks.''

An advance came out of nowhere, it seemed, past the bush designated by Luke and past the barn. Ben fired, looking for Bear Head, not finding him. Luke waited, then let loose with the revolvers. Gloria shot at them from alongside the camera. In the kitchen Myra began to shoot.

Pierce droned. ''They kept the men there, watchin' the fire. They laughed and danced and offered the men the liquor they had stole. The screams of the little girls were real high, like babies cryin'.''

The Comanches came on, solid, riding straight for the station, as though to smash it flat by sheer force of numbers. It was the all the defenders could do to split them. Ben fired low and ponies piled up and then Luke did great execution with his revolvers again, but it seemed useless.

They couldn't hear Pierce now, but they knew he was talking. He began shooting at last, his mouth still working.

In the kitchen, Myra held the shotgun on the sill of the window and waited until the last possible instant before loosing her vengeance. Nothing was left in her but rage to kill. If Manning had walked into the room she would have turned the weapon upon her husband. Everything had gone, all belief in a future, all hope of love and understanding and kindness. She wanted to see the Indian faces before blasting them, she wanted to count her dead.

They swooped by and then some of them turned and rode back. Ponies went down and now, instead of essaying a double mount, or any other escape, they ran for the shelter of the wrecked barn and corral. The real helplessness of the defenders came home to Ben when he realized he did not have time or opportunity to pick off these because of the pressure of the attack by horsemen still throwing themselves at the station.

Luke's revolvers counted steadily and Gloria fell away from the window at his command to reload. Pierce was pulling the trigger of his rifle and still talking. Once in a while there would be a freak moment of comparative silence and into it would fall a few scattered words in a dull, droning tone, but they made no sense to Ben.

He looked at Gloria. Black powder had dirtied her skin, but as a moonbeam drifted over her she was almost beautiful in her rapt attention to her job. She looked up, handed him a loaded Springfield, and for a second their glances crossed.

There was no recognition in her, nor did he imagine that he conveyed any message to her. They were two entities meeting death on the same planc in whatever manner they could manage. There was not much time left. Marksmen from the ruins were filling each window with bullets and arrows.

Luke said, "Someone got hurt in back." He ran down the hallway. For an instant there was a lull, except for the whirring well-aimed arrows.

Pierce's voice said, "Them little kids, cryin'. You don't know Comanches unless you seen 'em jumpin' and laughin' over a thing like that. And pokin' the prisoners to get the full benefit of their sufferin'. Even more'n what they do to you, it's the way they do it. They fed the men of the rancheria, see, after the buildings had burned down and there were no more screams, only burnt women and kids. They treated 'em fine that night, ridin' out, usin' the moon. They drove the cattle and the horses. . . . I should say *we* did, because I was with 'em and doin' my share of the work. The prisoners saw I was white and tried to talk to me. They were half-crazy. They thought I might help 'em. *Me!*"

The horsemen had completed their run and were wheeling to attack again. Luke came in and said, "Shotgun got an arrow through his shoulder."

"Is he out of it?"

"He can still shoot a gun."

"Manning?"

"Not a scratch. He was still shootin' 'em after they'd been gone for a mile."

Gloria was asking Pierce, her voice strained, "They killed all the women? Every one?"

He ignored her. "The sun was hot on the edge of the desert the next day. They were foolin' and laughin' and makin' friends with the men. They come to where that big Mex cactus grows. You know, the spiny cactus, like a tree. They tied the men to the cactus. Then they hamstrung 'em so if they did work loose, they couldn't walk. They sat around awhile and one of the men wouldn't yell enough, so they cut off his tongue and his eyebrows. All the time they laughed. Like it was the funniest and best thing in the world."

Luke said, "These windows are gettin' too hot." He poked a finger through a hole in his hard hat. "Cost me ten hard ones in Kaycee. Now look at it."

Ben said, "It's tough to get a shot at 'em." He was crouched beneath the window. Every time he showed himself an arrow or a bullet came whizzing over his skull.

Luke said, "It ain't easy. From now on, nothin' is easy."

"Don't let 'em get holt of you," Pierce was saying in that singsong voice he had acquired in the last hours. "You won't want to hear 'em laugh. I promise you, you won't like it when they laugh."

Callahan was trying to get down off the table. "The bugles! Don't nobody hear 'em? The bugles!"

He had a revolver in his hand. He staggered to a window and fired it and an Indian screamed.

Luke said, "He might as well die on his feet."

"Believin' in his bugle," said Ben.

There was an ominous pause. Now the rush would come in earnest. Bear Head was gathered to spring upon them. The horsemen retired and more of the dismounted figures crept closer and closer, covered by the fire of the men among the rubble of the barn.

Gloria said, "They killed *all* the women? I didn't think they'd do that."

Chapter 26

♦♦♦

Ben Tyler knew only that the firing would never stop. Gloria was on the floor, reloading, because, as Luke said, if they all happened to run out of shells at the same moment the Indians would be in through the windows.

"And doors," Luke added. He was calm as ever, wiping sweat and powder smudge from his face. "They'll have the roof burnin' real nice any minute, now."

The fire arrows were again arching, now against the night sky, with all the color and beauty of fireworks. Bear Head was moving in for the final blow. When all was flames, they could either cook indoors or make a sortie and try to die in the open before the Comanches could take them alive.

In the rear they heard Hump yell, "They got Shotgun."

Luke, nimble as a monkey, ran back, fired his revolvers for a moment to stem an attack. Shotgun was hit in the head with a musket ball and was dead on the instant, Hump reported.

The stage driver said, "They come right to the window and poked the muzzle through. Did they get Manning?"

"No," said Luke. "They didn't get Manning."

He went to the room Manning defended. The flimsy bulwark of the dresser was still in place, though riddled. Manning was methodically loading his assorted weapons while the Comanches gathered for another charge. The keeper of the way station lifted his head, blinked, returned to his work. He was, Luke thought, like a cornered animal, no more, no less. There was no light of reason in him, only the fear which made him continue to fight. It was enough for now, and Luke went back to the front room.

He said, "The two of them can't hold that end of the building."

"We can't hold this end," said Ben. "Not without you."

"That's right." Luke looked around. Mrs. Manning stalked the kitchen, gun in hand. Gloria was crouched on the floor beside a pile of shells, loading rifles. Callahan leaned against the wall, mumbling about bugles.

Pierce turned from the window. "They're gettin' ready, out there. I heard Bear Head's voice. He's behind the barn."

Luke said, "Well, the next time will be the big one. We'll be burned out, anyway, in a little while."

"The roof is too hot," said Ben. "No use goin' up there."

"If anybody's got prayers to say, get 'em ready." Luke didn't smile. "Comes the time when folks look to their God, I reckon."

"Holy Mary, Mother of God," Callahan began, then stopped and cried feverishly, "I tell you, I hear the bugles."

Pierce seemed to be holding himself together by the strength of his clenched hands. His face was haggard, his eyes sunken in his head. Yet, Ben thought, Pierce wasn't afraid to die. It was more than that.

Luke said, "That roof will hold for a while."

"It'll hold," said Ben.

"Bear Head knows what he's doin'. When he sees the fire won't work fast enough for him, he'll come in hard again."

Ben managed a shot at a bold Comanche who ran close with his rifle and knocked him down. The Indian attack was so heavy that it was impossible to defend any window fully. The fire on the roof crackled. There were fewer Indian yells now, it was all business.

Hump yelled, "Can't hold 'em off much longer here."

Ben ran back, stepped over the corpse of Shotgun and emptied a rifle at flitting forms who came closer and closer, hugging the ground, leaping and darting, throwing themselves prone again, in an effort to breach the rear windows. His concentrated firing pinned them down for a moment and he returned to his post in the main room.

Luke was moving, ducking, agile as the Comanches, trying to make them believe all windows were defended. If he had fears, Ben thought, they were buried deep. His gambler's mind worked nimbly, estimating the odds, considering every circumstance.

Pierce continued to talk to himself. His eyes were sunken, lines of exhaustion ran from nostrils to the moving lips, he shook his head from time to time like a wounded bear.

Gloria alternately fought and reloaded weapons. The stubbornness of her character and her faith in survival was never more evident. She supported Callahan as she leaned one elbow on a window sill and gave him another revolver.

Callahan said, "I can hear bugles, I tell you," and spat blood.

Pierce sagged for a moment, waiting for a loaded gun. He looked into the kitchen and saw Myra Manning firing at a skulker who had essayed the broken window through which Lamkin had been killed, and he thought that she was also lost, as he was lost. He was wandering in a desert and the mirage of Josie and of what he had wanted and of what he had expected was gone. He remembered such a vision, but he could not piece it together, could not reconcile it.

He felt, as though it were happening now, the sharp sticks of Comanche squaws poking at his private parts, he heard the shrill giggling of them, he remembered his desire to die, to kill himself. It had not endured, this wish, because he had been tough in his core.

Where was his toughness now? Left on the plains? Had it melted with the knowledge that Josie was gone, that now he knew her to be an enemy?

He could not fight through the cobwebs. He felt branded with the mark of the Comanche. He felt shame and defeat.

He took a gun from Gloria, staring at her. She had done him no harm, except perhaps in the matter of the farmer from Jersey. Why should she suffer a Comanche rape?

He saw Myra Manning wipe a hand across her brow.

The lost woman wouldn't mind dying, he knew, but he could only imagine her alive in Bear Head's hands. Even the men, Ben, Luke, Hump—none of them deserved what only Pierce fully understood would be their lot if caught alive.

His tongue ran again, without volition. "You don't know how they are. You don't know what they can do. Smart, they are. Every man has a different special part that hurts. They know, they can figure it out."

Luke said, "Leave it go at that. I don't wanta know." He picked a target and fired carefully through a window.

"There ain't much time. When they once get past a door or a window, everybody kills himself," said Pierce. "No use fightin' any more then, is there? *Is there?*" His voice pealed in the room.

Ben said. "I can't get a proper aim."

The stench of blood and death was on them. Callahan fired the revolver and was miraculously not hit as he peered out the window, saying, "I heard it. The bugle. The 6th is out there some place."

His murmurings were no stranger than Pierce's. "If you won't kill yourselves . . . I can't stand any more of their laughin'. . . . Money in a Kaycee bank . . . Scalps in a saddlebag. It don't add up, nothin' adds up. Two and two got to make four, don't it? . . . You got to have a sum, added up."

Luke said to Ben, "A couple of locos. You all right, hoss? You know what to do?"

Ben nodded. Luke meant they should be sure to kill the women first. It wouldn't be long, now, he knew. The ring of Indians was closing in and from the barn and corral the bullets and arrows sang steadily through the windows.

Pierce's lips were moving, but he was whispering to himself. Luke emptied the Starr revolver, swore when one of the foil cartridges failed to explode, reached for the Colt's .45 and aimed at a head too close to a window.

"Amazin' the way that roof holds up."

"It's a strong building," said Ben, but it was not strong enough, he knew.

Pierce said audibly, "A whore like Gloria. Money in a bank. It ain't enough. I can't think straight."

He stared at Ben. His eyes were maniacal now, and for a moment it seemed he would turn the rifle on the people within the way station.

Outside there was a wild yell, as though all the Comanches had given vent on a signal.

"It won't add up," said Pierce. "I can't get no sum. Why should we hear 'em laughin'? Why should everybody?"

He dropped his rifle and began walking toward the door. For a moment Ben froze. Callahan was mumbling about the bugle, Luke was intent on defense. Gloria and Myra were at their posts.

Pierce said in his off-key voice, "If I go out, they'll quit. Manning's right. Coulda saved a lot of trouble. It's no good, you see. She ain't there any more and that woman with Bear Head, she's somebody else. You see that, don't you? I got to make the sum add up."

He was at the door, his hand outstretched, when Ben realized fully the import of the move.

Pierce said, "The hell with it. I'm dog-tired anyway. The goddam hell with it."

Ben leaped across the room. Dropping his rifle, he caught Pierce's shoulder, yanked him around.

"No! Leave me go!"

On the instant, Pierce was changed into a mountain lion. Never had Ben struggled with a man so strong, so agile. He took blows that would have stunned a smaller man, he was slung against the table vacated by Callahan, almost strangled.

Pierce was insane, there was no question of it. Ben used leverage, tossing him, then had to catch him before he could open the door. They went down, rolled over. Luke took a swipe at Pierce, missed and had to go back to shooting painted faces away from the windows. Myra and Gloria were oblivious to the fight, so busy was the action.

From the rear come Manning's hysterical shriek, "They got Hump! I'm all alone! Help me, help me!"

This was no way to die, thought Ben. He put forth superhuman effort, nailed Pierce to the floor.

Pierce heaved like a tidal wave, throwing Ben loose. He faked a run for the door, then lowered his head and butted.

Ben stepped back. He brought up his knee under Pierce's chin. He hammered his hard fist down on the back of Pierce's neck. For a moment he feared that he had killed the man.

There was no time for self-recrimination. He reached for a rifle, found it empty, got another. He emptied it through a window at an approaching mass of Comanches.

This was the end, he thought, seeing Gloria and Myra with empty weapons, seeing Luke pull out his favorite .38 for a last stand. It was nearing the time when they should all make an end of it.

Then he, too, heard the bugle.

It was as Callahan said, keen, quavering, high up above the sound of gunfire. It held a note, then dropped and threatened, then soared again. It was the sweetest sound ever heard in the world.

Callahan was on his knees, blood running from his grinning mouth. He choked, "You didn't believe me. The 6th. They got here. That's my outfit, the 6th!"

There was a jumble of action. Ben saw the first of them come in, blue-shirted, firing short carbines, then the side-arms, then the saber. They wheeled and came back and then there was a second wave and the arrows and bullets stopped hitting through the windows as though by magic.

Then there was a wild cry, and all the Comanches began slipping away like blobs of quicksilver in the moonlight, retreating in swift and sure style without orders, each knowing what to do and how to do it. The cavalry re-formed, but there was no single group for them to fight, only twos and threes and single Indians who ran faster than was believable, for their horses.

Ben saw the headdress and the white horse for an instant, then it was gone, before he could aim, and anyway he was now afraid of hitting a cavalryman. He saw Luke's face, as much bewildered as relieved. He saw Myra Manning and thought that she looked frustrated, disappointed, as though dying was preferable to living, as she leaned upon the smoking, emptied rifle and stared out at the rescuers.

It was over in a matter of moments. An officer sat his saddle slouched and grim and the pennon-bearer was a length behind him. The bugle sounded recall.

Callahan was at the door. He got it open, staggering, coughing blood. "I told you! I knew it!"

He fell as he went over the sill and lay upon the earth and Luke was swift, getting between the sergeant and the standard-bearer with his tricornered pennon. A bearded man with a bag dismounted and was at Callahan's side in a moment. Luke maneuvered himself and Ben to block off Callahan's moonlit view of the pennon and Ben looked around, not understanding.

Then he realized the kindliness of Luke's intent. There was a number on the flag, but it was not *6*. It was a slanting brazen *4*.

Callahan said faintly, "I knew the 6th would make it."

The doctor made a quick examination, shook his head.

Callahan said, "I'm glad you came in time, Father. I'd not want to go without the blessin'. . . ." He smiled broadly. "Good old bugle. I kept . . . tellin' them. . . ."

He choked and a last blob of blood poured from him.

"Lung-shot," said the doctor. "He should have died before now."

The officer on the horse said impatiently, "Colonel MacKenzie, commanding 4th Cavalry. Can anyone tell me if that was Bear Head's bunch?"

Luke cocked his hat to the other side of his head. "Colonel, that there was the whole goddam Comanche nation."

Chapter 27

◆◆◆

There was a day for cleaning up, there was a military funeral for Callahan, there was a great burning of wreckage and offal. MacKenzie was gone, chasing Bear Head, possibly again over the Rio Grande on one of his swift raids, reckless of politics or anything but killing Comanches.

A detail had been assigned to the way station under a veteran sergeant named Flynn, who amazingly resembled Callahan. Horses had been provided to pull the two stages to their destinations, complete with drivers from the ranks who were happy to get relief from MacKenzie's pell-mell campaign.

Somewhere during this time Pierce awoke from a long sleep and lay on a bed, trying to remember. Gloria pieced it together for him, scornfully reminding him of his crack-up.

"Ben saved you. If it wasn't for him, you'd be dead and buried with the others under those trees. And I'm going to marry him."

"Yeah," said Pierce. "I went loco, all right."

She left him and he lay staring at the ceiling, which was marked with a few scattered bullet holes. They had got awful close to the window to put bullets in the ceiling.

He felt relaxed and cleansed. He began putting his thoughts in order. There were the scalps, he hoped nobody had done anything to them, he had to get over into Mexico and collect on them. There was Kaycee, and the bank. He could not remember how much money he had on deposit, but it was enough. He could take a long rest, this time. He'd worn himself plumb down to a nubbin.

Otherwise, how could he have gone loco? It had never happened to him before, except maybe on the desert a couple of times when he was thirsty he had seen some sights.

The main thing now was to get something to eat. He was weak as a goat. He swung his legs over the side of the bed. He found his pants and a shirt and moccasins. That would be Myra Manning's work, he thought, having his clothes handy.

He went out into the main room and the sun was shining. He heard Manning talking. His voice was loud and aggressive. There was a soldier in the kitchen and Manning was holding forth.

"Hump and Shotgun got themselves killed in the back rooms, there. Not me, I stayed low. I kept my guns goin' and never give 'em a clean shot at me."

Pierce saw the guns on the bar and on the tables, then. Manning had laid them all out in a row. They were on display for the gullible and Manning would make a nice thing out of it, Pierce had no doubt.

Manning, the Indian fighter, who had provided weapons and ammunition for the defense of Comanche Station, that would be it. He could explain the nicked ear as a momento of Comanche bow and arrow. He could be a big man, now.

The soldier escaped and Myra moved within Pierce's range of vision. Manning said loudly, "You ain't backin' me up, woman. You ain't bein' a proper wife to me, neither. I don't know what's got into you."

She went silently about her tasks. Pierce remembered Lamkin. Things were returning to him, he was becoming whole again.

"Why, people will come here special to see us. We're onto a good thing. All them graves out there, bullet holes in everything. You got to brace up, woman. We're the ones fought at Comanche Station!"

She looked at him with such loathing as Pierce had seldom seen. Then she drooped, literally, her shoulders sagging, her head down as she turned away. Manning grabbed her, shaking her, suddenly violent.

"What the damn hell's the matter with you, woman?"

Pierce went in silently on moccasined feet. He took hold of Manning's ear, the one which he had cut.

Manning screamed, going down on his knees. Pierce pinched until the blood ran, saying, "Mayhap we oughta trim the other one. Make 'em match."

"You got no right! A man's wife . . ."

"Why don't you get the law on me?" asked Pierce amusedly. "Or why don't you show us how you fight Comanches?"

Myra Manning said wearily, "Leave him alone, Pierce. He won't be any different, no matter what. He can't help himself. It's all right. He never could scare me."

She went to the root closet. She was digging up the plate box Lamkin had buried there.

Pierce said, "Get outa my sight, Manning. And keep it in your mind, I can get this way often as I want. Or wherever else you go."

Manning scurried from the kitchen. Myra brought the box to the table and put it down gently and said, "Luke and Ben are takin' it to El Paso. They're going to send me every picture. It'll be somethin'."

Pierce said, "If there was anything I could do, Miz Manning . . ."

"You must be starved," she said. "I got plenty food. Set down. I'll feed you right now."

He'd be all right when he ate and had a little more time, he knew. He would get around to thinking about Josie and how it was no good any more and no use to fret. He would begin figuring out the best season to come back and collect some more Comanche scalps. Nothing was any different now that he was himself again.

Another day went by and it was time to leave. Ben wandered around the station with Luke and it seemed a different place. The rubble of the barn and corral had been somewhat straightened in the labor of getting out the corpses and counting them.

"The Army has to count everything," said Luke. "It's a way they got. The dead and the livin' must be accounted for. This here is a place we'll see again, mayhap. No use frettin' about anything."

He was anxious about Gloria. He did not know how

much had taken place between the woman and Ben since the end of the fight. There had been so much confusion, hard work, hullabaloo, that nobody could keep track of anything.

Ben said, "It's real amazin'. So much happening in such a short time."

He was finally unsure of himself. He had not been able to do more than reiterate his desire to marry Gloria. Too many things and people had intervened. He expected her to walk out with her bag and join him. He was nervous.

Luke said, "Well, I'll tell you. If you live through a thing like this, you prob'ly got years to go. On that ranch. I'll go right down there with you and look it over. I know a place to buy some Hereford stock at a good price."

"Sure," said Ben. "That's right friendly of you."

Still there was a suspension of their intimacy which both recognized. They walked around the building to where the stagecoaches waited and Flynn was still asking questions, notebook in hand, making crabbed marks with a stub of pencil.

Gloria was packed, attired in a light dress. The serge was ruined, discarded in favor of Myra, who thought she might repair it, some day. Pierce came into the room and looked at her.

"Go away."

He said, "You been in and outa too many beds."

"It's no use, Pierce. You might just as well save your breath. You said it all before."

"You can't do it to that tenderfoot."

"Goddam you, Pierce, shut up!"

He was neatly dressed for the trip, shaven and smiling. He said, "But he's a farmer. What you gonna do with a farmer?"

She wished she could be calm and stare him down, but she couldn't. "Marry him, that's what. He's better than you. He can whup you, too."

"I ain't about to fight him."

"I'm going to have a ranch and cows and chickens and a kitten with a bow around its neck."

"You can't dance with no kitten. There's no hurdy-gurdy on a ranch."

"You foulmouth, filthy Indian killer."

"All them places you been," he said. "You want him to know about 'em? He will. People will tell him."

Tears started down her cheeks. "You can't dirty me up. I'm woman enough to make him happy. I got it in me. I can do it."

"Maybe. But what will he say when he learns? Never mind about me, he prob'ly knows that now. But what about all them you slept with for pay?"

"You stinking bastard!"

He shook his head at her. "You'll never make it."

He left her. She sat with her hands over her face, her knees together, leaning forward so that the tears would not splash her light dress.

In the big room, Ben saw Pierce approaching and set his jaw, trying to stifle his distaste for the man.

Pierce touched his skull and said, "You sure hammered sense into me when I went loco. Reckon we're even."

"Reckon we are," said Ben, his voice cold.

"No cause to carry it any further."

"O.K. with me."

Pierce grinned easily and said, "Damn funny. For a while, there, seemed like the world and everybody in it had changed a whole heap."

"You don't believe it?"

"Do you?"

Ben considered. "I expect only time'll tell."

The grin widened, then vanished. Pierce turned abruptly away and picked up his saddlebag with its burden of Indian scalps and went out into the yard. Ben followed and saw him toss the bag up on the boot and climb into the eastbound stage.

Ben moved restlessly. Gloria was taking a long time. Myra Manning came out, shading her eyes. She looked like an old and bent farm woman Ben remembered from New Jersey. She bade him good-by, reminding him about the pictures Lamkin had taken, accepting his reiterated promises about them.

Luke was still talking with Sergeant Flynn. The checkered suit was somewhat in disrepair, the hole was evident in the hard hat, but the gambler managed to appear debonair.

Enlisted men still worked desultorily around the place and one was arranging crosses on the graves in the little grove of trees. Too many graves, Ben thought, for such a small, out-of-the-way place. It was a cockeyed country, all right. But it was new and big, and today, in the sunlight, minus Comanches, it was handsome. He was young, he had life ahead of him.

He heard Gloria's step within and saw Myra Manning go to her. They briefly embraced, both somewhat embarassed.

Gloria said, "While there's life, there's hope."

"I wish you good luck," said Myra. "Real good luck."

"You had a bad break of the cards," said Gloria.

"I don't know what you mean." Myra flushed dully.

"You know, all right, dearie." Gloria's voice grew harsh. "If I was you, I wouldn't stick around this dump another hour."

"There's no place I want to go." Myra looked out of the window toward the graves in the wooded glen.

"Everyone to her own taste, as the old woman said when she kissed the cow." Gloria shrugged, her accents remaining hard. "Maybe we'll see each other again, dearie."

"If you're comin' through," said Myra indifferently.

Gloria picked up her carpetbag and came out into the sunlight. Her head was high, her cheeks touched with artificial color, her lips carmined. Sergeant Flynn left Luke and intercepted her, asking questions, making notes.

Luke lounged over to Ben and said, "That man can ask more questions than a coroner's jury."

His eyes on Gloria, Ben said, "Guess he's got reasons."

Luke took a last glance around. "It wasn't a bad place to make a fight. Funny thing. You, me, and her." He nodded toward the girl. "She said we'd pull out. And Callahan called the turn on the cavalry, even if he did have the wrong troop."

"And Manning had guns and bullets."

"Yeah, Manning." Luke was also watching Gloria now. "Well, that's life, a game of cards. You play the cards the way they fall."

"Man proposes, God disposes, my Uncle Tiger always said."

"This here'll be known as a big fight. Manning will tell whoppin' lies and because they counted a heap of dead Injuns, Manning'll be believed. Maybe some day you and me will forget what rightly happened. People will want to know and we'll make up things. It happens."

"It won't matter, by then."

"That's for sure." The sergeant was finishing with the girl and turning back to them for last-minute information. Luke stood stock-still, but Ben pulled away and went to Gloria, taking her bag.

She said, "Oh, Ben. Thank you." Her eyes were bright and her voice clear and firm.

"Wanted to talk to you," said Ben.

She looked him straight in the eye. "It was the way things happened. Excitement, I reckon. All that."

"That's all it was? You believe that?"

"I know," she said. "I couldn't make it."

"Couldn't, huh?" He felt stupid, but he was conscious of a deep-down relief.

"It wouldn't work out. Not on a ranch. I need noise, things happenin' alla time."

"Well, I'm . . . sorry, Gloria."

"I'm . . . sorry, too." She turned and walked toward the eastbound stage and he followed her. Pierce looked out at them, blank-faced as an Indian. Ben handed her up, and Pierce did not move an inch as she settled beside him, arranging her skirts. Ben stepped back, searching for words, not finding them.

She looked out the window. "I hope you find a nice kitten."

The stage lurched once, then pulled away, two cavalrymen on the box. A handkerchief fluttered, a cloud of dust arose and obscured everything. Ben walked back to Luke and the sergeant.

"You sure I got all the names, now?"

Luke said, "Miguel, Silo, Sligh, Adobe. Shotgun Beemis, Hump Foley. Wade Lamkin and your Sergeant Callahan. Them's the dead. 'Course, Adobe, he rightly shot hisself."

He winked at Ben, in high humor. "Still, he's dead as anybody else."

Flynn read from his list, "Survivors are Manning and Missus, Luke Post, Ebenezer Tyler——"

"Make that just plain 'Ben,' now, will you? I aim to be known that way from now on." He did feel relief. He felt as if nothing had happened and everything was ahead.

Flynn made the correction. "Gloria Vestal, Pierce . . . What's his first name, that Pierce?"

"Damned if I know," said Luke. Then he said, "Wait a minute. He has got a sort of a name, at that."

"White Eye," said Ben.

"White Eye, that's it. White Eye Pierce."

Flynn nodded. "I heard he lived with the Comanches." He wrote it down.

"You got everything, now?"

Flynn said, "I better have it. MacKenzie, he's tough. You people put up a hell of a fight here."

"Much good it woulda done if MacKenzie wasn't so tough," Luke said. "So long, Sergeant."

They went to the westbound stage. A bird was singing in the trees that sheltered the graveyard. Ben stood a moment, then turned and looked at the far, small cloud of the eastbound stage.

He clambered in beside Luke and returned the gambler's quizzical stare.

"Yeah. You were right."

Luke said, "Why, Ben, they just ain't our kind of folks."

The stage shook itself into motion westward.

Luke said, "Now I happen to know a gal in El Paso, Sadie Forest. Nice gal. You'll like her."

"You mentioned her before. Before we got to Comanche Station." How long ago had that been?

No time at all, he realized. The Texas landscape whirled crazily in his vision. No time at all and already a part of the past.